Akinyi

– RICHARD WOOD –

An environmentally friendly book printed and bound in England by
www.printondemand-worldwide.com

This book is made entirely of chain-of-custody materials

to Chris
best wishes
Richard
Christmas 2017

www.fast-print.net/store.php

Akinyi
Copyright © Richard Wood 2012

All rights reserved

No part of this book may be reproduced in any form by photocopying or any electronic or mechanical means, including information storage or retrieval systems, without permission in writing from both the copyright owner and the publisher of the book.

All characters are fictional.
Any similarity to any actual person is purely coincidental.

ISBN 978-178035-276-3

First published 2012 by
FASTPRINT PUBLISHING
Peterborough, England.

Chapter 1
Monday 7th September

I don't do first day of term.

The sudden wild rush as kids pile into school. Anybody would think they were keen to be back. They laugh, they punch, they push, they jostle. They get together in giggling huddles. They cling to each other and they laugh their heads off about their shared secrets. They talk big. Don't put it past some of them to act big.

And me?

I watch and wonder what happened to the summer and its holidays.

This first day was different, though. Not just because we had a new deputy head - Miss Lyon her name was - but because ... well, because I met a boy.

I'd met boys before, of course I had. Half the kids in our school are boys. Going by the din they make you'd think it was three quarters. Or more.

But this boy was different, and he was my first proper boyfriend.

The first few minutes weren't promising.

'Where do you think you're going?' said Miss Lyon.

It was lesson change-over time in the afternoon. Classrooms were emptying and the corridor was heaving.

The boy said nothing, just swung his weird black raincoat over one shoulder and strolled out of a classroom. He'd have pushed past her into the corridor if she hadn't stuck out an arm and blocked the door.

'Name?' she snapped.

The boy scowled and looked away.

'Smart,' he muttered.

'Congratulations, Smart. You just volunteered.'

'For what?'

Miss Lyon handed him a stack of notes. 'I need two messengers.'

She spoke softly and she smiled sweetly, but her body language told another story. Everything about it said 'I might be new around here, but try messing with me and I'll claw your heart out and feed it to the orcs.'

The boy with the raincoat squared up to her and for a totally unbelievable second I thought, oh my God, he's actually going to headbutt the deputy head.

I was stunned, but the boy wasn't and neither was the Deputy Head. There might be chaos all round them but they were focused. On each other.

Akinyi

Then the boy, with his funny raincoat and his scowl, loomed over me. I was an easy target, I suppose, being the only kid standing still.

'What about her?' he said. 'Why doesn't she do it?'

I could have scarpered there and then.

If I had, I'd have missed him, probably never set eyes on him again. Then he wouldn't have been my boyfriend.

And a few weeks later on one crazy Sunday evening he and I wouldn't have had a massive row. And when the school caught fire and the policewoman got stabbed at a football match I'd have been ... well, I'd have been upset, course I would, but it wouldn't have been the great big deal it turned out to be.

'Fine, why not?' said Miss Lyon and she turned to me. 'What's your name?'

'Akinyi, Miss.'

There was a gleam of recognition in her eyes and just a little smile on her lips. Oh, oh, here we go again, I thought. Her first day and already she knows who I am.

She had TV advert golden hair, parted in the middle and dropping in smooth waves to her shoulders. Her eyes were browny yellow. I saw friendliness in them, but I saw something different, too, and it wasn't something off a shampoo ad. It was a threat of sudden anger, even violence. Oh my, I'd seen some scary teachers in my time but she was something else.

'OK, you two. Take these notes round all the classrooms. You that way, Smart, and you this, Akinyi. Away you go.'

Akinyi

And she beetled off along the corridor.

As soon as she was out of sight, the boy had the cheek to dump his share of notes onto me. 'Have fun,' he said and walked away.

Just like that.

I wasn't standing for it.

'Hey!' It came out as a splutter as I chased after him. 'You needn't think I'm doing all these on my own.'

'Flush them down the bog then,' he said. 'I'm no messenger boy.'

I was amazed. He was thrilling. It was the first time I'd known anybody get stroppy when a teacher gave them a job.

'You wouldn't dare,' I said.

He was dangerous and I was tempted.

'Wouldn't dare?' he scoffed. 'That's a laugh.'

'We have to do what Miss Lyon says. She's the Deputy Head.'

'You might have to. Willowbank's top posh totty.'

'So?'

'Doesn't mean I have to. Kowtowing to teachers. Not me.'

'What's your problem?'

'All those kids staring at you.'

'Staring? How do you think I feel?'

Akinyi

Our eyes met. He challenged me, and I had this wicked feeling. A feeling of surprise - yes that's the easy bit, but there was something else, too, something I didn't expect in a million years.

It was joy.

You see, I'd never known anybody, specially not a boy, who understood. Most kids, if I even touched on what it felt like to be me, they looked away, changed the subject, caught sight of a friend they'd far sooner talk to.

This boy nodded. 'Must be tough,' he said. 'Being black and the Headteacher's daughter.'

'Yeah,' I said in a daze, 'it's not a bed of roses.'

I saw his knuckles tighten white as he gripped his raincoat. Suddenly I needed to giggle. I knew if I did, I'd frighten him off, never see him again. And I didn't want that.

'Face it,' I said. 'It's not like we have a choice. Might as well get it over with. You first.' I opened the nearest classroom door and pushed him through. 'Mr Chamberlain ...'

There was a roar from a teacher in outrage mode.

'Get out! Get out! Now!'

'Alright, alright. Keep your hair on.' My new friend shuffled back into the corridor.

'What was that all about?' I asked. 'What were you playing at?'

'Me?' He laughed, and I laughed, too. I couldn't help it. It was his blue eyes and his cheeky grin. 'Teachers take one look at me and go apeshit.'

'Do you often get into trouble?'

'Trouble? It follows me wherever I go. Always has.'

I recognised the grin. My dad said that in the old days cheeky grins like that tempted teachers into smacking heads.

He surprised me again. 'What about you?' he said. 'Ever been in trouble? What with belonging to the bossman?'

It was a familiar topic in my life. But always a cruel dig, never a cheeky grin and a proper invitation to open up.

Take it easy, I told myself. You don't want to go overboard. Then I thought who cares. Overboard is exactly where I want to go if this boy comes with me.

I smiled. 'You haven't even told me your name,' I said, and he treated me to it again - the grin that drove teachers insane and made my knees go all funny.

We dawdled from classroom to classroom. The notes were neither here nor there but we did deliver them. He often came out with the grin, other times with a dark scowl and a mutter. We had an ace time. I didn't want it to end.

Yet before I knew it, school was finished. Kids were pouring out of the gates. I turned for home, hoping and hoping that he'd follow me.

And he did. We sat on a garden wall at the end of my street. I'd never known anything like it. I'd only bumped

Akinyi

into him an hour ago and here I was telling him stuff I'd always kept buttoned, zipped and velcroed.

'My dad came here as headmaster of Willowbank when it was a grammar school,' I told him. I'm prattling, I thought, but I don't care. Just so long as he stays with me. 'It was exactly his kind of place. For years, hundreds probably, its kids were top in everything - you know what I mean.'

'A-stars in their exams. Little swots.'

I gave him a friendly push. I could do that. Already.

'Then it turned into Willowbank High School,' I said. 'With twice as many kids.'

'I bet that was a shock to your old man's system.'

'Tell me about it.' I was thoughtful for a minute. 'I don't think he's been the same since.'

'Loads of us Ashbrook scruffs to deal with.'

'I can see Ashbrook from my bedroom window.'

'I bet we make a right old mess of your view.'

Willowbank, where I live and where our school is, is on one side of a steep valley. You look downhill to the motorway and the river, both on their way into the city a mile and a half away. Ashbrook is this massive housing estate on the opposite hillside.

'I can watch the motorway traffic going over the flyover,' I said. 'Dad says they built that at the same time as the Ashbrook Block at school.'

'Ashbrook Block, that's a laugh. By rights it should only be us lot that get to use it.'

I ignored the bitter edge in his voice. I only wanted to laugh into his wonderful blue eyes.

Then suddenly it was over.

'See you tomorrow,' he said, and he ran away, along the top of my respectable neighbour's garden wall.

He wore jeans, a t-shirt and boots. Not a scrap of school uniform. As if he cared!

At the end of the street he turned and waved.

'Brendan,' he called. 'They call me Brendan.'

Chapter 2

After that it should have been back to normal. Normal and a bit boring.

Only - I'd met Brendan, and things would never again be what I used to call normal.

It was a fine September evening with a gentle breeze, alright for a bike ride. My friend George Newcomb called for me. I do know some boys. I've known George since we went to the same pre-school.

But when I say "know" I don't mean know the way I already knew Brendan.

Brendan. Lovely name, I thought. Suits him, with his blue eyes and his cheeky grin.

Brendan. I hummed his name into the breeze as George and I freewheeled down high-hedged lanes a mile from home in Willowbank.

It wasn't easy for George to get time off. His father didn't allow it. Truth was, George's father, in my not so humble opinion, was a bully. Not to say a silly old fart.

But this evening George had permission to be away from his homework for an hour and he whistled tunefully as we came to Nether Fencote. It's a tiny hamlet of four or five red-roofed whitewashed stone houses hidden in a dip in the hills.

It was a place George and I loved. The old stone church was our favourite. We knew where the key was kept. We leaned our bikes against a gravestone and went inside. The organ was dusty, but George was a brilliant musician.

In fact, I'd heard our music teacher, Mrs Siddle, tell him he was a prodigy. Even with missing keys he could squeeze a tune from the rickety instrument. I danced in the aisle and sang along.

The sun was low when we came outside. We locked the door behind us, giggling with our heads close together as we slipped the huge iron key into its hiding place on a stone shelf in the porch. Screaming swifts raced each other round the tower.

George perched on a gravestone, swung his legs and hummed.

I lay in the warm grass and looked up at the evening sky.

Brendan.

I smiled and sneaked a mischievous little peek at George. I've known him all these years, I thought. And I've never stopped to think that he's quite a goofy kid really.

Compared with Brendan, he's seriously goofy. With his thick glasses and his hair that won't lie down however hard he tries to give it the straight parting ordered by his 20th century dad.

Now Brendan ... the trendy almost shaved head, the skin so smooth any girl would envy it, the blue eyes and their see-if-I-care smile.

And ... and, that certainty I had, which set my heart racing, that his child-like innocence was only a small part of what Brendan was about. Along with it went something more exciting, more challenging, more dangerous that I'd ever seen.

Perhaps I'd see him again tomorrow. Roll on tomorrow.

Without warning, George was dragged backwards from his seat. As I sat up I saw a fattish, boy about the same age as me pin him to the ground, with one knee on his chest. A second boy, far skinnier, grabbed George's bike and took off along the lane. Not before a girl had snaffled his drinking bottle.

'Get this,' the skinny boy shouted. 'Twenty eight gears.'

George coughed and choked. 'You can't mug me. I haven't even touched you.'

The fatter boy squeezed his throat and told him to belt up. 'Wotcha got on you worth nicking?'

'Get off him!' I yelled.

It was pretty feeble, I know, but what was I supposed to do? It's not every day I get to see a real-time mugging.

I gave the boy a hopeless push. How useless was that!

'Cor, look who it isn't,' he laughed. 'Mr Mac's lass,' and he pummelled George even harder.

'Is he your friend, or what?' I turned to the girl and shrieked at her. 'Can't you sort him?'

The girl gave a scornful laugh as she drained George's drinking bottle in one gulp.

'Get off!' George wriggled, but he was helpless. The boy was as merciless as he was strong.

'You look posh and loaded,' he said, 'Singing and the flash bike. Turn your pockets out.'

'How can I when you're flattening me?'

The boy gave George's throat a squeeze before letting go.

George was desperate for something to offer, a bribe, anything to get this yobbo off his chest.

'The church,' he said. 'I can show you how to get in if you like.'

'What's in there?' the boy sneered. 'Hymn books and that rubbish.'

'It's only a little church. Only gets used once a month.'

'Well then, what's worth nicking?'

'You can't steal from a church.'

'Just you watch us.' I winced as I saw him squeeze George's throat again. 'Tell us what there is and I might let you up.'

'There's a statue.' George whimpered. 'It's worth millions.'

'Statue? What's one of them?'

Now the girl joined in. 'I know what it is,' she said, 'it's medieval.'

'You what?'

'Medieval, Dumbo.'

'What's that then?'

'There's a knight-in-arms lying on his back,' she said. 'With his dog to keep his feet warm.'

'How do you get in?' the boy growled.

'Don't be an idiot,' I said. 'We won't let you in till you let George stand up.'

'It has a massive door,' said George.

'With the original Norman stone porch,' said the girl.

'Norman? Who's he when he's at home?'

'I know where the key ... er ...' said George. 'Get off me, will you, before I choke to death.'

'Let him up, Legs,' the girl ordered.

The boy wasn't exactly charming about it, but he did let George stagger to his feet. Poor George, he looked quite silly. He rubbed his bottom with one hand and his throat with the other, and he tried to think of something manly to say.

'Give him his bike back, Marksy,' the girl said.

The skinny kid with the oddly shaped head did one more wheelie. Then he pushed the bike at George.

The girl was a real surprise. She was the boss. There was something about her. Something wild and free. The faintly olive skin perhaps, the quick, dark eyes, and the widely spaced front teeth. She was pretty in a natural sort of way. Not like the Willowbank girls, all eye-liner and lipstick.

Yes, she was very pretty

And scary.

George thought so too. He couldn't take his eyes off her.

'Don't want to take any notice of Legs and Marksy,' the girl said. 'They're harmless.'

'Harmless?' said George. 'He as good as throttled me.' He nodded at the boy who had pinned him so painfully to the ground. 'Why do you call him Legs?'

We all laughed, even Legs himself, though he wasn't too happy about it.

'A bit dense, aren't you?' said the girl. 'Cause he hasn't got any, that's why.'

'Cheeky bitch!' Legs muttered, but I noticed he didn't want the girl to hear.

And it was true. The boy's legs were short. And I'd seen what they did to George.

'I'm not dense,' George said. 'I'm a genius.'

'Come off it, George.' I groaned and pulled a horrible face.

Akinyi

George! Why couldn't he see this wasn't the way to talk to these kids? As if they were going to stand there and let him brag that he was a genius.

Sure enough, they smirked. Even Legs' face cracked into a proper smile.

'It's true!' said George. Their laughter had a rough edge of scorn. It upset him, but it didn't stop him blundering on. 'My dad says so. And the teachers.'

'Ooo, well then,' sang girl. 'It must be true.'

Legs got mad. He came for George, with a thump to the shoulder this time. It was a bony thump, and George staggered.

'Not exactly heavy weight champion of the world, are you?' Legs sneered.

'Leave him, Legs,' the girl snapped. She stood beside George, his body-guard. 'My name's Saisha. I know who you are.'

'Oh?' said George. 'How come?'

'You're that kid who plays the violin.'

We were on our way home now. George kept close to Saisha, pushing his bike and keeping it between him and Legs.

'My dad once made me go with him to a concert at the Town Hall,' Saisha said. 'You were in it.'

The lane brought us back into the valley, to the evening lights of Willowbank and Ashbrook and the roar of traffic along the motorway that slices between them.

'This is where we turn off,' I said.

'Bye,' said Saisha. She turned to George. 'See you, Genius.'

'Cool,' said George. 'That would be great.'

The two boys hooted and ran off down the hill.

'You what?' said Saisha.

'To see you.'

Legs and Marksy turned to watch. Me too. We all knew she'd bewitched him with her wild dark eyes, her gap-toothed smile. He fancied her. It wasn't news to the other kids. I could tell they'd seen it before, but I felt a pang of jealousy.

Then I remembered Brendan, and I treated myself to a secret little smile. Silly George.

'Tell you what,' Saisha laughed, turning to join her friends in running down the hill, 'you can come with us any time. Bring twenty quid from your posh house.'

Her laughter turned scarily shrill.

Chapter 3

Year 11: the Big One. Years of preparation over at last. Years of nagging from teachers and from fretting mums and dads.

Course work, homework. Practicals, tests, mock exams, study leave, homework.

And at long last GCSE proper.

I knew what I wanted, five or six A-stars, two or three more As. Next year it would be A Level Physics, Biology, Chemistry and Maths in the 6th Form. On my way to uni and then to teacher training.

My dad expected it. My teachers expected it. I expected it myself. People had always told me I was clever and I knew I was a worker. You didn't get any street cred for that in our school, but I knew how to rub along with most kids and keep my eye on my dream.

My dream? That was something I kept well hidden. My secret dream that one day I would return to Africa to be a teacher among my own people. Until I met Brendan I didn't know anybody who would understand that. Not that I gave them any chance. There are some things best kept to yourself, and wanting to be a teacher is one of them.

It wasn't long before Brendan had my secret out of me. One whole day to be exact. I spent it daydreaming, wondering when I'd see him. And after school, there he was, picking me up at the gate. His eyes were as blue, his grin as cheeky and his raincoat as weird as I remembered.

'Fancy a walk into Ashbrook?'

I was really nervous and I came across as a total doozy. 'Got loads of homework.'

'Never been to our side of the bridge, have you?'

'My chemistry module. And an English essay. I can't afford the ...'

'We have electricity and gas, you know. Cars, buses, bikes. We have two legs and one head. And we don't bite - well, some of us have been known to take a nibble at the odd ear hole.'

He was fantastic. I'd have gone anywhere with him. 'Come to mine first and I'll change out of my uniform.'

'Your old fella wouldn't like that.'

'He's a pussycat,' I laughed. 'He sometimes scratches but he doesn't bite.'

'I'll hang around outside.'

'There's no need, honestly. He doesn't get home till 6 at the earliest. Two hours.'

Akinyi

Ours is a detached house with high-ceilinged rooms looking through sash windows onto sloping lawns. Front and back there are well-stocked borders and fruit trees. No thanks to me, I might add. My dad does the gardening. It's the only break he allows himself from school work, school work, school work.

'I knew you'd have a ten mile garden,' Brendan laughed as he followed me up the drive. 'And how about that, no burglar alarm.'

'Come in.'

'I'll pass, thanks.'

'Pretend it's my house, not his.'

I led him by the arm. He was shy. He felt out of place. His eyes were everywhere, taking it all in.

First left off the corridor inside the front door is Dad's study.

'This was our family's drawing room,' I said. 'We still sit in here if we have visitors. See how my dad has messed it about. He's turned it into his computer studio-cum-office. Look at that ugly metal filing cabinet.'

'Antiques,' said Brendan. 'A jewellery safe. And I bet you can play that piano.'

It was in the bay window, and I lifted the lid and ran my fingers over the keys.

'The grand piano is Dad's,' I said. 'I play the clarinet. Sometimes, though, I wake in the night and hold my breath. It's my dad playing softly and sadly for himself.'

We were both caught by my sudden sadness. I was embarrassed and for a minute I didn't know quite know where to look. Then I nodded towards the room's one softening touch. It's a framed photograph above the work desk of an auburn haired woman in her early forties. Her calm brown eyes, her freckly face and her smiley lips, they just give you that sense of somebody who's used to being in charge.

'My mum.'

Brendan frowned.

I laughed. 'You can't expect to know everything already.'

'Go on then, tell.'

'My adopted mum, of course.'

Brendan looked uneasy.

'What?' I prompted.

'What's niggling me is what I'll do if your mum jumps out of that picture and catches me in here.'

I took his raincoat, held both his hands and looked into the blue eyes.

'Mum and Dad adopted me as a baby in Kenya,' I said. 'Until Mum died, adoption wasn't something that upset me.'

'Your mum died! When? How come? I don't know what to say.'

'Everything you've said so far is perfect,' I told him, and I meant it. 'Do you know what most people's line is? Time is the great healer, they say. Life goes on. The shock will pass. You'll forget.'

'And it's not true?'

'No way, it's all rubbish. Whenever I look at that photo I want to cry. I still think it's incredible that Mum is dead. Dead! That's crazy. It doesn't make sense. She was always so alive.' I pulled away from him. 'Sorry. I shouldn't dump this stuff onto you. Do you still want to take me to Ashbrook?'

He nodded.

'When we get there you can dump some of your hang-ups on me,' I said.

We were alright again by the time we crossed Willow Bridge. Mind you, Ashbrook freaked me out. Ridiculous, I know. I was 15 years old and had lived in Willowbank pretty well the whole of my life, yet Brendan was spot-on when he'd guessed that I'd never been into Ashbrook. I bet I wasn't the only one. There were loads of kids at our school who never crossed the bridge.

Brendan thought it was a big laugh.

'Look at these straight rows of red brick houses,' he mocked. 'Can people live in joined-up houses? Do they earwig each other through the walls when they sit on the toilet?'

'Brendan!' I giggled. 'You're gross.'

'Disgusting, isn't it? You're right. Why don't they get the man servant to sort out the peeling paint? And why have all the houses got satellite dishes? You don't mean that people watch football on the television? Eee and look at these tiny gardens! There's hardly room for the swimming pool.'

He danced round me. He pointed and laughed.

It was true that my eyes were drawn to the houses with boarded-up windows. There were plastic bags lying in the gutters and torn polythene caught up in the hedges. I felt sick when I found myself staring at the clutter of parked cars. Some were bumper-to-bumper, others blocked the pavement. One or two stood on piles of half burned, rotting wood and broken bricks because their wheels had been lost.

'Lost?' Brendan hooted. 'Yeah, that's right. Lost.'

'Are you saying someone stole their car wheels? Why would they do that?'

My question, apparently, was so funny it didn't need an answer.

Chapter 4

Anita, Brendan's mum, was amazed that he had brought home a black girl. I knew it the moment we met. That fleeting frown, that skittery loss of eye contact, that moment of panic. I was very young when I got the message.

A second was all it took for Anita to recover. She was shy and she was quiet, but she was warm and friendly. She was Brendan's mum, and I was fascinated.

'Your mum is brilliant,' I whispered. 'It's only from mums you get such ... what do I mean?'

'Acceptance,' he said, and I was amazed by his understanding. 'I've been a pain for Mam, but she's still here.'

Anita brought in a tray of tea and sandwiches.

'Akinyi is the Headteacher's daughter, Mam,' Brendan told her.

Akinyi

Anita put her hand to her mouth. Then she reached out and touched my face with gentle fingers. Her eyes - they were the same as my mum's, strong and comforting, yet where mum had a laughing face Anita's was strained and hardworked. And no wonder! I didn't know it yet, but I soon would, that it was Brendan who had brought all those strain lines to her face.

'Are you alright, love?' she said quietly. 'Coming here, I mean?'

I smiled uncertainly. 'Well, yes, I think so ... as long as you don't mind.'

'Course she's alright,' Brendan scoffed. 'I've told her you don't bite, Mam.'

'She has a right to know, our Brendan. About you. It's only fair.'

'Tell her then, Mam. Be my guest.' His eyes met mine, and they were bright with mischief. 'Dumping time. Fasten your seat belt.'

Anita sat down between us and gave Brendan a good shove to make us some space.

'He's all innocence, Akinyi. Watch him. Believe you me, he's the devil. He was a toddler when he learned to use those blue eyes to get out of trouble. When he realised that kids went to school he couldn't wait. He even tried to sneak in when he was only just 4 and had to be collared by the teacher. One day the kids had a party. Our Brendan went to school with them that afternoon, cheeky monkey, and got into his first fight.

Akinyi

'The headmistress came to see me. "You'll not believe this, Mrs Smart," she says. "Oh, I'll believe anything," I thought. "Try me," I says. He'd only gone into the classroom, hadn't he? Plonked himself down at a desk to make a clay model. Got into a fight with the kid whose desk it was. Knocked this kid's teeth out. That's all.'

I looked at Brendan. Would he deny it? I was tense.

Him? He was completely laid back. Hadn't even taken his eyes off the TV screen.

'So there you are,' Anita said. 'His first week at school and he's at home, suspended.'

'That'll do for starters,' Brendan chuckled.

My mouth was dry with anxiety. 'Have you been suspended since then?' I asked.

'Oh, not more than half a dozen times,' he said.

Well! I was amazed. What about my mum, I wondered, what would she have made of me strolling home one day with Brendan in tow?

No one had switched the TV off. It showed African babies with swollen bellies. 'What can you do to help?'

'Up yours, mate,' said Brendan, and he switched the presenter off in full flow. 'Him and his smart-arse questions. What bright answers has he got?'

'It's not his fault,' I said.

'Then why doesn't he do something about it?'

'You feel so helpless, don't you?'

'Do you?' said Brendan. 'How come?'

'It's a huge problem. What can I do, little me? There's nothing I can do.'

'Excuses. You can just hear them, can't you - everybody who's watching the programme, all whining the same thing. Who? Little me?'

He was doing my head in. I was going from one shock to another. 'Brendan,' I said, trying my best to keep calm, 'you can't imagine how bad I feel looking at those babies. I feel seriously guilty, don't you?'

'Maybe you should, Akinyi. Let's face it, you could have been one of them.'

I gasped. Brendan had given me it from the shoulder, just like that, and it was what I needed. He made my mind up.

'Right,' I announced. 'That settles it. Putting it off until I'm a teacher isn't good enough.'

'Do something now, before it's too late.'

That was when I told him about my African dream. He was walking me home along Ashbrook streets and this time I didn't even notice the boarded-up houses and the cars with no wheels. I was walking through the bush country along the red dust paths under the vast, cloudless blue skies of my Africa.

'Your mum was great with me,' I said. 'I don't know about mine.'

'That doesn't sound too friendly.'

'Oh, Mum was lovely, don't get me wrong. We were friends. She taught me to swim. We played together. We sang and danced. We went camping and we went shopping. We read stories.'

'Stories? You mean nursery rhymes and fairy tales?'

'Didn't your mum read you those?

'Do me a favour.'

'Mum was still reading with me and telling me stories when I was 10 or 11. My friends would have taken the mickey something rotten if they'd known. So I never let anyone see how close I was to Mum.'

'You said she wasn't as wonderful as my mam.'

The faraway excitement of my imagination dipped into a frown. 'She was lovely but I'm mad with her.'

'Mad? I don't get that.'

'Not fair, is it? I mean, Mum couldn't help dying, could she? Thing is - she spent hours bringing me up as a happy little kid. Then she left me to reason it out for myself that my real mum and dad were Africans, probably poor people ...'

'From Africa's Ashbrook,' said Brendan.

He was amazing. He was fantastic. It was those glimpses of understanding I'd never had before. And, lurking with them, an almost brutal frankness.

'I wonder.'

'Did they die?' he asked.

'I've asked myself that loads of times. I don't know.'

'Did they give you away?'

Akinyi

I couldn't speak for a minute, and when I did there was a catch in my voice.

'Brendan, you're so funny,' I said. 'This is stuff people don't even mention. If they do, they go on tiptoe.'

'OK, I'll whisper it on tiptoe. Did they give you away?'

I was laughing and crying at the same time.

'How do I know? And if they did give me away, why did they? Kenya was where Mum and Dad met. They went to be teachers in a Nairobi school. They married there. When they found they were never going to have a baby, they adopted me. Then they brought me to England. Why? You tell me.'

I reached out to hold both his hands and gazed into his face. He'd already given me so much and now I was asking him for the impossible.

'You'll have to worm it out of your old man, the head bossman.'

I pulled away. I knew it was unreasonable, but just for a minute I was disappointed in him.

'If only it was that easy,' I grumbled. 'He's the last person I'd want to talk to about this stuff.'

That wasn't fair either. There's millions of lovely things about my dad. He lets me get on with my own life - most of the time anyway. He isn't bossy. He doesn't interfere. So long as I've got my school work organised, that's all he cares about. And he knows, because I've told him often enough, that I know what I want and where I'm going.'

But there's a really scruffy side to me as well. I've had my ears pierced and given half a chance I dangle stuff from them, specially in Rasta or African colours. I have two clips at the top of my right ear, so I look like quite a with-it kid, though I'm not really like that at all. Most kids think I'm swotty and dead boring. They haven't seen my bedroom, and luckily enough, neither has my dad. Fair do's, he never pushes his nose in there, so he hasn't seen the floor messed up with my clothes, the drawers and my wardrobe and my cupboard all open and stuff spilling out.

'You're seriously mixed up, you are,' said Brendan as if he could read my thoughts. 'There's more to it than you've said.'

I looked at him through tears. And for the first time he reached out to touch me, put his arm roughly round my waist. And I was very happy.

'I like you, Brendan,' I said, looking into his eyes, working hard to smile. 'Nobody has ever ...'

We crossed Willow Bridge in the valley bottom and started the steep uphill walk under the motorway flyover, with traffic booming above us. Pulses of sweet-scented, foul-tasting diesel inflamed my nostrils and the back of my throat.

'Just before Mum died she told me about the road to the lake in the west. Lake Victoria. The biggest lake in Africa. Talking to you has made me realise stuff.'

'Like what?'

Akinyi

'Mum must have known she was going to die. Maybe she wanted to leave behind a special something from her Africa, something that would last me for ever. Mum loved the place names, Brendan. She rolled them round on her tongue.'

'Tell me one.'

'There's a road from Nairobi through the Great Rift Valley to Naivasha and Nakuru. There's a lake, and it's pink from shore to shore with flamingos.'

'Cool.'

'The road keeps going west to the Kisii Highlands. There are plantations of banana trees. The road is red murram.'

'Don't know what that is.'

'It wraps your car in a cloud of flying dust and bounces its springs. Keep going and you're into the land of the Luo tribe. My name is a Luo name. Akinyi. It means I was born in the morning.'

'Born in the morning. Yeah, I like that.'

'The Luo live beside the Lake. Mum told me it's as wide and as blue as the sea.'

'And that's what you dream about. The road to the Lake.'

'I knew you'd understand.' I looked into his face. 'And that's where I'm going one day. To be a teacher.'

'In the land by the Lake.'

We sat on my neighbour's wall.

'First,' Brendan reminded me, 'you're going to raise some serious money for those starving kids.'

He put his arm round my waist again and pulled me to him. Talk about excitement! The pounding heart, the swoon, the moment of rapture! All that romantic stuff. I turned my face to his, smiling, ready for his kiss.

Instead he pushed me roughly away and stood up.

'Oh, Jesus!' he said. 'Frosty.'

Out of the shadows of our drive came our Head of Year, Mr Winter. Oh yerks, talk about naff timing.

'Evening, Akinyi,' he said casually as he got into his car. 'Just passing, Brendan?'

Brendan headed in the opposite direction. Fast.

I felt sick with disappointment. Lousy timing doesn't come into it, I thought.

'Brendan.' I called for him. I was desperate. 'Come back. He was only visiting my …'

Brendan had reached the end of the street.

'Brendan,' I called again. 'I already have some ideas.'

He'd gone. Darkness had fallen and I was talking to myself.

'A Fun Fest,' I muttered. 'For my favourite charity. Build Africa.'

Chapter 5

It's not just the headteacher's daughter bit that's done my head in. It's the adoption thing as well. That's why I don't have many real friends.

And that's why it seemed like a miracle when Brendan appeared from nowhere in my life. You'd think there'd be tons of reasons why he couldn't understand me, would run a mile from me. Adopted out of Africa. Headteacher's daughter. Posh voice. Big house on the Willowbank side of the valley. Never been in trouble with a teacher. Want to be a teacher, for God's sake.

Yet he understood me right from the start. Don't ask me how I knew. I just did.

Then he rejected me. Ran off without a backward glance. In the night I woke up with that feeling of rejection that had made itself at home in me ever since my mum died. Maybe it was there before she died. Maybe it started the day some kid at primary school asked me why I was black

Akinyi

and I went home and said to my mum, 'Mum, how come I'm black when you and Daddy ... ?'

That day something clicked in me and I started wondering oh wow I wonder if I belong here.

Don't ask me where it was, this feeling. In the back of my mind? In the pit of my stomach? In my knees, when I sometimes felt I couldn't be bothered to get going into a day.

Instead of a bubbly charmer with the curly hair and coal-black eyes and stunning smile everybody had gushed about, I became watchful and suspicious of people. And I didn't commit.

That's what our Head of Year, Mr Winter said, the same guy who blew it for me and Brendan by suddenly jumping out from behind a bush - not really, but it might as well have been a big thick bush because we never saw him coming - anyway, that's what he said to me one day when we were having a chat.

Everybody called him Frosty, by the way, which in some ways he was and other ways he definitely was not. Not for me, anyway. He was my Head of Year all the way through high school, and we had quite a few chats.

'Maybe it's because you don't commit, Akinyi,' he said when he was sorting out some hassle I'd had with another kid. Or kids. And for the millionth time.

Frosty meant to be kind with what he said, but it made me more self-conscious than ever. You don't commit, I told myself, and I watched myself and found it was true. I was careful with everybody - except George, and I'd known George from the year dot - and people thought I was standoffish. They thought it was because I was the Headteacher's daughter and thought too much of myself, but really it was because I was scared. Scared that if I got too close I'd be rejected. Again.

Like my African mum and dad rejected me. I don't know how or why, but they must have, mustn't they? Then Mum. She went and died. It was beyond me to understand that.

But ...

Well, another thing Frosty said, and he said this to make me feel better, 'One way or another you're a feisty character, Akinyi, and you'll get by.' A funny kind of compliment, wasn't it?

But there you go. The following day, Wednesday 9th September, feisty Akinyi tells her knees to get out of bed and get by and get on with this Fun Fest idea. Little knowing that in time it would be at the centre of the mayhem caused by the school fire and the murdered policewoman.

I didn't hang about. I went to see a funny man. His name was Thirza. He was a teacher at our school. The kids weren't sure if that was his first name or his surname, but everyone knew him and everyone called him T. Not just behind his back, straight to his face.

He taught Art and he was a magician. He made things disappear from one hand and appear in the other. He filled a jug with water and tipped it upside down to show there was nothing in it. Illusions. Unbelievable card tricks. Levitation. And he listened to the kids, taught them his patter, seemed not to mind their cheek.

Just the man for my Fun Fest.

I popped into his after-school Art Club. There were kids of all ages there, from 6th Formers doing amazing canvass abstracts to Year 7s splashing water about. Music was my thing. I hadn't been to the Art Club before. The noise hit me first.

Then I saw this massive workbench. It spanned the front of the room. On top of it T had built a wall of books. I reckoned it must have taken him years. They walled him into his seat. They could buzz as much as they liked, those kids. They could jump up and down, but they couldn't get at him in his seat.

And they accepted it. They chatted with him over his barricade.

'Yes, T, no T. Aw! do I have to, T?'

If they felt like it, they lobbed him a present. Over the wall of books. Chewing gum or some artwork they fancied having him look at.

When they saw me the kids fell silent for a moment. Then the noise and movement started up again, and I could hear the familiar whispers. It was always the way.

'It's Akinyi.'

'A what?'

'Akinyi - don't you know anything?'

'Can't miss her, can you?'

'She's a right ...'

'Akinyi, it's Akinyi - Mr Mac's daughter.'

'Her name's Akinyi.'

It was the chaos that sickened me. I turned away. Some other time perhaps.

One of T's small boys blocked my escape, 11 years old, bright, innocent, not a care in the world.

'Wanna see a great drawing, Akinyi?'

Good teachers that I knew would have ticked him off. Sharply, too. Sit in your seat this instant. Face the front. Put your hand up. Unwillingly, I followed him to stand in front of a tall easel.

'Wicked, innit?' he piped. 'Just wait till it's finished.'

It wasn't a drawing. No way.

It was a life-size oil painting of a football fan. A man in his thirties, maybe early forties. Draped across his sweating bare chest was a Union Jack. Onto his shaved skull he had daubed lurid red, white and blue stripes. A pink scar slashed diagonally across his right cheek.

He was amazing. His eyes blazed his fanatical commitment.

Commitment to what, I wondered. A football team? Or something uglier, more angry and more scary?

She had given him a huge boot, propelled into violently ugly focus, almost in 3D, against a blurred background of thousands of gaping mouths.

She? How did I know the painter was a she? Because she had made him brutal, with his sweating chest, his shaved head, and his pink scar.

Brutal - and sexy.

For all the lurid violence the artist had put into his face, she couldn't disguise her admiration for its slender shape, with its arched eyebrows as delicate as a woman's. And those I'll-die-for-you-or- I'll kill- you eyes!

'Awesome, innit, Akinyi?'

'Awesome isn't the word,' I breathed. 'It's stunning.'

'He's one of the Boot Boys. They call him the Gaffer. I'm going to be like him one day. Behind the goal at the Rovers end.'

'Whose painting is it? I asked.

'One of the 6th Form. I reckon he's one of the Boot Boys firm, don't you?'

'I don't know what that means,' I said, 'but it's a wonderful picture.'

'I'll do one like that one day. When I'm one of the Boot Boys.'

'What's your name?'

'Liam, Akinyi.'

'Oh well, thank you for showing me the painting, Liam.'

Now I was the one they buzzed round. T was behind his barricade of books but I was an open honey-pot.

'Look at mine, Akinyi.'

'Over here, Akinyi.'

'Mine's better than his any day. T says ...'

'Just sit down,' I protested. 'I've come to see T .... er, Mr ....'

'David and Megan, go to your seats.' Invisible behind his sad book wall, T issued his orders. 'Carrie, that's twice I've told you not to splash Lily's work. Leroy, you must concentrate or your Noah's Ark won't be a patch on last week's flying saucer.'

The buzzing cloud dispersed. Kids sat at their desks, hands stretched high, beckoning me to them. There was a moment's peace before the murmur of voices began again. They rose to a hum, then to the unchecked babble that had greeted me when I opened the door. But now I looked with widened eyes and saw method in T's spectacular madness.

'I'm sure you're overdoing the blue, Joshua. Use more water.'

'OK, T.'

'How are the trees coming along, Emily?'

'The trunks are OK, T. The branches, though - they're all wonky against the sky.'

'Show me.'

A girl padded to the front and reached up on tiptoe to hand her painting over the wall of books.

'How does he know?' I said. 'How can he possibly tell what you're up to?'

Akinyi

Liam frowned as if I'd spoken an off-the-planet language. 'Sorry?'

They accept him as normal, I thought. It's weird. They actually think he's a good teacher.

Suddenly, standing beside me, there was Saisha.

The tough girl who had dominated her rough friends as they bullied George. The girl who had worked her own more subtle charms on George. Smitten him, to be precise. And here she was, shimmering out of the noise and bustle of the Art Club, tall, beautiful and strangely ... what was it? Strangely confident, strangely sure of herself.

'Didn't expect to see you here, Saisha,' I said cautiously.

Saisha shrugged 'You'd like to see my clowns,' she said.

Her self-confidence - wow, it was quite something.

'Finished. Look.'

A troop of painted, costumed circus clowns sang, played and danced in their powdered wigs and lavish make-up. From their positioning, their movement, their gleeful, winking expressions I could tell Saisha had often watched them in real life.

'Go on then,' she said. 'Say something.'

She knows I'm wrong-footed, I thought. And it was true. I was thinking about those rough boys at Nether Fencote Church. How one of them had mugged George. How Saisha herself had coolly drained the drinking bottle on George's bike. Yet here she was calmly showing off her after-school painting and being as nice as pie.

'Which one is your favourite?' I said.

It was an awkward enough question but Saisha glanced at me with affection and flushed her pleasure with a proud smile.

'The Fool. One day I'm going to be like him. I'll travel with the circus and learn to be a magician.'

'You're really good at painting,' I said. 'I can tell the Fool is your favourite.'

'He's my best friend.'

Without warning, her mood darkened.

She dipped her paint brush into her dirty water jar and made an ugly smudge. It was on the white-faced clown, with his red ears, his gaudy costume, his ruffled collar and pointed hat.

'Who's that?' I asked.

'White face, the chief clown.'

'It doesn't make sense. What are you doing, spoiling him that way?'

'He's T, of course.'

'Oh.' I winced.

'My dad.' Saisha hardly moved her lips.

I looked sharply at her. I mean really sharply. My face went red hot, and I hissed. 'What?'

'Sssh, you heard. The nutter behind the heap of books.' I was queasily familiar with the hinted cry for help. 'My old man. That's him - the clown.'

'Oh my God, Saisha! I didn't know there were two of us. With dads at school, I mean.'

'Oh well.' Saisha shrugged. 'You do now.'

'But those kids you were with ...'

'What's up with them? They're my mates. They live near me.'

'You want to watch it. One of those kids half killed George.'

She laughed scornfully.

'You shouldn't call your dad a nutter either.'

Our eyes met. Hers are a deep dark brown, I thought, nearly as dark as mine, and they're streetwise and cunning. She isn't going to blink first.

'Don't you want to be a teacher?' I asked. I knew it was a stupid question before the words were out of my mouth. 'Like your dad?'

Saisha laughed and she did blink first.

'Course not,' she said. 'Gonna run away with the circus.'

I wouldn't put it past you either, I thought.

'Well,' said Saisha. 'You came here to see Mr T.'

'Did I?' I was startled.

'And you're wondering how you're supposed to speak to him when he's done his disappearing trick behind that wall of books.'

True enough, I thought. I'm also wondering how his daughter got to be a leader in a gang of rough boys.

And why has nobody knocked his stupid wall down? Why, I could do it myself. Now. Sweep the books off the workbench, bring him face to face with the kids he's supposed to be teaching.

I shuddered. He would be horrified. Petrified.

And suddenly, there he was, standing beside me. I blinked my surprise. It was that same shimmering trick Saisha had played a moment or two earlier. Now you don't see me, now you do. How weird was that!

I only knew him as the jolly chap who made witty remarks and entertained the kids with funny games and magic tricks.

Like the trick of teaching a class from behind a barricade of books.

I'd never noticed a keyhole of tension above the nose bridge of his glasses. Their round lenses changed the shape of his deep-set eyes, giving him a haunted look. However did he get his reputation as a funny man? I had a glimpse of how jaundiced Saisha felt to be at school with this man as her dad.

I shouldn't have come, I thought, and I was suddenly so nervous I half forgot what I wanted to say.

'I wanted to ask you, sir, if you'd take part in our Fun Fest,' I began, but my voice trailed away as I went right off the idea.

Too late.

'I've heard about it, Akinyi, and I shall be honoured,' said T.

Heard about it? How could he possibly have heard about it? I'd only just dreamed the idea up.

I couldn't dream up a quick excuse for changing my mind. I had no choice but to go ahead.

'I've seen lots of your tricks, T, and I wondered if you could do your sword swallowing routine.'

'With fire, Akinyi? Would you like fire, too?'

'With fire? That would be brilliant'

He drummed two finger nails on his front teeth and pointed one finger at me.

'Not a word. It's our secret, OK? My daughter will be my assistant. As you say - brilliant.'

I'd got what I came for and more, but I went away puzzled and uneasy. Not once had T's sad face hinted at fun. Close-up, something about him really scared me.

And his Saisha? She's as screwed up as I am, I thought. Could we be friends?

Chapter 6

Concentration was not George's strong point, but he did best when I was around to keep him going. After school on Thursday we practised at his house, he on his violin, I on my clarinet.

It was a specially complicated piece, which his tutor had set him on purpose. To stretch him. To get the best out of him. It was way beyond me, but George was so good he could play it with his eyes closed, and I could tell he was getting bored.

'Being a prodigy,' I said. 'It's a doddle for you, isn't it.'

He yawned and put his violin down on his bed.

'I'm sick of people telling me that stuff,' he said. 'You wouldn't like it if you had to practise for hours and hours.'

He opened his laptop, and I smiled as I saw him scroll to the football pages.

Akinyi

I played on. 'Your father will be on your case,' I warned him.

'Shouldn't poke his nose in then, should he,' George chuntered. 'No slacking. Practice makes perfect. The more you practise, the luckier you'll be. Practice, practice .... I'm sick of practising.'

'I'll play this solo section. Then you'll have to join in or he'll be here in seconds.'

George shuffled the paper.

'Rovers won on Saturday,' he said dreamily. 'Again. Billy Meadows scored two.'

'He must be quite good, is he?'

'Played four, won four, drawn none, lost none. Scored 9, one against.'

'Is that good?

'Two hundred and sixty five minutes played since that one goal against. Undefeated at home for over a year. Seven yellow cards, one red.'

'You love all that stuff, don't you?' I said. 'Football statistics.'

'One day,' said George, 'I'm going with the boys to a match.'

'That'll be nice.'

'There's a gang in one of the bottom sets. You know them.'

'I can guess the ones you mean. Red and white striped shirts.'

'Rovers tops.'

'And they wear snazzy trainers.'

'And they have a song.'

'Yes, I've heard it. They're hopelessly out of tune.'

'They couldn't care less about that. We *are the Ro - vers Boot Boys.*'

'Sorry, George,'I laughed. 'You're in tune. You'll never belong.'

'To be with those boys and to sing with them when they go to see the Rovers …'

'One of the Boot Boys firm,'I said, dead casual. 'Led by the Gaffer.'

George looked up from his lap top screen and gaped at me. 'How … ?'

I smiled fondly at him.

'Poor George,' I said. 'Just think what your dad would say if he knew your dreams.'

I can't be bothered with this hard practice piece, I thought, not my scene anyway, and I switched to a light-hearted dance tune. Too bad if George's father came snooping.

George. Since I'd met Brendan I was looking closely at George. All our lives we've been close, I thought. We were at pre-school together and at primary school, and in the same class at high school. When we played on the floor together George pulled my curls and kissed me whenever he felt like it. Now he looks at me as if I'm some kind of distant beauty.

He wouldn't even dare touch me now, I thought, and I was quite sad.

It was as if he'd read my mood. With a sad sigh he shut the laptop and picked up his violin.

'Practice makes perfect,' he said.

As George drew back his bow to play the opening bars, out of the corner of one eye I caught a movement. I played a couple of bars. Then the movement distracted me again and I had a full view this time. A girl walked past the gate at the front of George's home. Again she appeared, and this time she took a long hard stare up the drive.

There was no mistaking her. It was Saisha, the girl we'd met at Nether Fencote.

The girl I stumbled across in the after school Art Club. She called him the nutter behind the heap of books. Her dad. I remembered her voice. It was dark with anger and frustration. Yes - and pain.

George noticed her, too.

'Oh, my God,' he said. 'She told me I'd to bring twenty quid next time I met her.'

'She was with that skinny kid with the weird-shaped head.'

'And the rough one with short legs and massive muscles. Twenty pounds!'

'And you didn't say no,' I said. 'I bet she's come to collect.'

George's face was hot. 'I bet she has.'

And to prove it, here she came. Striding up the drive as if she owned the place.

The front door bell jangled.

'Quick!' said George. 'Get playing.'

Frantically, he stuck his violin under his chin and began to play. Not a minute too soon because oh!oh! his bedroom door opened and in marched his father.

'A young person to see you, George.'

'Young person?' said George. His surprise sounded so fake I was sure his father couldn't be fooled. 'Who?'

'You may have a few minutes together, but remember that only with practice will you be good enough to achieve your ambitions.'

George went downstairs, and I followed him. I was wondering what next. Some kind of disaster or a bit of a laugh?

'Alright?' he said as if he was chilled when he saw Saisha.

'Alright,' she said, with a defiant glance at George's dad, who was running a suspicious eye over her.

George led the way into the garden. Saisha and I raised eyebrows at each other and followed.

'He'll know me again, won't he?' she said, 'Genius's old man.'

'This is our orchard,' said George. 'Apple trees, pear trees, plums. I climbed that tree this summer to pick the highest fruit. Those bushes are gooseberries. If you eat too many, they ...'

'Don't tell me,' said Saisha. 'I know. They give you belly ache.'

'Vegetables over there - onions, sprouts, leaks.'

'George's mum won first prize at the summer fete for one of her marrows,' I said, though I was pretty sure she wouldn't exactly be fascinated.

George pushed open a wooden gate.

'The geese live here. We'll have to run in case they ...'

'They don't bite,' Saisha scoffed, but she joined George and me in dashing as the gander flapped and hissed and the goose joined in the fun of paddling after us.

'That's William,' I giggled as we squeezed through a beech hedge gate and forced it shut behind us.

'We call him the Conqueror,' said George. He was proud the geese had put on a show.

'And she's Matilda, right?' said Saisha.

George looked at her in surprise. Saisha stuck her tongue out at him.

'No need for the gobsmacked bit,' she said. 'I'm not just a pretty face, you know.'

At the top of the garden was George's father's tool shed.

'It's a combination lock,' said George.

'I can guess the number,' said Saisha.

And she did. I was quite impressed. George's surprise was amazement.

'How ...?'

'Saisha's dad's a magician,' I said. 'I bet he taught her.'

'No-brainer, isn't it?' said Saisha cheerfully. 'When you've called your goose William the Conqueror, it doesn't take Mastermind to guess your combination lock is 1066, the Battle of Hastings. What's inside?'

'You can have a look if you like.'

'Might as well. We've come this far.'

It was her turn to be surprised. She who had played it super-cool now stared in silence at the display of George's father's proudest possessions.

Along the full length of one wall there's this metal shelf. It's never particularly interested me, and now I wondered what the big deal was for Saisha as she worked her way along it, running her fingers over each of the neatly lined-up tools. Every one was state of the art and expensive, greased and labelled.

'He's a bit organised, your old man.'

George was smug. Then his face soured.

'Organised and bossy,' he said.

'Chainsaw,' said Saisha. 'Circular saw. Does he need both? Hedge trimmer.' She read the label on an unopened new box. 'Six-piece 18 volt cordless pack.' She blew through her teeth. 'Six hundred and sixty nine smackers and eighty two pence. So it's peanuts, that twenty quid you promised us.'

George was embarrassed. 'I've been meaning to say ...' he began.

'Don't worry, Genius,' she told him kindly. 'I never thought you could.'

It doesn't add up, I marvelled. She's a teacher's daughter. She's bright, really bright. She knows about Norman churches and about William and Matilda. She's warm and funny and kind. Yet she wanders about the countryside at the head of a gang of rough kids and talks their street-wise talk.

And she eyes up George's dad's tool shed as if she fancies raiding it.

George puffed out his chest. 'Oh, well you know - twenty pounds, we can afford it, of course. It's only twenty pounds. It's just a matter ...'

'Of getting your hands on it. Never mind. There's stuff here worth more than five or six hundred, never mind twenty. Alright if I help myself, is it?'

George shifted from foot to foot in panic.

'Well, I'd have to ask my ...'

'Not now, mind. Some other time.'

'Of course.' George took off his glasses and rubbed their lenses with his fingers. He's sweaty with relief, I thought. 'Some other time.'

'I mean what I say,' Saisha told him, with a threatening flash of those wild eyes. 'You promised, and I'm coming back some other time.'

And I already knew her well enough to suspect she really did mean it.

Chapter 7

Head of Year 11 was Mr Winter. In his own way he was popular with the kids. We only called him Frosty behind his back. It was not that you liked Frosty. You just knew he'd be fair and he'd do his best to understand where you were coming from.

And if you needed the hard word ... well, you'd come to the right place because Frosty didn't hesitate to lay it on the line for you.

Even if you were the Headteacher's daughter.

Like the time this kid called Basil Whitaker threatened to thump me. 'I'll pick my spot, Akinyi smarty pants,' he said, 'and I'll plant my fist on your fat nose end.'

So I got my retaliation in first and he and his friends took his bleeding nose to Frosty. Oh, oh, my dad had to come to Frosty's office for a warning.

The year heads were busy people and I knew the best time to catch Frosty in his office was early on, before school got properly going that Friday morning. He had a big desk and a big seat behind it and he could sit there being pompous when he wanted to. Or, like now he could wave you to one of the padded seats he kept in front of his desk for cosy chats. We sat down together and he listened while I took off on my Fun Fest idea.

He ran his fingers through his wiry hair and raised one eyebrow. He was famous for the wicked stunts he could perform with that single eyebrow. And he could use it to scare the pants off you.

'A Fun Fest ... To raise a lot of money for ... who did you say it was for?'

'Build Africa. It's a charity working for African kids. They'll help us set up a link between Willowbank and a school in Kenya.'

'You've never done things by half, Akinyi.'

'Listen, sir. Can I have a plug-in to the next Enrichment Week? I just need a few hours - an afternoon say. Enough time for some musicians, a comedian and ...'

'Whoaa, slow down.' Frosty flicked through his diary. 'Let's assume that I can wangle you a bit of the Activities Day ... Tuesday afternoon before Half Term. That's October 20th. We have a space to fill there. And what else are you signing us up for?'

'George Newcomb and I can play a violin and clarinet duet, accompanied by Mrs Siddle.'

'Glad to know you're leading from the front.'

'Then there's the Steel Band.'

Akinyi

The eyebrow did its thing. 'I've heard one of those. A fine old racket they'll make, so that ticks a box, I suppose.'

'One of the teachers is a magician. Mr Thirza. I don't mean to be cheeky, but everybody calls him T.'

'Yes, the staff don't do any better, either, sorry to say.'

'He can swallow a sword, you know.' I frowned, thinking about that pile of books. 'He can make himself disappear.'

'You've obviously had a word in his ear. And he's said he'll do the honours, no doubt?'

I nodded. 'And throw in a surprise or two.'

'You could sell snow to the Eskimos, Akinyi. What else?'

'I haven't got much further. I need to know you and my dad are up for it.'

'You realise, of course, that there's the small matter of GCSEs this year. What's your father going to say when you tell him that instead of doing your Biology homework you're Twittering and You Tubing about your jamboree?'

'Six weeks. We've got six weeks. We can do it.'

'You might need Mr Thirza's magic to help you pull it off at that short notice, Akinyi.'

'Are you up for it, sir?'

Frosty leaned back in his chair, hands behind his head. 'Three conditions, Akinyi. One - the Headteacher agrees.'

'I'll handle that.'

'Thanks but no thanks. If we're embarking on this adventure, Akinyi, we do it properly. No favours. No pressure on Mr Mac - I mean the Headteacher.'

'Condition 2?'

'I need more detail. In particular, who are the other people whose arms you have in mind to twist.'

'Give me three or four days and I'll be back to you.'

I stood up and headed for the door.

Frosty didn't move. He spoke quietly. 'There's the small matter of condition 3, Akinyi.'

I knew Frosty, and I recognised a problem when I heard it.

The playful eyebrow was flat. 'You're not going to like this,' he said.

I waited, one hand on the door, sensing trouble.

'It's about you and Brendan.'

I frowned and I could feel myself starting to get seriously nervous. I edged back into the room.

'I think it would be fairest if I brought him here so that I can say this to both of you.'

'Like what?' I whispered. 'What's to say?'

'I'll bring him here, shall I?'

I sat back down in Frosty's office, waiting, wondering.

Frosty was a one-off. Ever since I'd come to Willowbank High from the primary school he'd been my Head of

Akinyi

Year. OK, so we'd had our moments, but he'd given me way more help than grief.

Like when it began to dawn on me that I was different. That I'd been adopted. That I was African by birth. That perhaps I'd been rejected by my natural parents.

Frosty is brave. I trust him, I thought as I sat there in his office, but what's he playing at?

Brendan slouched as Frosty ushered him into the room. His head was down in sullen defiance, always his way with teachers.

'Take a seat, Brendan,' said Frosty.

I stroked the chair beside me, encouraging him with a smile to chill and sit with me. He stayed on his feet, and he screwed his raincoat up in one tight fist.

'I hope you're getting settled into your last year at Willowbank, Brendan,' Frosty said. He sounded laid back, but he'd gone to the big seat behind his big desk and it was obvious our cosy chat was history.

'Should be Willowbank and Ashbrook,' Brendan muttered.

'Fair point.' Frosty nodded. 'And I'll get straight to mine. You two have got to know each other pretty quickly. So you'll know, Brendan, all about Akinyi's Fun Fest plan. Right?'

Brendan gave him a hardly noticeable nod. 'And before you bother mentioning it,' he said. 'I know she's taking nine GCSEs. So?'

I shifted on my chair. I didn't know if I could handle sitting here while these two alpha-males took pot shots at each other about my life.

'So this,' said Frosty. 'You two need to cool things.'

Hot blood flared in my cheeks. I saw the pallor of Brendan's face surge into an unpleasant red.

'Cool what?' he snarled.

I reached out to offer him a soothing hand but found only the raincoat.

'It's alright, Brendan,' I said.

'Cool what? We haven't done anything.'

'Not strictly true, is it?'

'You're a teacher, mate, not a copper.'

I would never have believed that anyone dare speak like that. My eyes shot in alarm to Frosty's face. There, believe it or not, I saw only calm. He was as laid back as ever. If anything, he was mildly amused.

'It's my business to make sure you both do as well as you can at school,' he said. 'You've work to do and exams to pass.'

'She does, you mean. Don't pretend you care what I do. And I couldn't give a monkey's.'

'Thank you, Brendan,' said Frosty. I could have sworn I even detected a chuckle. 'That's exactly my point. You see, Akinyi does care about her exams, and, for your information, her father cares more. If she concentrates on her school work, she'll pass a whole hatful, go into the

6th Form and on to qualifying as a teacher. Or a lawyer or a doctor. She has enough on her plate with this Fun Fest.'

My face was hot as I felt Brendan's gaze switch accusingly to me.

'You think that stuff makes sense, don't you?'

He glared. In the once-innocent blue eyes I saw scorn. The baby-smooth face was twisted into hatred.

'Interfering busybody. He should get a life.'

He stormed from the room.

I felt numb. I could hardly bear to look at Frosty.

'Exams and uni,' I muttered after a silence. 'We might as well have been talking some obscure foreign language.'

Chapter 8

A whole day dragged past, and I didn't even catch sight of Brendan. I was still fed up when I got home that evening. There was supper to make. First I sat down to a couple of hours of homework.

English. We'd talked in class about life and its difficulties. School. Friendship and betrayal. Mums and dads. Embarrassing moments. Moods. Bad hair days. Everybody knew what was coming. Go home and write about it. Teachers are so predictable.

For once, it suited me fine. Life and its difficulties. I didn't need any help from Google or Wikipedia. My fingers took over and gave the keyboard a good rattling.

Not long ago one of my so-called friends called me a hard-faced black bitch. And guess what. She's got a point.

I think I've become hard-faced since my mother died. Her death was so cruel that at first it didn't sink in. I've read this stuff in novels and women's magazines. You know the kind I mean. "Every time a door opened I expected my darling Henrietta to walk in as always, her face alight with love and laughter. Whenever the sun shone I looked out into the garden and it was with a shock that I realised she would never water her magnolias again."

I know that's slushy rubbish, but it was true for me. Coming home from school was the hardest. I always took it for granted that Mum would be there, and the empty silence of the house smacked me in the face whenever I let myself in.

I think that when Mum died and I was left to live alone with my dad I dug a deep pit somewhere in the back of my mind and shovelled into it all my feelings that were not stone-faced. In went any curiosity I had started to feel about Kenya and my birth parents. In went the horrible pain at the loss of my mum. On top, and occasionally showing above the surface of the hole, was my sadness that I couldn't do relaxed and friendly chat with my dad. He is a tired and sad old man and I should look after him better. He deserves a warmer and more comfortable family home. Mum gave him that. I can't.

For the first time I hesitated. This next bit might not make much sense, I thought, but my fingers were already on the move.

My pit containing my deepest and softest feelings would still be sealed if something wonderful hadn't just happened. I've fallen for a boy. His name is B, and he is lovely.

Polite and well-mannered? Er – no. At least not in the ways I've been brought up - say please and thank you, be nice, keep your bedroom tidy. (Not that mine is anything to write home about.)

Hard-working, then, and well-behaved at school? Nope, sorry.

Can I take him home and introduce him to my dad, the Headteacher? Well, put it this way. I'd like to one day - maybe - perhaps, but don't hold your breath.

Again I paused and again my fingers flew.

The loveliest thing is that B talks to me and I can talk to him. He tells me about his family and his childhood, including many painful moments, and he's encouraged me to tell him about the pain I buried in my mind until he came along. I've told B about my mum. I've told him that ever since I can remember Mum and I laughed. We made music together and she sang. B's mum has never done that with him. It wasn't stiff, formal music like my friend George's father makes him play. Mum read stories and poems to me and taught me the old-fashioned nursery rhymes and fairy tales.

One day, when I was only 6 or 7, I came home from school and sang her the song we had learned in class. I still remember the words, and I remember the thrill my song gave Mum.

Down by the riverside the green grass grows

Where Mary Nelson washes her clothes.

She sings, she sings, she sings so sweet,

She calls to her playmates across the street.

Playmates, playmates, won't you come to tea?

Come next Sunday at half past three.

While I sang Mum played along with me on the piano. Soon after that I started on the clarinet, and though I don't have much talent Mum was my best fan.

After school one day - by then I was at the High School - when I came up the drive to our front door my dad opened it for me.

Akinyi

Mum had been poorly in bed for a few days, and I was ready with the tales and the jokes of the day and the suggestion that I would play her some get-well-soon melodies on the clarinet. I was surprised to find Dad at home. He normally works till 6 or 7 in the evening. His face was grey and sad. I knew something was terribly wrong. We sat in the front room. That was unusual, too. Dad explained that the doctor couldn't help Mum any more and she was going to die.

Do you know what I did? I locked myself in the bathroom. I didn't cry. I didn't feel sorry. I didn't feel anything. I sat in the bath, shaved my legs and played some rubbishy music on a new CD player one of my uncles gave me. I actually let that meaningless gadget blot out thoughts of my own mum, who was dying in the next room.

Later, Dad called me into their bedroom. Mum's face was ghastly pale and she was staring at the ceiling.

"I've called the doctor," my dad said. He held Mum's hand. "There doesn't seem to be any pulse."

I saw with a horrid lurch in my stomach that he was helpless, and I grew up years in one moment.

"Mr Winter told us in Biology that you can hold a mirror to the patient's mouth," I told him.

I found a mirror in Mum's bedside drawer, and he held it to her face.

"No sign," he said.

We sat together in numbed silence till an ambulance man rang the front door bell. I didn't see my mum again. When this kid told me that her mum had burned her arm on their brand new electric hob, I imagine I didn't show enough interest. At least you've got a mum, I wanted to scream.

I could stop now, I thought. But no, on I went.

And do you know what? B and I have fallen out. There are things going on his head that I can't get hold of. Mr Winter said he was worried that I was getting distracted from my work. B was furious and said some pretty rude stuff. I was caught in the middle and made a mess of things. Then B was furious with me, too, and he shot out of the room. He's disappeared.

So it must be true. I am a hard-faced bitch and I wouldn't bank on ever being soft again. Especially if B doesn't come back.

I read through my work. I went to *Select All* and my finger hovered over the *Delete* key.

Shock, I told myself. And you haven't got over Mum yet. Not to mention B. You've had to grow up quickly. You're decades older than your mates.

Mmm. Not so sure about that. Decades more screwed up maybe.

I pressed *Delete*.

Chapter 9
Sunday 18th October

Partying fans poured through the streets to the football stadium. An hour before kick-off the pedestrian underpasses that took the crowds across the abandoned railway tracks were already dams. Rovers fans, with their striped red and white tops and scarves were in the noisy good humour of Premier League aristocrats on a run of good form. Sneaking among them came the Blues. They kept their heads down to hide their secret hopes that the Lady Luck would make this a historic day for them and their small town, small club.

Inside the ground, behind the home goal teenagers and young men sent out blasts of tuneless song.

'We are the Ro-vers Boot Boys!'

The firm spread out their marquee banner with its single word daubed in blood red - *ROVERS*. They stamped their boots, and the deep roar of their excitement thundered through the stadium.

The stadium rocked to a fanfare of enthusiastic chants as the announcer bellowed the names of the Rovers players. Shrill whistles greeted his attempt to give a fair hearing to the lowly opposition. The noise was at its loudest as the teams swaggered onto the pitch.

Kick-off time. The ball ballooned high into the floodlights against the gloomy October sky. As they jumped to meet it, two players clashed heads, tumbled to the floor in a heap of tangled limbs and lay still. There was a second of incredulous silence. It dawned on forty thousand Rovers supporters that the opposition had a team, too.

The party mood turned ugly.

Chapter 10

It was a Sunday evening, five weeks after Frosty's interference, when Brendan came to find me.

It should have been a lovely surprise. I was desperate to meet him again. Had been for five long weeks. Desperate to patch up our misunderstanding and to laugh together again. For the first few days, at morning breaks and lunch times I'd ghosted about the school in a pathetic search for him. Couldn't find him anywhere. It was hopeless. I used to imagine that he was following me, toying with me, making sure to stay out of sight. I'd even turn round really suddenly and charge back the way I'd come. It was a dead loss.

I gave up.

Then there he was on a Sunday evening of all times.

Trouble was I had rehearsed all afternoon with Mrs Siddle, the music teacher, and George whose amazing music talent I was relying on to be a hit at our Fun Fest in two days time.

Akinyi

I was still locked into the mind-blowing harmonies we'd been weaving into a pop melody. It was brilliant stuff. It was going to be a massive hit with the audience, we were sure of it.

We were laughing. Hugging ourselves with excitement as we came out of school. I thought for a second George was going to kiss me. And I was carried away enough for that second to think, what the hell, I don't mind if he does. I laughed into his face. Ready for it.

Then ... oh, oh! Brendan emerged from the street shadows and I ran head-first not into his arms but into our biggest bust-up so far.

I was wearing my jet black hair shoulder-length, drawn back from my high cheek bones and my dark, dark eyes. It had cost me a bomb, that hair do, specially for the Fun Fest, and I was proud of it.

I wasn't laughing any more. I knew full well that in the orange street lighting I looked dangerously arrogant.

I knew, too, that nothing about me fazed Brendan.

'You'd better not two-time me, Akinyi,' he said.

His smooth cheeks darkened into a deep scowl. He terrified me, but I squared up to him.

'I'm not even one-timing you,' I said, and I was really sarky. The meeting I'd longed for spiraled out of control. 'You haven't been near me for weeks, in case you haven't noticed. I've looked for you everywhere and you've avoided me.'

'Left you to get on with passing your poncey exams. And your Fun Fest.'

'That was your idea as much as mine, remember. Thanks a bundle for dumping it on me.'

'So? Gives you your chance to mess around with sad Newcomb.'

'You might think he's sad, but we'll be proud to have known him one day, when he's a world famous musician.'

'If he's so brilliant, how come he isn't getting on with his school work, instead of pratting about?'

It was a good question, and I should have told him so.

'Look who's talking,' I snarled instead. 'How many times have you told me you've caused nothing but trouble for your teachers since you were in the infants?'

'Me? I'm different.'

'No, Brendan, that's my line.'

We were right into each other's faces. We were beside my neighbour's wall, where we'd laughed together on our first day. And where he'd have kissed me if Frosty hadn't come blundering out of a meeting with my dad.

'He's a total wimp, that kid,' said Brendan, 'yet you're not bothered about being seen with him. I'd be embarrassed.'

In the dark shadows beyond the pool of orange street light, kids nudged themselves and giggled. At least one of them was lurking so close I was unnerved and had to spin round to drive him off.

'Whey! Hey!'

Akinyi

A spurt of scornful laughter, then a snarl from a girl's voice.

'Shut it, Marksy. Get out of there.'

Saisha.

And those two friends, no doubt - Marksy and Legs.

This is the last thing I need, I raged. I don't want to be their lousy spectator sport,

'He might be a wimp,' I said furiously, 'but I bet one day you'll be glad you knew him.'

'Oh yeah, course I will.'

'Don't give me your sarcasm, Brendan Smart.'

Brendan flared. For a second I thought he might hit me. I glanced in panic into the dark shadows between me and home.

'What planet are you on Akinyi? The bloke's a loser. Do you want to be with a loser or do you want to be with me? Loser!' he sneered, and he swaggered along the street. 'Loo-oozer!'

'Shut it Brendan.'

He turned on me again and brought his face up to mine.

'He's a loser. And you hang out with him, Akinyi, so what does that make you?'

I will not look away again, I told myself. Not for him. No, not even for him.

'You're so full of yourself, Brendan. OK, so you think George and I are losers. One day you'll be begging to be mates with him. You'll be sitting in some grotty pub and he'll appear on Sky News. "Look," you'll brag to all your sad nobody friends, "it's my mate George." Oh yes, you'll tell them, alright, that you were at school with good old George.'

Now I was the one swaggering, taking off Brendan's cocky walk and macho patter.

'Me and George right? Best mates. Oh, yeah, I knew him before he was famous. We go back years, right. You'll be so full of it. You'll use George because your own life will be so sad and pathetic. Who'll be the loser then Brendan? You'll be the loser - and a user and a waster.'

I'd gone too far. I was too smart for my own good. I hated myself for this stupid scene. I ached to call it quits. To reach for him, to hug him.

No chance. His face was hard and his eyes contemptuous.

'That's what you really think isn't it?' he sneered. 'Of me.' He didn't wait for a reply. 'Thought as much.'

He slouched away, looking cool, just like he couldn't care less.

I watched him for three seconds. Tears were streaming down my face. Then I took a deep shuddering breath and dared myself to call after him. The words were only an impulse away. "Don't go. Please. Don't go away again."

Instead, I dashed the tears off my face and I went totally ballistic.

'Nobody decides for me who I see and who I don't,' I yelled.

'Pity you didn't tell that to Frosty.'

He didn't even bother to look back.

And the worst thing was I knew he was right. I stormed homewards.

I hoofed heaps of freshly-fallen beech leaves ahead of me.

I sobbed. I snuffled. I called myself all the silly cows that ever lived.

Chapter 11

The city's helicopter was up, and a dozen police cars sounded their sirens. Rovers had lost, that much was obvious. And there was trouble. Big trouble.

Ambulances howled as they nudged through escaping spectators and bumper-to-bumper traffic. The damp air seeped violence.

In the Music Room, looking down onto the main hall of the Willowbank High School a heavy woman posed straight-backed, head high, at the piano.

Mrs Siddle was performing for the packed and rapt concert hall of her dreams. Her right hand picked out a melody, her left dwelled on the chords. She was a soprano. Years of shouting at kids and singing thankless demos for kids had put a guttural rasp into her voice. She could still lay on the tear-jerking melancholy, though. And she knew it.

'*Come all you maidens, young and fair,*

Akinyi

All you that are blooming in your prime,
Always be 'ware and keep you garden fair,
Let no man steal away your thyme.'

Chapter 12

I was busy re-living my row with Brendan. I was furious with him. And furious with myself.

Plus I was furious with Frosty, who had poked his nose in where it definitely wasn't wanted. Oh, I understood well enough what his thinking was. Headteacher's daughter - GCSEs - his job to make sure I passed my exams with flying colours - not proper for a Year Head to stand by while the Headteacher's daughter got tangled up with a dodgy character from Ashbrook - shocking influence - anything might happen. Blah-di-blah.

Well, anything *had* happened. I'd found a boy who understood me, that's what - and his mother who accepted me with the kind of warmth that was a distant memory in my own life. They didn't run away when they found out how screwed up I was about stuff.

About school and its Headteacher. About my dad - both my dads. About my mum. About both my mums.

Akinyi

Funnily enough, come to think of it, I never worried much about my African mum. Hardly gave her a thought, in fact. That wasn't fair, was it?

When I glanced out of the kitchen window and saw that the school building was glowing in the dark, I thought for a long second that it was a TV scene. Then I realized that was ridiculous, so I switched off the kitchen light and I still couldn't get my head round what was happening. I could make out smoke rolling towards me. As I looked it got suddenly thicker, and a huge puff of it billowed against our kitchen window. It blotted out my view of the garden and the orange sky of the city beyond.

And then it clicked. My God, it was the school. On fire!

The phone rang. My dad answered it. My dad can do the grim-faced look, but this time I instantly knew from his grim-faced silence that I was right. Something horrendous had happened. At the school.

Stunned, he dropped the receiver. Left it dangling by its wire from the wall. I picked it up and listened for a second. Nobody there. I slammed it onto its wall hook.

Then we dashed out, both of us, heading the way nobody ever headed, down the garden, over the fence and across that holy of holies, the school cricket pitch.

Miss Lyon was waiting on the school yard. The school hadn't taken long to pin a good-fun nickname on the Deputy Head with flowing golden hair and yellowy golden brown eyes. She was the Lion. Of course she was.

'This is as close as we can get,' she said, 'without getting barbecued.'

Akinyi

My dad is terrified, I thought. Hardly surprising, since fifteen years of his working life look like they're going up in smoke. Like never before, I'll have to look after him.

I clung to him as we shivered in the darkness. There was a chilly autumn drizzle, but we hadn't given ourselves a moment to grab an outside coat. There was nothing to do but look towards the thump of water-pumping engines, the floodlights, and the blanket of smoke rolling out of the school.

We couldn't even shuffle closer to the building where Dad had been boss for all those years. A fireman blocked our way. He poked his torch first into my face, then into my dad's. Then he whipped back to me.

Nothing different about that. I knew all about such double-takes. I'd known them since I was knee-high, and I knew exactly what the fireman was asking himself. Why is the Headteacher chaperoning a black kid? He was too polite to ask, and I, from years of hard-nosed practice, left him to get on with wondering.

'Station Manager Dafyd Evans,' he said. 'Ashbrook station.'

Dad's carefully groomed silver hair is usually quite distinguished. Not that night, it wasn't. In the torchlight he'd gone old-fogey grey. He has broad shoulders, and he draws them back the way he was trained in the Army. Not that night. That night they'd slumped. Instead of being a really tall man, he was dwarfed by this fireman.

It was agony to see him caught like a scared rabbit in the blinding torch light.

'How much damage?' he asked.

Dafyd Evans spoke with a gently poetic Welsh voice. Just what I needed. It gave me that little bit of hope.

'Eight seventeen it was, when we were called. We reached the school at eight-twenty three and met Miss Lyon at the gate. I called up two more pumps, and they arrived from the city at eight forty. We've just located the seat of the fire.'

'Where was that?'

'First floor, long narrow room on the left at the top of the stairs. Looks down onto the hall. Looked, I should say.'

'The Music Room,' said the Lion.

'Oh, my God!' Dad whispered. 'Mrs Siddle isn't in there, is she?'

We all watched Dafyd Evans' back as he walked away to speak into his radio.

'It's a hell of a mess,' he said turning back, 'but we're pretty sure the building's empty.'

Arc lights flooded the entrance hall. Even from this distance we could tell it was a disaster area. I edged round the fire-fighter to peer through a tangle of hoses. My dad flat-footed behind me in his misery.

The front door was smashed.

'Sorry we had to break our way in,' said Dafyd Evans.

Things had been tossed out onto the steps. Surely, that was a display board dangling from its frame. And a scattering of torn and drowned paintings. I recognised the pitiful remains of a magnificent display of Sixth Formers' work. T's Art Department had given me a conducted tour of those paintings, pottery and sculptures only three days earlier, their bit for my Fun Fest.

I was choked.

'It might not look like it to you, but we'll soon be in control,' Dafyd Evans said. 'It was touch and go, mind you.'

'All that revolting water.' My dad murmured his agony.

'Could have been worse, Mr Macdonald. Two more minutes and the fire would have been through the hall roof. You'll soon get it back to rights.'

'Only by closing the school, I suppose.'

'That's not on,' said the Lion.

Tears of gratitude pricked my eyes, as the Lion, brave and decisive, took my dad's arm. Though she was new to the school, had hardly known him six weeks, she was already the only person who could get away with that.

She's the best teacher in the school, I thought. As good as Frosty. She doesn't get uptight about how to treat the Headteacher. When it suits her, he's just another parent. She can do that and still give him his headteacherly respect. And when she thinks something needs saying, like she does now, out she comes with it. My dad's supposed to be the boss, but right now he's looking for her to show the way.

'If someone lit this fire,' she said, 'we won't give them the satisfaction of closing the school.'

Akinyi

'Lit the fire!' My dad stared from her to Dafyd Evans. 'Are you suggesting ...?'

'Too early to say for certain, Mr Macdonald.' The fire-fighter shrugged. 'We got here just in time for the flashover.'

He saw that he needed to explain. 'Your Music Room filled with thick smoke, see, and a lot of heat. Probably quite quickly. Then the window above the hall gave way. Oxygen rushed in. Up went the flames. Like a ball of fire across the hall ceiling. We were there just in time to get jets onto it.'

'Quite quickly?' said the Lion sharply. 'How quickly?'

'Twenty minutes, twenty five maybe. If I was a betting man I know where I'd put my money. You know kids nowadays ...'

The Lion was in his face. 'Kids?' she said. 'Who said anything about kids?'

The fire-fighter backed off. 'No offence. We often get hoaxes, specially on the Ashbrook Estate. We drive to the scene and run into an ambush of flying bricks and bottles. Kids every time.'

'We'll keep an open mind. If it was a kid or kids from this school you can be sure we'll find out who.'

Dafyd Evans nodded, but he didn't fool me. I knew he wasn't convinced.

'Twenty minutes you said,' the Lion reminded him.

'Difficult to say exactly, you know, Miss Lyon. But it's been a quickish build-up. Twenty, twenty five minutes.'

Akinyi

'So you're saying it started at what? Gone half past 7?'

'Our dogs will be on the scene tomorrow, sniffing for an accelerant. We'll know more exactly when we've fully investigated, but I'd say well after half past. Ten to 8. Maybe as late as eight o'clock.'

A man appeared from the darkness. 'Evening, Mr Mac - Miss Lyon,' said Frosty. 'Guessed I'd find you here.'

'Just passing, I suppose?' said the Lion.

She hid the smile that I saw light up her face in the hellish glare of the flames and the arc lights. Not quickly enough, though, to stop me rumbling how much they fancied each other. Some secret to have spotted!

'Heard the news from the city, Mr Mac?' Frosty turned to my dad, raising the famous eyebrow.

My dad's vacant look said it all. He was miles away, hadn't even heard the question, never mind the news.

I spoke for him. 'We haven't watched the TV,' I told Frosty. I gestured into the dancing shadows. 'The fire ...'

'Understandable,' he said. 'There's a full-scale police alert. A policewoman was killed at the Rovers football match.'

It was a shocking moment, and I was already numb from the fire, so it didn't sink in properly. My dad had got the message. He dug his finger nails into one side of his grey face. Even the Lion was at a loss. She stared at Frosty with wide eyes, one hand across her lips.

'My fault.' Dafyd Evans muttered. 'Didn't realise you weren't aware.'

'It never rains ... and all that,' said Frosty. 'We can only concentrate on our own problem. We can't rely on much help, at least for now. I've walked round the school with Martin Philips, the community constable. We did our best. Checked doors and ground floor windows, darkness permitting. There's no sign of forced entry. Martin says his forensic colleagues will have some ideas by the morning, and CID will divert some attention to us if and when they can. It's everybody on murder alert for them.'

'Can't blame them, can you?' said the Lion.

'At least we have Martin,' said Frosty. 'He's phoned Mrs Siddle and gone for a word with her at home. He may need to take her to the station. If there's space. In the meantime, I suppose there's no legitimate reason for anybody else to have been in the Music Room on a Sunday evening?'

'Oh good heavens!' my dad bubbled. 'Akinyi, you and George were with Mrs Siddle all afternoon, I assume.'

Frosty turned to me. I'd known him for four years and I knew it wasn't just the eyebrow. His whole face was lively. He could do the favourite Uncle Frosty look, straight from a children's colouring book. Next moment you saw the hard edge of the stare that made kids tremble, as if he was a policeman or a private eye, not a teacher. It logged every twitch and read every thought.

'I knew you were rehearsing with Mrs Siddle, Akinyi. I didn't think you'd pitch camp for the weekend,' he said.

'It was our last chance before Tuesday's Fun Fest.'

'What time did you leave?' said the Lion.

'Probably - it was quarter past seven.'

'All of you?'

'Sorry?'

'Did the three of you leave together, you and George and Mrs Siddle?'

'No. Mrs Siddle stayed behind to feed her dog.'

'Damned dog,' Frosty growled.

'Fill me in,' said the Lion. 'Her dog is news to me.'

'She has a terrier,' I said. 'A Jack Russell pup. Pirate.'

'And she brings it into school.' With that eloquent eyebrow, Frosty might as well have shouted his scorn on prime-time TV.

'She's always had a dog and let it follow her everywhere,' my dad said. 'Evenings and weekends. I don't allow staff dogs on the premises in school hours. Mrs Siddle understands that.'

The Lion's controlled face gave away fewer of her thoughts and feelings than Frosty's single eyebrow did.

'So you and George left the building together,' she said.

'Which way did you go?' he eyebrowed.

'Down the staircase to the entrance hall, out through the front door.'

'See any smoke?' said Frosty.

I shook my head.

'Smell burning?'

Akinyi

Again.

'Notice any suspicious characters hanging about?'

My lips must have tightened a millimetre. To Frosty that was as good as a signed confession. He pounced.

'Met somebody in the street, didn't you?'

I squirmed. I glanced at the Lion and at my dad, and I knew I'd screwed up.

'Yes.'

'Brendan?'

Hot anger spread through my cheeks and down my neck. I've already told Brendan this evening that I'll see whoever I want, I thought. Now I'm going to have to tell Dad and Frosty the same.

'So what?' I squirmed to hear my voice grate like an out-of-tune violin.

His voice was the opposite, sonata sweet. 'Still around, is he? I thought we'd come to an agreement.'

'Might have.' I packed the words with defiance and glanced sideways to see what my dad thought.

'What's this, Akinyi?' His face was full of hurt and reproach.

'Nothing, Dad.' I blocked him with a snarl. 'Don't worry about it.'

Frosty cut in. This was not the time for family tiffs. Now he poked his nose right into my business.

'Brendan - walked you home, did he?'

'He wanted to, but I wouldn't let him.'

Frosty waited.

I didn't want to, but I had to back down. 'We fell out.'

'He didn't like you being with George. Right?'

'Exactly. You stopped me seeing him ...'

'Seeing him? Who are we talking about?' Poor Dad was lost.

Frosty ignored him. 'So that you could concentrate on organising the Fun Fest and getting on with your exam work,' he told me.

'I'm sorry,' my dad butted in. 'Could someone fill me in?'

'Mr Winter stopped me going out with Brendan,' I snarled. 'He's an Ashbrook Estate boy, so naturally I could get pregnant at any moment.'

Dad looked more lonely, more wounded than ever.

'Akinyi,' he pleaded, 'how could you - the thought never so much as crossed ...'

'I wish I'd never agreed to stop seeing Brendan. He doesn't think it's fair and neither do I.'

'So you had a humdinger tonight,' said the Lion.

I nodded. 'Sort of.'

'And off he went in a huff?'

'I'll make up with him first thing tomorrow.'

'Was anybody with him when he left you?' Frosty asked.

'No, but it wasn't just Brendan. There were some other kids hanging about.'

'Their names?'

'I can't be sure. They stayed in the shadows. Maybe a strange boy and a moody one with short legs. Kids from Ashbrook.'

Along with Saisha, daughter of T the Art teacher. I kept quiet about her. I'd have it out with Saisha in my own time.

'And a girl, but I didn't see her,' I said.

'Jonathan Marks and Leonard Longley,' said Frosty.

'Arsonists?' said the Lion sharply.

Frosty shook his head. 'Friend Brendan, however ...'

I sucked my teeth. The Lion glanced at my dad, and he nodded his permission for her to take Frosty aside and whisper in his ear. I wasn't standing for that.

'If it's Brendan's character you're assassinating,' I said, 'I have a right to hear.'

The Lion glanced at Frosty. 'I don't know what Brendan has told you, Akinyi,' he said. 'About his form.'

'His form?' What was he talking about? 'Try me,' I blustered.

'Brendan is a burglar and an arsonist,' said Frosty.

His voice was matter-of-fact. Take it or leave it. There was nothing to debate.

'Convictions?' snapped the Lion.

'You'll find his file makes interesting reading. It's a year or so since he was last in court. Broke into a warehouse. Stole goods worth a few thousand pounds. Started a fire causing two hundred grand's worth of damage. Convicted with half a dozen similar cases taken into consideration. Three years probation.'

Silence.

'An interesting young man,' Frosty went on.

He met my eye. Dead level. No funny eyebrow. No blink.

Just look at him, I thought. Telling me I told you so.

'And he was here tonight,' he said, 'out of sorts with the Headteacher's daughter. I think a community constable chat will be in order in the morning.'

'Right,' said the Lion. 'Set it up with PC Philips. Brendan's parents, too, of course.'

'His mum,' said Frosty. 'And step dad.'

'And the probation officer.'

I was appalled. 'It can't have been him,' I protested.

I might as well have saved my breath.

'Let's see how the firemen are getting on,' said the Lion.

'There's so much to arrange.' My dad jerked his hands to the sides of his face.

He looked bewildered and exhausted.

'Brendan was with me. Then he went home. I'm sure of it,' I said.

The Lion and Frosty hardly gave me more than a glance.

They were so certain. They knew so much more about the world than I did. I was scared. And irritated.

In fact, I was furious.

I didn't look into Dad's eyes. I couldn't. I knew I'd see unbearable disappointment and pain. He was my dad, and his heart was breaking, but I had to abandon him.

First, I'll go home for my outdoor coat, I thought. Then I'll walk into Ashbrook to find out the truth from Brendan.

And warn him.

Chapter 13

It didn't take long for me to have second thoughts. It was when I'd crossed Willow Bridge and plunged into the dark streets of Ashbrook. I crossed the road to avoid the threatening shadows and the ugly laughter of men and boys loitering beneath a flickering street lamp. Their joints glowed in the dark, and that whiff … well, who knows what it was, best not go there.

What would Brendan and Anita make of me turning up at this hour of the night?

With Brendan I'd walked hand in hand through the streets and arrived at his house warm with laughter. Some chance of laughter when I turned up at 10 o'clock at night! It wasn't even as if I had in mind to say sorry for the row we'd had.

I did want to say sorry. But not yet. First I wanted to check out this talk of "form". What was it all about? Did it really mean he was an arsonist? An arsonist who would set fire to our school. Our school. My dad's school.

Akinyi

Oh God, I hope not. It's not possible. Is it?

He was the first friend I'd ever had who understood. I mean really understood that I was an outsider. That I didn't belong. That it was hard to be the Headteacher's daughter ... and at the same time not his daughter at all.

Burned the school - I couldn't bear it if it was true.

As I walked along Brendan's street I had to duck and put my hands over my ears. A helicopter clattered overhead, picking me up in its dazzling searchlight.

Why were they zooming in so low and so late at night? It was as if they wanted to freak me out.

And they were succeeding. They were doing my head in.

The front room light was on and I could hear the TV. At least I wouldn't dig the family out of bed. That was a relief.

I rang the doorbell and waited. Anita clawed back the curtains and peered out. Who can blame her, I thought. Who wants uninvited guests at ten at night?

Anita rattled a door chain and spoke through the smallest of openings. Her voice had a grittiness of hostility I hadn't heard before.

'Who is it this time?'

'It's only me, Anita. Akinyi. Can I come in?'

'Akinyi! Now what's happened?'

'Can I come in and talk? Just for a minute. With you and Brendan.'

'What about?' Anita grumbled, but she freed the chain and opened the door. 'We've just got back from the station.'

'And she doesn't mean bus.' It was Brendan's voice, harsh and raised to make himself heard above the TV.

'It's alright,' I said. 'I won't be a minute.'

'He'll be at school tomorrow morning, Akinyi love. What are you doing out here in Ashbrook at this time of night? Don't tell me you're on your own, are you?'

'I am, yes.'

'Couldn't you have waited till tomorrow?'

I was still on the doorstep. I hugged myself against the chill of the night and thought it was a good question.

'Please, Anita.'

'We've told the cops everything we know.'

Brendan was slumped on the sofa in front of the gas fire and the TV. He hadn't even a "hi" for me. He had the volume turned up full blast, and he was chewing gum.

He blanked me.

I felt sick, while the TV blared.

'Sit you down, Akinyi,' Anita said.

I couldn't wait, and I sat as close to Brendan as he'd let me.

'Brendan,' I pleaded. 'Couldn't you turn it down a minute? Please.'

'Take your pick,' he said. 'It's the telly or the helicopter.'

I was shivering, I was scared and I didn't know what I was doing there. I did know that in a minute I'd lose my cool.

'Look, Brendan, there's been a fire at school.'

Bull's eye. I felt his slouching body stiffen.

'A great big fire.'

He sat up.

'They're wondering how it started.'

From the glass-topped table he grabbed the remote.

'They think it was on purpose.'

Brendan poked the off-button and the room was silent. For a panicky moment I wished I could duck back into the meaningless din of the TV.

We waited as the helicopter made a run along a nearby street. The silence settled.

'You said they,' said Brendan. 'Who's they?'

'Well, who do you think? My dad, of course. The Lion. Frosty.'

'I see,' said Anita quietly. 'A cop gets killed and her mates run our Brendan into the station. There's a fire, so Bingo, now it's the school's turn to come knocking.'

I put a hand - I couldn't resist it - onto Brendan's knee. He didn't push me away.

Silence.

'They say he has the form, Anita,' I said, hardly above a whisper.

Silence. Horrible, clock-ticking, pin-dropping, hostile silence.

'And that makes it right for them to come here every time, doesn't it?' Anita was weary. 'In case you haven't noticed, Akinyi, our Brendan's gone straight for weeks. Since you've known him, in fact.'

'I'm glad. But ...'

'And the only reason why the police let him out of the station tonight was because he told them he spent the evening with you. You happen to be the Headteacher person's daughter. They were impressed by that, I can tell you. Oh yes. They tried to check with your father on the telephone, but they got an answering machine.'

'Surprise, surprise,' said Brendan. 'I don't suppose it's every night his school catches fire.'

'They let our Brendan go when his probation officer turned up,' said Anita. 'Anyway, they'd picked up so many kids from the football match they hadn't got time to do much more than push them all around a bit. Brendan couldn't have murdered the woman. I told them till I was blue in the face. It's no good asking our Brendan. He plays dumb. That's a trick he learned from his father.'

I squeezed his arm. 'Speak, Brendan,' I said. 'Murdered somebody. That's ridiculous. You couldn't.'

'Of course he couldn't,' said Anita. 'He wasn't even at the football match. Were you, Brendan?'

'No, of course he wasn't,' I said. 'And even if he had been, why would he kill a police lady?'

Brendan stared at the blank TV screen, saying nothing.

'The dumb trick even at home.' Anita only just controlled her rage.

Brendan stood. 'It's chucking out time at the pubs,' he said. 'I'll walk you home.'

Anita saw us to the door.

'You're just like my dad,' I smiled at her.

'How's that, love?'

I touched her arm. 'You're tired,' I said. 'Tired and sad.'

Scared, too, I thought.

'You're the first person to have a good influence on him, Akinyi. Since he was a toddler.' There were tears in Anita's eyes. 'I had such high hopes.'

'Waterworks time,' said Brendan. 'We're out of here.'

He took my arm and pulled me gently away. It wasn't much but it was the best moment of my disastrous evening.

'Frosty says you have form, Brendan,' I said as we walked along the street.

'It's his job to know, so why not?'

'What is that, Brendan? Form?'

'Form?' he snarled. 'It's when they come knocking at your door every time a house gets burgled. That's form.'

I hesitated. 'Frosty says you've done stealing and burglary.'

'And the rest.'

Akinyi

'The rest?' I said. My voice was hoarse. 'Is that fires?'

'Yeah, I've done fires.'

I hesitated again. It was painful. I was scared to know the answer.

'Brendan,' I began. 'Did you ...?'

'No, I didn't.'

I sighed. 'Frosty ... and a policeman. They're coming to see you tomorrow.'

He laughed. I stopped him under a street light and checked his face.

'Are you laughing, Brendan?' I said.

'Course I am. Why not?'

'But ... the police. They want to talk to you. They think you set fire to the school.'

'I heard you, Akinyi. And I laughed.'

'How you can laugh when you're in trouble like this?'

'Trouble? This isn't trouble. Trouble's when you've done it.'

'But, Brendan, they're going to ask you ...'

'I can tell you what they're going to ask me. They've asked it all before.'

On the flyover the motorway was quiet. So quiet I could hear the river as it rushed beneath Willow Bridge. Brendan climbed onto the stone parapet and spat into the darkness below.

'Now then, Brendan my lad,' he said.

I laughed. He was good.

'Hey,' I said, 'you'd make a good policeman in a school play.'

'Now then, Brendan, my lad, who were you with tonight?'

'And what's the answer?'

'Hey up, that's not fair. You didn't tell me I had to do the answers as well.'

'OK. Then I'll answer for you.' I put on his young man voice. 'I was with a girl and two boys. Their names are …'

'Whoa! Knock it off. I don't know any names.'

'Of course you do. You were with me for starters.'

He shook his head. Now he wasn't laughing. 'Not that I know of,' he said.

'But, Brendan …'

'Can't help you.' He strolled along the parapet. 'There were some other kids around. Can't remember who.'

'Brendan …'

'This is how it goes, Akinyi. Listen.' He jumped off the bridge wall and stood with me. 'OK, says Frosty. You won't mind if I guess. Guessing, I say. That'll get you nowhere. You and Akinyi have a fight, he says. She leaves you. What did you do then? Came home, I say. Arriving at what time? he says. Dunno, I say. Like I told the cops, there was no need to notice.'

'But, Brendan, is it true?'

'True? What do mean, true? I haven't said anything yet.'

'Will your mum be with you?'

'Course she will. Cops can't talk to me without her. I'm a juvenile, aren't I?'

'And what does Anita say?'

'My mam? She knows what to say. She tells the truth. Stone cold. Why not?'

'Go on then. What does she say?'

'Ask her.'

I giggled. 'I can't do the voices the way you can.'

'It comes with practice.'

'Right.' I took a breath. 'Anita, what time did Brendan get home? And I've stopped joking, Brendan. I want the truth.'

'OK, joke over. Now tell the officer the truth, Mam. Well, says Mam. He wasn't late, I do know that. Eight. Quarter to. Quarter past. She's had enough, has Mam. She unfolds her arms. That always means somebody's going to catch it. Then she goes into orbit. I don't believe our Brendan is stupid enough to be around when a policewoman gets done in, she screams. Or to light another fire. He knows the cops would take him away this time. I've told him. Any more trouble, my lad, and I'm having you put into care. I can't take any more of this. I'm already under the doctor with my nerves. Depressed. That's what he says I am. I need a quiet life, the doctor says. Our Brendan knows that, and he's promised me to go straight.'

'Brendan, you're sick.'

'What, me? What have I done?'

'Laughing at your own mum like that. It's not fair.'

He leaned over the wall and spat into the river.

'No, you're right,' he said. 'My mam means everything I've just said. She's had enough. More than.'

We were thoughtful as we sauntered up the hill into Willowbank.

'It's been rough for Mam, life in Ashbrook.'

He was quiet and I gave him time.

'Not like my Grandma. She was Rosebud born and bred. Terrace house. Right down in the city. She knew everybody. Down there, when the law came knocking Grandma knew she had back-up. Neighbours. Friends. Family. None of them were far off.'

I tried to imagine it.

'Here, Mam's on her own, even if her useless Eric is at home. First sniff of trouble and he sneaks off to bed. Leaves her to get on with it.'

'I'm sorry I was horrible to you earlier,' I said. 'I'll stand by you now whatever happens.'

The laughter really was over, and he snapped at me.

'Whatever happens, what's that supposed to mean?'

'Brendan, I only ...'

'Teachers and cops. Now it's a fire, and it's them you believe.'

'But Brendan, I'm not a teacher. I'm not a cop either.'

'It's the same every time. Frosty had a go at us and you sided with him.'

'I want to stand beside you. I've just said it. Whatever happens.'

'I've done nothing wrong, so what can happen?'

We were at the drive to my house.

'Will I see you at school tomorrow?' I asked.

'I'm usually there.'

I was helpless. I hadn't meant to upset him. Just the opposite. But somehow I'd stirred up his rage. Again. In the space of two seconds.

It was impossible.

And now he disappeared along the street, and yet again I'd lost him.

Chapter 14
Monday 19th October

The fire had shocked me, and Monday morning's daylight did nothing to help.

A thousand kids picked their way, wide-eyed, along smoke-grimed corridors to sit at smoke-smeared desks in classrooms with blackened windows. Instead of the usual carry-on of pushing, jostling, laughing and shouting, kids were stunned, even the boys. They could normally find something to joke or to scrap about, but this was something else, a bit like groping your way around in the dark.

We had to stay with Form Tutors for the first hour.

Except me.

Frosty appeared in our class. 'You're needed in the Headteacher's study, Akinyi.'

'Nothing's happened to him, has it?' I asked nervously. 'Is he poorly?'

'No, no, he's fine Akinyi. Nothing that a good night's sleep wouldn't put right.'

'Well then, what …?'

'It's the police. They need a word.'

We hurried along the corridors. The police? I didn't like the sound of it. I'd never spoken to a policeman in my life.

Frosty pooh-poohed my anxiety. 'You'll be fine. Just stick to the truth,' he said.

Charming, I thought. That's supposed to make me feel better, is it?

'The truth? About what? What truth?'

Frosty was already tapping on my dad's office door. He opened it and ushered me in. A raised eyebrow, a knowing wink, and he was gone, leaving me to wonder and to wait for my dad to explain.

He stood up from behind his desk and nodded at a thin man, who stood, too, and offered me his hand. I didn't take it. I was too busy looking to my dad. When's he going to tell me what gives, I thought.

'This is Detective Chief Inspector Cardew, Akinyi. I've given him permission to ask you some questions.'

'There's no need to be alarmed, Akinyi.'

I was miffed to see that the policeman was quite at home, thank you, inside the dark suit, with its waistcoat, white shirt and closely fitting tie. Calm and confident. Unlike my stressed-out dad.

Akinyi

'You're wondering why you're here,' Detective Chief Inspector Cardew said.

'You could say that,' I nodded and agreed.

'It's not a mystery, Akinyi. Sit down.'

He nodded to a chair close to his own. Our knees weren't touching but it was a close thing. I tried shifting away without making it too obvious. Cardew crossed his legs and sat cat-on-mouse still with cradled hands in his knees. The skin on his hands was so pale I could see a network of veins, and his fingers were slender, with cared-for nails.

My dad stayed in his headteacher chair, hiding his own fretfully shifting fingers behind his headteacher desk. He looked on with tired eyes and that creased grey papier mâché look from last night's shock.

'You were in the school a few minutes before it was set on fire,' said Cardew. It was a simple statement, expressing real interest. 'Your father and I have agreed that it will be in order for us to talk things over together here - rather than at the police station.'

It was his quiet self-confidence I didn't care for. There's a machine-like smoothness about it, I thought. Maybe my dad was like that once. Never again, I'm pretty sure of that. Not after this fire.

'You wouldn't prefer the station, would you?'

Oh, oh, the humorous bit now. A little joke, with the faintest hint of a smile. It was meant to remind me he was the big policeman and could call the shots.

I looked at my dad for a bit of help, and he shook his head. I silently clicked my tongue and tut-tutted. That's my dad, I thought irritably. He looks what he is, a man who's been up all night.

'So you and I will have our little chat here,' the Detective Chief Inspector continued, 'where your father can be sure that you're alright. OK?'

I looked at my dad again, and again he gave me his weary nod.

'Let's see how we get on, shall we?' Cardew smiled. A real smile this time. 'I want to check a few facts. You were in school yesterday afternoon.'

'Yes.'

'Practising your music with one of your teachers, Mrs Siddle. Can you remember what time it was when you left?'

'Of course I can. It was only yesterday.'

The two men shared a quick glance, a same-wavelength smile, oh so serious on my dad's part, gently amused on the Detective Chief Inspector's. I couldn't help noticing that where my dad's forehead was cramped with tension, Cardew's had the smoothness of a much younger man. He was in control of his life. Yet I had a feeling they weren't far off the same age.

'It was 7.15. Mrs Siddle told us it was time for home, and we left, George and I.'

'George Newcomb?'

Akinyi

'Yes. We're working together on a music piece for the Fun Fest tomorrow afternoon.'

'And very talented the pair of you, I understand.'

'Thank you.'

'So you left at 7.15. What about Mrs Siddle?'

'She stayed behind.'

'To feed her dog. Am I right? What happened when you left the school building?'

'I went into the street.'

'Where you met Brendan Smart.'

'We had a chat and then I went home.'

Cardew waited with that little smile. Obviously he knew more and was watching.

'Well, we had an argument.'

'Thank you, Akinyi. And then you went home. Did Brendan go with you?'

'Not likely. We'd just had a massive row.'

'Did anybody see you go home?'

I shrugged. 'I doubt it. Why would they?'

'Did Brendan go home, too?'

Again I shrugged the question off, making out I didn't care either way. 'I suppose so, yes.'

'But you didn't see him go?'

'No, I was busy stropping off in the opposite direction.'

Akinyi

'You didn't look back?'

'I wanted to but I didn't.'

'So you don't know if he went down the hill towards the bridge and the road home to Ashbrook ... or if he turned back into school?'

I wondered if I could stare him out.

Hopeless. He met my eye with that smooth confidence. I had to admit that, for all I knew, Brendan might have gone in either direction.

Cardew looked down at his lap, just long enough to flick a speck of dust from one knee of his smart suit.

'As it happens, your father can confirm what time you arrived home, Akinyi. Brendan's movements on the other hand ...' Looking up, he changed tactics. 'How did you first meet Brendan?'

I was seriously put out. To talk about Brendan with a policeman was bad enough. In front of my dad ... well, some things just aren't on, are they?

'It's ironic, really, that it was the Lion who introduced us,' I said carefully.

'That's Miss Lyon, one of my deputies,' my dad said from his observation post on the sidelines.

Cardew nodded. 'Tell me about irony,' he said. 'It's one of those concepts that have passed me by.'

Yeah, right. 'You seem to know most things,' I said sulkily. 'I bet you already know that Mr Winter tried to split us up. One teacher brings us together. Another splits us up. That's irony.'

'Ah, and how did Miss Lyon bring you together?'

'She needed two messengers to take a note round the classrooms.'

I thought my little smile was secret enough, but no - he spotted it.

And I spotted him spotting me. Got you, I thought. Now I know for sure that you're practised and clever. And dangerous.

'A good moment, was it?' he said.

'Yes it was, actually. Since you ask.'

'You went together, I take it?'

No way was I about to share with Cardew and my dad that mind-blowing moment when Brendan suggested we should flush the notes down the bog and go home.

'Look,' I said rebelliously. 'Why are you asking me this stuff? I thought I was here about the fire.'

Cardew studied me with his gentle calm. 'Humour me,' he said.

There was nothing weak about him, just that he wouldn't let go.

'It can be annoying, I know,' he said, 'but I do like to form the picture as clearly as I can,'

It wasn't too pushy, but I didn't find it friendly either.

'Picture?' I grumbled. 'What picture?'

'You and Brendan. I'm learning a lot about you both .'

'Do you think we lit the fire?'

Akinyi

'Probably not both of you, no.'

He was poker-faced. The words were cold. I could be looking into a dark hole, I thought. Maybe there's nothing behind his smile and his smooth face. No sympathy. No understanding. Just a clear, cold brain sussing me out. Is it possible that he really believes, even for a moment, that I might make a shambles of my father's school?

And Brendan? Well, there was no need to wonder if the Detective Chief Inspector suspected him. After all, he'd have the details of Brendan's famous form at his finger tips. Wouldn't he just!

'You were telling me how you set off round the school with your exciting new friend,' he said.

I didn't like it. What right, if any, I wondered, have I to tell this policeman to get lost, I'm not playing any more?

'He was nervous,' I said unwillingly.

'That's interesting. I didn't have him down as the nervous type.'

'That stuff isn't his scene. Knocking on classroom doors. Kowtowing to teachers. Hundreds of kids staring at me, he said. I soon put him straight about that.'

'Oh? How, in particular?'

'How do you think? They stare at me all day and every day, don't they?'

'How's that?'

'Oh, come on! There's loads of Afro Caribbean and Asian kids at Willowbank, but I'm the only African kid in the place. And you'd better believe I'm the only one whose dad is the Headteacher.'

That shut him up. Yet all he did was wait. It wasn't fair. I was the one niggled by the silence, while he seemed to get a kick out of it. And at last I was the one who sighed impatiently and spoke.

'I told Brendan he didn't have to be scared, and he told me nothing scared him.'

'You believed him?'

'Perhaps. I didn't know. Anyway, I told him I was setting off with the notes, and away I trotted like the good little girl I am.'

'Do you think he's a good-looking young man?'

I scowled 'What!'

Was he joking? Did he seriously expect me to tell him, in front of my own dad, how much I fancied Brendan? And if so, why?

'What do you think?' I said.

'Beauty is in the eye of the beholder, Akinyi.'

He was seriously getting up my nose. Why did he never commit himself? I wanted to tell him. Your problem, Chief Inspector Cardew, I'd say, is that you don't commit.

I gave him a dirty look.

'Go and behold him then,' I said.

Cheeky!

'Akinyi!' That was my dad having a little go at me.

Cardew smiled, but I didn't trust him.

'I'm an old man, Akinyi,' he said. 'Tell me what you see.'

'People who don't know him mis-read the signs, and that's what I did.'

'That's honest. And interesting. Tell me what you mean.'

'I thought he needed looking after. Come with me, I said, and I'll show you what to do.'

'And the signs you'd misread?'

'I thought he was shy.'

'But?'

'I had the feeling he hadn't often chatted up a girl. Not one like me, anyway.'

I could feel my dad's gaze fixed to my face and I shifted irritably in my seat.

'Not that I know a lot about boys. Except for George.'

'So Brendan is no George?'

'The other way round,' I sniffed. 'George isn't a patch on Brendan. He's gawky but he doesn't know it. He swaggers, and he shows off, while Brendan ...'

I stopped. My face was hot. This conversation was seriously embarrassing. I'd had enough of it.

Detective Chief Inspector Cardew gave me a moment.

'While Brendan ... ?' he prompted.

He's getting his picture alright, I raged. Not a picture of me. Oh no, it's not me he's painting in his police artist mind, but Brendan. I understand that now, and I'm going to stuff him. I'll make him see my Brendan, not the Brendan he's manipulating me into painting for him.

And while I'm at it, I'll take my chance to tell my dad. I'll show him my Brendan. I'll blot out the Brendan of his headteacherly imagination.

They want a picture, so the picture I give them will be my picture. And let them use that, if they can, to stick alongside his form as proof that he lit the fire.

'I've told you,' I snapped. 'We could talk to each other from the start.'

'What did you talk about? Give me an example.'

I sighed, raging again. I can't get anywhere with this policeman. Has he any right to pry into my business this way?

I glanced at my dad, who smiled and nodded his encouragement. I had a nasty impulse to take a swipe at him.

'For example,' I said, 'I told him what I'd never said to anybody before, that I'm the Headteacher's daughter. I normally leave people to stumble into that little conversation stopper in their own time.'

Dad's smile vanished. He looked ready to drop, and I was ashamed of my spite.

'It was a shock for Brendan and he felt awkward,' I said. 'Just for a minute. Then he realised that maybe he didn't

Akinyi

need to run away after all. It was a good moment. I was pleased with myself.'

I paused, and I treated both men to a stroppy smile. 'And I still am.'

I met my dad's eye, and stared him out. That was a doddle, compared with trying it on with the policeman.

I looked at Cardew, sure I'd said enough.

'Will that do?' I asked.

He dipped his head. 'Feel free to go on.'

'Have I helped you paint your masterpiece?'

He rubbed his nose, and again he waited in silence.

'Will you go to Brendan's class and arrest him when we've finished?' I said. 'Or will it be me you arrest?'

'I don't think we're quite ready for an arrest, Akinyi, do you?'

'I'll go back to my class then.' I stood up.

'Think for a moment or two before you go. Is there anything else you want to tell me?'

I wasn't keen, but I sat down again.

'About Brendan or about Sunday evening?'

'You tell me, Akinyi. There may be something you still want to say. After all, it's Brendan you've got yourself involved with, not just any Ashbrook boy.'

'So?'

'So let's say he's a lad with an interesting record. You are the Headteacher's daughter, and you've been sucked into something outside your understanding.'

People kept ramming it into my face. Winding me up. Frosty. The Lion. And now this police Detective Chief Inspector.

'I wouldn't have missed what I've learned from Brendan and from his mum and from Ashbrook,' I said. 'Wouldn't have missed it for anything.'

I've had it up to here with these two old men, I thought, one a freaky policeman-witch doctor prying into my life, the other my clapped-out old dad sitting by and letting him get on with it. I straightened my school skirt and sat up in my chair. I was ready to walk out.

'He was the first person I've known who understood what it was like for me to be ...'

I looked at Dad again, and I hesitated to bring him yet more pain.

I wasn't surprised that Cardew didn't hang about. He still had hopes of getting me to dish the dirt on Brendan.

'For you to be what? Black?' He spotted that I winced, and he leaned on me. 'Adopted?'

Maybe I winced again, but inside I was calm now. In a minute this would be over. For once I could hold my head up, pleased that I hadn't betrayed Brendan. Pleased that I'd justified myself to my dad.

'I've never been ashamed to be adopted,' I said, 'but Brendan is the only proper friend I've got. And ...' My

Akinyi

eyes filled up as I looked at my dad. 'He asked me why my parents left Kenya.'

I really cried now, and it was because I was happy to speak of how Brendan understood me and how he supported me.

'To him it sounded like paradise, with sun and sea and giraffes, and I laughed about the Kenya he had made in his mind.' I stood up and went to the door. 'And now I'm damned if I'm saying any more to either of you.'

The two men shook hands.

'We'll keep in touch, Mr Macdonald.'

Cardew opened the door for me. He held out a hand, and it looked like a limp handshake. I wasn't fooled. His grasp was as firm as a heavy warning.

Chapter 15

I had to hand it to the kids in my class. They'd turned things round in the hour I was away. They'd swept the dust from desk tops into black bags. They'd mopped the floor, and they'd wiped the smoke grime from the windows. They were pleased with themselves.

Away they went to second lesson, laughing and clowning as per usual. For me that was Music with Mrs Siddle - not, of course, in the Music Room that day.

Poor Gloria Siddle!

She was a star when you were alone with her. With Gloria's help I'd become quite a mean clarinetist in the school orchestra, and I could get by among the altos in the choir.

But oh dear, her lessons with the class. As Headteacher's daughter, I had to watch every move I made. Kids could make life hell if I was a goody-goody. Otherwise, quite frankly, I'd have had a go at them long since. It wasn't as if somebody had forced them to take GCSE Music. They could have gone for any one on a list of other subjects instead, such as Art, Business Studies, French or IT. The usual options system.

And now GCSEs were looming.

Yet they fooled about in Gloria's lessons. It was unbelievable, the things they got up to.

Incredibly, George was the worst.

Obviously, with talent like that he went to a tip-top tutor outside school, but really his progress was down to Gloria. She homed-in on him as soon as he came to Willowbank from the primary school. In less than two years, as a tiny Year 8, he starred in her concerts, up there on the stage with the white shirt and black bow-tie 6th formers. She took him to the Town Hall for city events. She rehearsed with him in the evenings, at weekends and in the holidays. The two of them sometimes included me, but I wasn't fooled. I knew well enough George and Gloria were the box-office superstars. He was her little angel. He soaked up what she taught him. He went out of his way to please her.

Not in class.

In Gloria's music lessons, George the angel flew out of the window and George the devil took over. His noisy ambition was to top the other boys' worst behaviour.

Long before the fire, I'd been agonising what to do about those lessons. I pinned George while we were working together for the Fun Fest. He was pathetic. To my face he couldn't agree more. Oh yes, of course he'd support me. He'd knuckle down to work in the next lesson.

Along came the lesson, and there was George strutting his stuff as if we'd never spoken.

His favourite trick was to count how many times Gloria would send him out of class. He was as pathetic as that.

'George Newcomb, leave the room.'

'Yes, Miss. One.'

'George Newcomb, you naughty boy, stand outside the door.'

'Me, Gloria? Two.'

Each time, he left the room, stood in the corridor for ten seconds and then strolled back to his desk. And Gloria, well, she was hopeless enough to let him get away with it.

I couldn't live in my dad's house without knowing that Gloria could choose from any number of teacher-tricks to nail him. She could make him sit right beside her at the front. She could make sure he really did stay in the corridor. Out there, away from the support of his big-mouth friends on the back row, he'd shiver in his shoes. He'd be scared stiff that the Lion would find him and drag him into her room. Best of all, she could ban him from the lesson till his father promised he would behave. George was like a little kid in short pants when his father was around. Anything was better than being nobbled by his dad.

But no, it was as if Gloria was programmed into this pointless loop of kicking him out every five minutes. Result? A class of brainy kids were as good as nowhere with GCSE music theory.

Surely, I thought, the fire has knocked some sense into them.

Forget it. Two boys pitched into an arm-wrestling match, and their mates swarmed to watch. Gloria spoke to their backs. They egged on the he-men. They placed bets. Gloria lumbered to her desk, opened her register and spiked a name with the end of her biro.

'Kieran Clarkson,' she yelped. The noise level dipped half a decibel. 'Yes, it's you I'm talking to, Kieran Clarkson.'

One of the elbow-wrestlers glanced at her. 'Me, Miss? Hang on a minute, Miss.'

'Come out here at once, Kieran.'

'Half a mo, Miss.'

'Immediately, boy.'

'Aw, Miss!'

The noise level rose.

'He can't come out now, Miss. Not in the middle of a match.'

'He's the champion, Miss.'

'Never been beaten, Miss.'

'You could beat him, Miss.'

'With your wrestler's muscles, Miss.'

The class yelled. I kept my head down. My face burned with shame. I don't have it in me to take these bear-baiters on, I thought. I'm a wuss.

'You wouldn't get up in a hurry from under Gloria, Clarky.'

Hilarious approval. I squirmed on my seat.

'I'm waiting for you, Kieran,' screamed Gloria. 'Out here immediately with your manuscript pad.'

In a moment of doubt, Kieran glanced at her. His opponent didn't need asking twice. He smashed Kieran's forearm onto the desktop. Kids cheered. The desk swayed and crashed to the floor in a shower of grubby textbooks, crumpled crisp packets, chewing gum and sweaty trainers.

'Clarky's lost,' they howled.

'Not fair,' Kieran shrieked.

The winner's supporters buried their hero in back-slapping bodies. Kieran's crowd jostled. A fist flew. Everyone was yelling.

In the pandemonium it took a moment for anyone to notice that the Lion had prowled into the room.

The volume control spun to pin-drop silence. Someone scraped up the crashed desk. The arm-wrestlers shuffled to their own seats. A sour smell seeped into the classroom air, the sweat-pong of silly boys scared they had pushed their luck too far.

It was Gloria who broke the stunned silence. I just couldn't believe her attitude. She had the cheek to get on her high horse.

'Yes, Miss Lyon?' she said, nose in the air, as if she'd never had a moment's trouble with a class of kids in her life. 'Can I help?'

The mighty mound of her back cranked up into her humped shoulders. The idea that the Deputy Head needed to rescue her from a class of kids! She was humiliated.

The Lion's lioness eyes brooded on the threat of violent punishment. She ran them over the class, including me, one last time before she left. The silence lasted long enough for her to get out of earshot. Then the volume was turned up again.

'You're for it now, Miss. It's the slipper for you, Miss. In the Lion's den.'

'On your bum, Miss.'

'Your big bum.'

'Your enormous great big fat bum, Miss.'

Gloria drew herself up in a pathetic attempt to give them the same glare she had conjured for the Lion.

'Leave the room, you impertinent boy, George Newcomb.'

George was swaggering to the door amid catcalls. He was turning to raise a goal scorer's salute. It was the applause he longed for.

Then I stood.

'Shut it!"

Yes, I thought, seized by a second of panic, this is me. Yelling. Demanding to be heard.

'Just shut up a minute, will you?'

It's no good asking why, after plucking up courage for weeks, I'd chosen this moment. I was on my feet. There was no going back.

It's no good asking how decided what to say. I'd dreamed about this. Dreamed and daydreamed it. I wasn't talking off the top of my head either. The words came out pat, as if they'd composed themselves in my subconscious mind.

My face burned, but the moment of panic passed. My mind was cool.

'I've had enough.' I heard myself, I knew I was right, and I allowed anger to drive me on. 'I'm not standing for any more of this crap.'

And I told it the way it was.

'If you're shocked to see me putting myself on a pedestal to lecture you, well you're not half as shocked as I am. But you'd better believe this. I'm not about to apologise to a single one of you lot. Somebody has to speak out. Somebody has to bring a bit of sense to this crazy class. And if Mrs Siddle is too old and too defenceless to do it, and nobody else has the guts, then it'll have to be me. That's right - your own favourite Headteacher's daughter.'

A boy laughed a sneering laugh, and I felled him with a contemptuous glance.

'It might not be cool to say so, but pretty well everybody in this class does well at school. Most of us have our GCSEs in mind and we want as many passes as possible. I certainly do. Next year I'm going into the 6th Form and after that I'm going to uni.'

I took a shifty look round the class. Nobody talks like this at school, I thought. It's not cool to brag about being clever and doing well. You only confide to your special friends that you want to be a doctor or a lawyer ... or, heaven help you, a teacher.

Too bad. I wasn't going to stop now.

I plunged on.

'I have my clarinet,' I said, 'and I pick up some music theory from that. Probably enough to scratch a dismal pass mark. An E. Grade D if I'm lucky. You, Megan and you Carlo, why don't you wake up? How are you going to explain one GCSE F at your Oxbridge interviews?'

They were all ears. What a relief. What would I have done, I wondered, if they'd given me the Gloria treatment? Catcalls, whistles and jeers?

They didn't. Eyes down, they listened. It was the E and the F that got to them, I thought with a little smile. I should have thrown in a G.

The exception - wouldn't you know it - was George. He paused by the door as he was prancing out of the room for the Nth time. His lips moved in sympathy with me and I saw that his face was glowing with adoration. What an idiot! I could have spat.

'This is our second year with Mrs Siddle, and OK, we've had some laughs. Mostly it's been a total nightmare. I for one need to use these last few months to scratch together enough music theory to be sure of a proper pass. Grade C maybe. I'd have liked an A or a B. That's out of the window. Mrs Siddle is a good teacher, and I vote we give her the chance to start teaching us.'

I sat. There was one long moment of sheepish silence. Then a girl coughed. A boy adjusted his chair. People opened their bags. Manuscript pads appeared.

'Oi! Re-match,' protested Kieran, and he braced his forearm on his desk top.

He was too late. His cause was lost. His mates were consulting Gloria's blackboard scribbles and waiting for her to speak. One of his friends pushed him away and told him to get his head down.

'You're a bunch of pansies,' Kieran snarled. 'It's only Music anyway. See if I care. I'm going in the Army.'

'That's it, Clarky,' a girl called across the room. 'Get yourself shot in Afghanistan.'

My heart was thumping till it hurt. I was mixed up. I didn't care even if the boys did follow Clarkson back into idiotic clowning. I didn't care if Gloria spoke or she didn't. It was delayed stage fright. I trembled all over my body. I tried to make myself small. Had I made an idiot of myself? Were this lot whispering about me?

Perhaps they were furious. Maybe they thought I was a spoilsport, a teacher's pet. Probably they'd never speak to me again.

Akinyi

Gloria was shattered. She looked as if she needed a good month's sleep. She slumped in her desk and left us all to wait and watch and wonder till the bell rang for break.

Now I couldn't bear to hear what the other kids thought. Gossip and gloating. They were bursting with both, and I'd let them get on with it. Brendan was the only person I wanted to see.

I was first out of that classroom, and I ran to find him.

I needed to tell him what I'd done, to hear him say I was right. I wanted things to be good between us again, the way they were before I let our Head of Year ruin my life. To admit I'd betrayed him to the Lion and Frosty. Tell him about Detective Chief Inspector Cardew.

I wanted him to tell me that he and his mum would smile with me, the way they did before I spoiled things.

Kids were fascinated by the assembly hall, its black hole and its busy workers. Picking through rubble. Pumping scummy grey water. Examining charred posts, fiddling with twisted window frames and dangling wires. Duty teachers fussed among them, shepherding everybody out. No Brendan there.

Miserably, I thought of last night's quarrel and how he'd avoided me for weeks before that. Where could he be? Staying at home, perhaps, or wandering about the town as he'd done as a kid. I looked across the valley to Ashbrook and I was tempted .

Do I dare? It's only across the bridge. Shall I ...?

Then I saw a wisp of smoke.

Akinyi

It came from behind a wall between the staff car park and the kitchens. As I ran, I realised there were two smokers, and behind the wall I found Brendan ... and Gloria.

Chapter 16

Gloria! Brendan here with Gloria! What!

As soon as he saw me he dropped his cigarette. He ground it into the grass with his boot. I didn't know he was a smoker. I hadn't smelled it on his clothes or his breath. Certainly not in his house, which Anita kept spotless. There was no way she would put up with fag ash on her carpets or smoke getting into her curtains.

Surprise, surprise, Gloria was not best pleased to see me. She gave me a snooty stare and shuffled to her car.

Brendan and I smirked at each other. Neither of us knew how to start. He'd hidden his short hair under a black woolly hat pulled down over his ears. For the first time, I noticed how chilly the day was and wished I could snuggle up to him.

'Gloria's lost Pirate.'

'Really?' I said with totally false interest.

'Yeah. He ran off last night. He's done it before. Gloria's gutted.'

'Of course. I ...' I dried up.

'Last night ...'

'Sorry I ...'

We both giggled. He put his arm round me and I pressed my face against his shoulder. That was better by far than words. We sat side by side on the wall, swung our legs and felt happier. There was a lot of talking to be done, but no hurry.

Then the Lion appeared.

I felt sure she would pick Brendan up, but no - it was Gloria she wanted. They talked. Gloria tossed her head. She slammed her car door. She flat-footed across the car park two furious strides behind the Lion. They disappeared into school.

'Gloria's for a bollocking,' said Brendan. 'She gave Jonny Marks a clip at registration this morning, and he legged-it home. '

We went towards the school together, holding hands. From behind the beech trees along the school wall the police helicopter suddenly roared overhead. I shivered with a guilty sense that it was tracking me.

Brendan didn't do guilt.

'We're here, pigs,' he shouted. 'Why don't you land on the cricket pitch and round us up for DNA testing?' He waved two fingers. 'Gloria's having a bad day,' he said. I was still freaked out by the helicopter. He'd already forgotten it. 'What with the pup and all.'

I stopped him. Till then I'd been so full of the relief and the happiness of joining up with him again that I'd forgotten how amazed I was. Now I couldn't wait.

'Brendan' I said. 'What are you on about? Are you spying on her?'

'Who? Gloria?' He laughed. 'We're mates, Gloria and me.'

'You and Gloria mates? Yeah, right. That's totally unreal.'

Brendan teased me with his baby smile. 'We go back a long way,' he joked.

I just couldn't get my head round what he came out with next.

'She's been having trouble with the Lion. That do in your class this morning wasn't the first.'

'She told you about that!'

'The Lion has poked her nose into too many lessons.'

'I don't get it, Brendan. How come you know this stuff?'

He enjoyed stringing me along, and he laughed again. Then, in a scary second, his mood switched.

'You're in the Lion's pocket,' he said. 'Ask her why she picks on Gloria.'

'That's absurd.' I couldn't help sounding like the Headteacher's daughter. Again. 'It's not Miss Lyon's job to pick on her colleagues.'

'OK, so what's with all the visits to Gloria's lessons?'

'They're a mess, if ours is anything to go by.'

'Dunno about that. Gloria has nightmares about her classes, and the Lion makes things worse.'

'That's crazy. She's a good teacher, the Lion.'

'Never said she wasn't. Look at it this way, though. Say your dad has a bunch of rowdy kids, right? The only time they belt up is when another teacher comes into his room. How do you think he feels?'

I was struck dumb.

'Dead right,' said Brendan. 'He'd have nightmares.'

'It still doesn't make sense. You don't even like the best teachers, never mind an old biddy like Gloria. How do you know all this?'

'When I first came to this school,' Brendan said, 'first thing I needed was somewhere to hang out for a smoke. Found that quiet corner at the back of the staff car park. Early on I came across Gloria. She goes there at break to see Pirate. Walks him. Gives him a drink and things. While she's resting she lights up, of course.'

The threatening Brendan had gone again. He chuckled, gently taking the mick.

'You wouldn't expect me to hide from a harmless old woman, even if she is teacher. The first day I stayed where I was. Sat on this wall with her car hiding me from the teachers. Had a quiet smoke.'

'Then what?'

'Waited for her to have a go at me. I would have moved on to find a different spot. She didn't, so I didn't.'

'She never gave you a detention for being out of bounds ... ?'

'She's a nice old bird. For a teacher.'

'Or told you that smoking's against the rules?'

Brendan scoffed.

'But teachers are supposed ...'

'Yeah, yeah.' He teased me with his maddening smile. 'It went on till we had a cold snap. Gloria found her old banger's locks frozen and Pirate trapped inside. She was in a bad way. So I sorted it for her.'

'What do you mean sorted it?'

'Heated her car key with my fag-lighter and that melted the ice in the lock. She had the shakes, so I lit her a fag. Like I say, we're mates.'

Compared with the way Brendan was looking after Mrs Siddle, I felt the feebleness of my own effort.

'I tried this morning to stop our class giving her a really bad time.'

'She told me what you did, and she wasn't happy. Your mates don't deserve you. Specially that pathetic Newcomb.'

'Tell me about it. The way he carries on. It's just weird. He's the best musician in the city, yet ...'

'He's a prat. If he wants to raise hell in a teacher's lesson, why doesn't he pick on somebody who can give him a run for his money? Tell you what. The day you tell me he's run Frosty ragged, I'll sign up as the first and only member of the Wanker Newcomb Fan Club.'

I remembered how a gutless silence had fallen onto the big-shots of my Music class when the Lion came in.

'It should have been you that took my class to the cleaners this morning,' I said.

'I've told Gloria - what she needs is a good thick stick. I've chopped her one out of a hedgeback in Fencote Woods. Next time he gives her any lip she should welly him with it.'

I smiled. 'She can't do that, Brendan. It's illegal. She'll get arrested.'

'It's illegal to give Marksy a smack, but he's asked for it and she's given him one.'

I nodded towards two figures hurrying along the school drive.

'Isn't that one of your friends?'

Brendan stiffened. He grabbed my hand and began to drag me towards the front door.

'Marksy - and his old lady. Told you he legged-it home because Gloria tapped him.'

'We can't follow them into school ...'

'Who can't?'

'But the duty teachers have thrown everybody out.'

'Follow me.'

Akinyi

Like a stray dog sensing it's to be put down, Jonny Marks trailed behind his mother. Like a naughty little girl expecting to be told off by Teacher, I followed Brendan.

Mrs Marks stalked past the temporary signs which told visitors to go round the back, and she hammered on the Lion's door. Brendan didn't hesitate either.

It wasn't Mrs Marks's style to wait for the Lion to invite her in. She jerked Marksy's arm. She dragged him behind her, so that he staggered exactly at the moment when Brendan kicked him on one shin with his boot.

The door slammed but not before I heard Marksy's agonised yelp. That kick gave me the same sickening feeling I'd had the evening before. I was walking through Ashbrook again. Begging Anita to let me into the house. Standing before Brendan as he chewed gum at the full-blast TV.

'Brendan!' I sounded like his mother. 'Why did you kick him?'

'No need to be soft on Marksy.' He whipped round on me. 'You should have seen the cheek he gave Gloria this morning. If he and his old lady land her in bother for smacking him I'll do more than kick his leg. That goes for your mate Newcomb as well.'

He stomped away, but I grabbed his hand and we hurried outside.

'You don't have to stomp off,' I said. 'I want to be nice to Gloria. And I'm doing my best to make it up with you.'

His face was a mask.

'Another thing,' he said. 'It wasn't me who lit that fire.'

'OK, OK,' I said. 'I've been trying to tell you I know that.'

'You told me yourself. They think I did. Frosty Winter and the Lion.' His anger simmered. 'Last night you thought I did.'

'Be reasonable, Brendan!' I was getting irritated at the thought of losing him in yet another bust-up. 'If you tell me you didn't do it, of course I believe you.'

'I saw red last night when I heard the school had been burned. First the woman cop, then the fire. What next? The first I knew about it - and this is the truth, take it or leave it - was when you turned up at our house.'

'OK.'

'I met Marksy and Legs Longley outside the Traveller's Rest, down by the bridge. They were hanging about. I didn't tell them to come with me but they tagged along anyway. That's how it's always been. A lass called Saisha was with us. She's a good kid.'

'Saisha? I know her.'

'She has a bit more about her. Marksy sucks up to me, and I thump him. Legs lives not far from us. We've always been mates. Started school at the same time. He came with me on some of my jobs.'

'What jobs?'

He ignored me. 'Not all of them, not by a long shot. He's got miles more sense than I have - knows when I'm getting into bother and makes himself scarce - I don't blame him.'

'Brendan! I don't get it. What jobs?'

'Legs didn't light the fire. Marksy was rabbiting on, making himself out to be a hard case instead of a mammy's boy. He said we should break into the school and scrawl some graffiti in the bogs. What a hero. Hasn't the guts to light a tab-end, never mind a dirty great fire.'

I probably looked as stunned as I felt.

I was helpless. Out of my depth.

'Look. It's me they're coming for,' Brendan went on. 'Not Marksy or Longley, not Saisha. Those three were there, same as me. For all the Lion knows or Frosty, any of them could have broken into the school and started the fire. That Saisha, she has more brains than both of them put together.'

'Yes, I know her. I've seen her with ...'

'Well, you can bet your life nobody's knocking on her door. Forget it. Then weedy Marksy's old lady goes crying to the Lion because Gloria has given him the clipped ear-hole he should've had yonks ago.'

From the stormy look on his face, I guessed he was thinking about barging back into school to sort Mrs Marks out single-handed. I tugged his arm.

'Then you met me,' I said.

'I was chuffed when I saw you.' A quick smile, and then his face clouded. 'And pissed off that he was with you.'

'I've known George since we were babies.'

Brendan grunted.

'Now we do music together. I can't help that.'

'So I went home. I can't help that either. The cops were there to say hello. Took me to the station for a chat about the policewoman.'

'What about Marksy and Legs?'

'Legs hates Marksy. As soon as I left, you can bet Legs scarpered. Probably went home to see his kid sister. It was her birthday yesterday and he was moaning because he had no money to get her a prezzie. Not even a packet of salt and vinegar.'

'What about Marksy?'

'I bet he took off home to his old lady. Half an hour later, the school's on fire. Those lads didn't light it. You didn't light it. So who else?'

'Brendan, I'm so sorry they're blaming you.'

He shrugged. His anger had gone, but he was still bitter. 'Teachers and cops, it's how their minds work. Who knows how to start a fire? Brendan Smart. Who has form for burglary and fires? Brendan Smart. Who was on the spot? Oh wonderful - Brendan Smart. Now, all we need is a motive. Well, knock me sideways, he's just had a ding-dong with his girlfriend. And who might she be? The Headteacher's daughter, bless her cotton socks. It's what they call an open and shut case.'

'You make it sound so cruel. And so hopeless.'

The bell had long since rung for end of break, and at last a teacher shooed us into school.

Chapter 17

My head was full of crazy thoughts, and French with Miss Butler wasn't one of them.

Immersion was Miss Butler's thing.

'You will only learn French,' she said, and she made funny little shapes with her bright red lips, and spoke with a French lilt, 'if we speak it and listen to it. So your French lessons from now until your exams will be in French.'

She meant it, and she was good at it, too. Her efforts were wasted on me that day.

Brendan. Did he light the fire?

What sort of spineless question is that, I asked myself. I told him only a few minutes ago, didn't I, that I believed him when he said he didn't.

Pathetic. Disloyal. Those were some of the more polite names I called myself.

Makes no odds, I thought, they don't make the question go away. Brendan himself told me. Everybody thinks he lit the fire. Everything points to him. He has the form.

The form. What sort of disgusting idea do you call that? Hostile. Unforgiving. Like the Lion and Frosty, so unchallengeable.

A boy has form, and this form changes questions into answers, doubts into certainties. Two plus two. Here's how it works. Start with a fire. Add a boy with form for lighting fires and what have you got? The boy who lit the fire, of course.

I felt sick.

This is what I can't face, I thought. If Brendan lit the fire, what does that say about his feelings for me? He might be shy of meeting my dad. Fair enough. He might struggle with the idea of going out with the Headteacher's daughter. I can forgive him that, too. It's not as if I haven't had that stuff since I was knee-high.

'Your daddy's a teacher, you're a sissy' - primary school talk.

'Your dad's assembly was a load of rubbish' - my high school friends.

'Your old man knacked me today, the bastard' - Ashbrook kids.

So what? I have a Grade A in swanning through such hassle.

Deliberately to set fire to the school, though. Surely, he wouldn't have, couldn't have. I might not always show it, but Brendan knows I love my dad. He knows my dad has nothing, apart from me and his school.

So if it wasn't Brendan, who was it?

His friends. What about them?

The one who half killed George at Nether Fencote Church, the one they call Legs. And Marksy, the one whose shin Brendan kicked. Brendan says he's sure we can forget them. But why? They were outside the school last night. What if they ... ?

Yes, yes. This must be what happened. Brendan tells them to get lost. They're still full of big boy talk. Burglary, graffiti, who-hates-school-most, that kind of stuff. One eggs the other on. They outdo each other. Neither wants to be the first to back down. Next thing they know is they've ...

Oh, come off it! How could anybody bring themselves to light a match and deliberately start a fire?

But look, it's simple, isn't it? All I have to do is tell the Lion and Frosty.

'Those two boys,' I'll say, 'get hold of them. Catch them unawares. Visit them at home, the way I did last night with Brendan and Anita.'

I'll do it. I'll head for the Lion's office as soon as this lesson is over.

Come on, why wait?

For the first time in my life I was beaten by schoolwork. I couldn't stand it a moment longer.

Akinyi

The class was immersed in French with Miss Butler. Mademoiselle B, now I came to look at her, was in her glory. She looked and sounded just like a French woman. She drew the class along as they studied her pretty red lips and tried to match her lilting pace. Her questions flew thick and fast. Their answers followed, more determined than clever.

I put my hand up.

'*Oui, Akinyi, tu veux dire?*'

'Please can I go to the toilet, Miss Butler?'

Titters shredded Miss B's delicate atmosphere.

'Akinyi, *je préférerais ...*'

'I'm really sorry, Miss Butler.'

I swept my belongings together. I flung my school bag across one shoulder and dashed for the loo. The shock of cheating a teacher made me tremble as I ran a comb through my expensively straightened hair and pouted in the mirror at my lack of make-up and the dark green dowdiness of my school uniform.

The corridors were empty. They echoed my guilty footsteps. I passed the Headteacher's door and felt too guilty even to glance at it. Through the entrance hall. It was taking shape again as workmen swept up fallen wall fittings, and 6th Formers binned the remains of their wonderful displays.

I couldn't even think what would happen to my dad's stress level if he knew I'd run out of a lesson.

Akinyi

Here was the Lion's office, door ajar. I held my breath and listened. Some poor kid was getting the hard word. And it wasn't Marksy.

Mrs Marks had left, then. What had Marksy told the Lion? What had the Lion prised out of Marksy? Perhaps Marksy had owned up. Perhaps Brendan had been told already that he was in the clear. Then there was no need for me to speak to the Lion.

I tiptoed away.

Lounging on the front steps, as relaxed as a tourist on a beach - wouldn't you guess - there was Brendan.

'Didn't expect you yet,' he said.

The staffroom window had a view down the drive. The Headteacher's window had a view down the drive. Half a dozen classrooms had a view down the drive. Brendan didn't give them a thought. He simply took my hand and shepherded me and my pounding heart out of school.

'Whose lesson have you legged, wicked girl?'

'I might ask you the same.'

'Nothing to it. I saw Frosty with a cop. I knew where they were headed. To pick me up from class.'

'Oh, oh. Don't tell me.'

'I scarpered.'

'Brendan!' He was so casual I couldn't believe it. 'You mean you haven't even been to your lesson …'

'Course I haven't. Would you?'

'Me? Brendan, I've never missed …'

'Alright, alright, I know. That's you. But if they want to lean on me they'll have to catch me first. Which they will do, but not yet.'

'And the Lion? Has she been to see you?'

'No.'

'That means when he came with his mother Marksy didn't admit lighting the fire.'

'Marksy? Course not. Why should he?'

'Oh, this is hopeless. I was sure it must have been him - and those other kids hanging around last night.'

'Fairy tales! Let's have a sarnie for dinner.'

'It's Cajun chicken baguette on the special menu today ... OK, I'm coming with you.'

Brendan mocked me with his grin.

'One minute you leg a lesson, the next you're legging dinnertime. You'll get the taste for it.'

Chapter 18

We crossed Willow Bridge. The motorway traffic growled above us on the soaring fly-over. We scrambled over a downtrodden fence into a wasteland of mud, crushed bricks and smutty ragwort by the river.

This was the main footpath for the Ashbrook kids, and soon they came past, going to the fish and chip shop for dinner. You could tell the Year 7s and 8s. They ran, jumped and raced. They'd been in school all morning and couldn't wait to have a bit of fun.

The bigger kids sauntered in twos and threes. The girls had their heads close together in confidential chat. The boys swaggered and insulted each other from a distance or idly kicked a flat football.

They had one topic of conversation and it kept them occupied in angry grumbles or contemptuous laughter.

School.

School and teachers.

Akinyi

Suddenly they were chased by the helicopter. It clattered over the Willowbank skyline, dropped over the school, the motorway and the river, then buzzed the Ashbrook side of the valley.

The youngest kids scattered along the stream-side path, screaming in mock panic and joyful scorn. Some stuck their fingers into their ears, others swatted the air around their faces as they ducked and weaved. A gang of boys used a thick bush as cover and strafed the invader with anti-aircraft guns.

'Cops are sick in the head,' said Brendan. 'Deliberately winding us up. All they want is trouble - and us in it.'

'Someone's killed a policewoman,' I said, feeling prickly. 'The police can't allow that.'

'Oh, they won't, don't you worry. They never do when it's another cop.'

Downstream from the bridge, the Willow turned into a broad pool. The estate kids had hung a rope from a sycamore. Boys were already swinging on it. They dragged it up a steep muddy bank, then launched themselves out over the water.

Boys egged each other on to go for a full crossing of the pool in a single Tarzan leap and swoop. None of them did.

'It's called Mog's Swing,' said Brendan, 'after the first lad to swing all the way, I suppose.'

The kids had seen me, that much was obvious. The Headteacher's daughter, no less, and she'd latched onto one of their own. They didn't know what to make of it.

Akinyi

Beneath the sycamore they rubbed shoulders as they as they ate their chips and drank their coke. They dragged on cigarettes and blew smoke towards me. Exaggerating their laughter.

I was lumbered with my bag of schoolbooks. There was nowhere I could get rid of it. I adjusted it on my shoulder, irritated by its heavy awkwardness.

Knots of girls tightened themselves against me. Boys jostled and flipped stones out into the pool. Ogling me from the corners of their eyes, they guffawed that bit more raucously.

And they challenged each other, with louder jeering laughter than ever, to go for the full Mog's swing.

Brendan surveyed the scene like a moody emperor.

He wishes we'd gone somewhere else, I thought. We need to talk and laugh together, get over our rows. How are we going to do that in front of half the kids in Ashbrook? It's not on.

To make matters worse, Jonny Marks turned up.

He saw Brendan and trotted along, babbling. 'I didn't shop you, Brendan, honest!'

Brendan glowered. 'What you on about, Marksy?'

Marksy didn't stand much above Brendan's shoulders and he had a bullet-shaped head. I was half repulsed, half fascinated. His eyes were colourless mudflats with red banks. His nose was sore. It wasn't helped by the way he sniffed creepily and wiped it, outrageously double-jointed, on his elbow. His mouth was a damp slit, which floundered in a jaw whose muscles seemed to have collapsed as if he'd had his teeth taken out. He was like a little old man, who couldn't wait to grovel for Brendan.

'See, Brendan.' He bent to roll back one trouser leg and show the beginnings of a thundercloud bruise. 'I knew what you meant and I never said a word.'

Brendan lurched towards him as if to take the little old man by the throat, but Marksy nipped behind me and used me as his human shield.

'Brendan! Brendan! I never even mentioned it, honest. The Lion leaned on me to shop you, Brendan, but I never did.'

Both of them shuffled round me.

'Great fire, Brendan, all that smoke and that great hole at the back of the hall. Pity they didn't close the school, though, eh?'

He looked me as if I was to blame. Then it dawned on him that he'd dropped a clanger. His cheeks bubbled. His mouth slobbered. His eyes darted in search of an escape. He was as devious as he looked. He knew there was no way he could outrun Brendan, so he latched onto me for protection.

'See that swing?' he said. 'I've swung across the river, you know - me.'

I burst out laughing in spite of myself. 'Really?'

'Yeah. There's not many can do it, but I did once, didn't I, Brendan? You were there, weren't you, Brendan?'

'You dropped Gloria in it with the Lion, and I'm gonna ...' Brendan swatted Marksy with his raincoat.

'Have I to show you?' Marksy appealed to me like an infant to his mother.

'Marksy,' Brendan said. 'get on your frigging swing. Go drown yourself, will you.'

Marksy's relief was pathetic. Out of Brendan's range, he slowed. He trailed to the swing, glancing back, full of second thoughts. He scrabbled his way up the banking, looking back at us. Honour wouldn't allow him to drop the rope and run for it - yet.

'He's a little git,' Brendan said.

'He didn't admit the fire,' I said. 'In fact, he ...'

'OK, I know,' Brendan snarled. 'Next time the Lion or Frosty leans on him he'll brown trouser himself and grass me up. Please sir, please miss, I saw Brendan Smart in the school with a box of matches.'

'Poor little kid,' I said. I forgot I had him down as my number one suspect arsonist. 'He doesn't mean any harm.'

'Should have been smothered at birth.'

'I'd like to see you swing across the river,' I called.

'He can only go half way,' Brendan said sulkily. 'Anybody can do that.'

I put my hand on his arm to soothe him. 'And you?'

'Me?' said Brendan. 'All the way, of course. From Ashbrook to Willowbank. Same as Mog.'

'I'd like to see you.'

'You're on. Straight after Marksy's had his go.'

Akinyi

He handed me his black raincoat and his woolly hat. He did his crabwise slouch to the top of the bank, where Marksy was gripping the rope. Smokers and stone-flippers turned to watch.

'You know what to do after this, Marksy, don't you.' It was an order.

Poised to make his swing or run for his life, Marksy dithered.

'If you saw me light the fire,' said Brendan, 'pick up Legs Longley - and your old lady while you're at it. Get to the Lion and give her chapter and verse.'

'Er ... Brendan?'

'If you didn't see me light the fire, then button it.'

'Yes, Brendan.'

'Swing then, you little turd.'

With an ugly jerk, Brendan sent Marksy flying on the rope high over the Willow.

Astonishment rippled through the onlookers. A sigh. Oooh! A gasp.

It was easily the biggest swing they'd seen Marksy make, that was clear. He hugged the rope, thrashed his legs and leaned too far back. His head flopped. If he'd had his balance right he'd have cleared the pool and joined Mog in the land of legend.

Of course, he didn't. Reaching his highest point far out towards Willowbank, Marksy panicked, let go of the rope and hit the water flat on his back.

As if from another world came a gust of hot air, the roar of fast tyres and the stench of hot engines on the motorway.

Then Marksy's head popped up. He spluttered and he yelled. You didn't have to be a mind reader.

'I'm telling on you, Brendan Smart, so don't think I'm not.'

His head sank into the water, then bobbed up again. He spluttered. He coughed. He panicked.

'I'll tell my mam what you did and I don't care.'

He beat the water with arms, head and shoulders. He disappeared and came up again.

'You needn't be surprised if she goes straight to Mr Macdonald.' He swallowed river water. 'You're an arse ...'

Sonist, I thought.

For a Gold Star Life Saver I was decidedly offhand about fishing Marksy from the river.

'That kid can't swim,' I said.

'Better pull him out,' said Brendan, just as casually.

He was right. None of the other kids were about to help. Obviously, they thought it was up to Brendan and me.

'Fetch some rope,' I said.

'Rope? There's no rope round here.'

'Funny. If there was no rope how did Marksy land in the water?'

'Oh, that rope.'

'You're not a boy scout, are you? What will you cut it with?'

'Look the other way. This is not for nice girls like you.'

And he was right.

From a pocket of his black raincoat he produced a nastier knife than I'd ever so much as dreamed of.

Chapter 19

It had an oddly attractive yellow handle, made of rubber. For just a moment I hoped it was a spoof.

But the blade, when Brendan held it up, was long and thin and tapered. Electricity shot through my whole body. I tasted a spurt of blood, and when I put a hand up to my mouth I realized I'd bitten my bottom lip.

Bitten it hard. Really hard.

'No way, Brendan! That's mind-blowing.'

'No need to get steamed up. OK, so it's a knife. Big deal.'

He scrambled into the tree. I wanted to sit down, I felt so shaky.

Then Marksy screamed.

I shrugged. I knew it was crazy. I knew I should say this far and no further. I should make a stand. No, I should run for it, get out of this place. I should tell Brendan that I'd had it with him. For good.

Instead, my common sense went awol. I was carried away by the sheer crackpot excitement of being with him. I couldn't help myself.

I had just about enough contact with a glimmer of sanity to make a feeble attempt at justifying myself. Why be self-righteous? I thought. In the circumstances, Brendan's horrendous knife is life-saving, not life-threatening. Ditto his climbing skills, even if it's true that he's honed them on cat burgling adventures.

He swarmed along the branch. My bottom lip was dangling, the bitten one, and I must have had a stupid gawp on my face. He slashed at the rope and dropped it at my feet.

No going back now.

I hardly knew what I was doing as I ran down to the water's edge.

Marksy had splashed and thrashed his way to a tangle of undergrowth and rubbish in mid- pool. There he could cling to what looked like the rust-pocked bumper of a wrecked car. He abandoned his insults and saved his breath for waterlogged pleas for help.

The grass bank dropped sheer into black water. I didn't like the look of it, not one little bit. It was about as far removed as I'd ever been from the warm clear blue waters of the school swimming pool, where I'd taken life-saving classes. I hesitated.

Brendan hurtled down the bank, Marksy squealed, and I took my shoes and socks off.

Akinyi

I dropped through the grey scum at the edge of the pool and gasped as its iciness seized me up to the waist. I kept my head above water because I'd got back enough sense to be pretty sure I didn't want to swallow any of that stuff.

Specially not with a split lip.

Didn't want my hair to go all frizzy again, either. Not for at least one more day.

On the high banking above Mog's Swing, the kids closed in to watch.

With the rope round my waist, I swam out towards Marksy through the oily sheen on the pond's surface. As I swam close, I weighed up my best chance of bringing him to the bank.

'Help!' He thought he was going to die. 'Help!'

I swam round him, breaststroke, and I kept well clear of his clutching arms.

'Help.' He shrieked and let go of his car bumper. 'Get me out of here.'

He sank and I dog-paddled closer. As he came up and lunged at me, I dodged, so that again he swallowed water and went under. He was all but done for, and I was ready for him.

'Look,' I said as he floundered into view. 'Isn't that your mammy coming down the bank?'

He turned in search of his mother.

'Got you, Marksy.'

Akinyi

I grabbed him under the armpits and rolled him onto his back.

'Pull, Brendan,' I called, and part swimming, part towed, we came to the bank.

Other kids were ready to help now the story was all but over. They and Brendan hoiked Marksy out of the water like a bag of supermarket shopping. He lay on his back, chest heaving, gawping at the sky.

Then he staggered to his feet. He was dripping and frozen, but he had enough left to give Brendan one more mouthful. Or he thought he had.

Brendan thought otherwise. He stuck two fingers onto Marksy's heaving chest and shoved him. 'Sod off home to your old lady.'

Away Marksy trundled, bullet head down, double-jointed elbows sticking out. Brendan reached for me with both hands and pulled me onto dry land.

'Maybe I have a chance after this,' he said.

'A chance? What sort of chance?' I said. 'Seems to me we're going from bad to worse.'

'Yeah, but you don't know Marksy. Not like I know him. He and his old lady will go squealing to Frosty. First they'll say I pushed him into the river.'

'In a way, that's true.'

'Whatever. Then they'll say I lit the fire. Frosty's a clever sod, and he knows Marksy. He'll ask how they know, and then he'll dig out of Marksy that he followed me

Akinyi

home. That's proof that I was nowhere near. Getting the little toe-rag out of the river was the best thing.'

'How do you mean - followed you home?' I said.

'Follows me all over,' said Brendan. 'He was watching you and me last night. When we had our barney.'

'He followed us? How do you know?'

'Always.' He stood, as all the kids did, guilty, but gaping at my sodden knickers and my goosefleshed legs.

'My cardigan,' I said.

He handed me it and I used it as a towel.

'It's been lovely. And now my skirt. I'll have to dash home before I freeze.'

'Your coat,' he said.

He wrapped it round me, draped his own precious raincoat on top, slung my school bag over his shoulder and took my hand.

'It's shorter to my house,' he said. 'We'll run.'

Staring kids fell in step behind us as we jogged up the hillside into Ashbrook.

'He's got this thing about me,' said Brendan. 'And he fancies you.'

'That's his hard luck.'

I was freezing but I stopped him on the cracked-flagged pavement. He held me with his strong warm body and, third time lucky, we kissed in front of I didn't care how many goggle-eyed kids. I pulled back and we gazed at each other in speechless amazement at how lovely it was. Warm and tasting of something ... I couldn't say what, because it was my first time ever.

His, too, I was sure of it.

Then I spat blood from my bitten lip, and I was furious again about that knife. I half pushed, half punched him away.

'Why do you have to spoil things by carrying a knife, Brendan?' I said. 'I'm amazed at you. Is it yours?'

'What if we meet some yobboes when we're downtown together?'

'You aren't going to show them your knife, are you?'

'What if they give you a pile of racist crap? What if they try beating me up for going with a black lass? What if they want to rape you because you're black and looking for a bit of easy white meat?'

'Brendan! That's gross.'

'Here we go again. We're back to last night, aren't we?'

'If we are, it's not my fault this time.'

'Oh yeah? It's mine, I suppose, for wanting to look after you when we get into a scrap.'

He sneered, and I had the nastiest thought. This is a row we'll never make up. We come from different worlds. I'll never understand him. I should have run as soon as I saw that knife.

'I want you to know this, Brendan.' I lowered my voice and threatened him. 'Nobody needs to play the knight in shining armour between me and racists or yobboes. I can look after myself. And I can do it without any knife.'

He smiled his taunting smile. 'Come here,' he said.

My clothes were wet and I was freezing. I wanted to run.

And I wanted him to do what he did. He pulled me close to keep me warmer.

'You don't fight violence with violence,' I said into his shoulder, and I felt him stroke my hair. 'If I thought it was the right way I'd have had loads of fights in my time.'

'OK, so you'll be alright when we're out one night and meet a gang in the dark.'

I laughed. He was impossible. I was impossible. We were making peace in spite of everything. Life might be good again after all.

'Am I standing out here freezing to death or are you taking me to your warm house?'

We ran.

'I'm sure your knife's illegal,' I panted.

'Oh, well, next time you can cut the rope with your teeth.'

'It's against the school rules anyway.'

'So is biting.'

I admitted defeat. Totally. As if he gave a monkey's about the school rules. I just knew he would laugh his scornful laugh, and when he did I was glad.

We arrived at his back door.

'Having a good time's against the school rules,' Brendan scoffed.

I ran a finger along his nose, gazing into his blue eyes.

'Are you sure Marksy followed you home?' I whispered.

'I didn't see him. Didn't need to. He was there, that's all.'

'I still think' - beating a fingernail tattoo on the end of his nose - 'he could have lit the fire.'

'And you ...' Brendan tattooed my sore mouth with kisses. 'You're freezing to death.'

'Everybody who adds it up,' I said, 'reaches the same answer. Brendan Smart.'

And nothing changes their mind, I thought, and I felt chilled to the bone. Brendan's the one with the so-called form, they say, and there's no more to be said.

Well, Akinyi, I told myself, chilled to the bone you might be, bloody mouthed and appalled, but if you play your cards right there's one thing you can do to keep him out of trouble.

Nick that awful knife.

No sooner thought than done. I slipped it from his raincoat pocket and slid it between the pages of one of the books in my school bag.

Chapter 20

I had a wicked afternoon. Anita spoiled me rotten.

First, she ran a hot bath and I soaked up the warmth I needed to stop my teeth chattering and my head-to-toe shivering. On a bed Anita spread out a full change of clothes. We smiled and felt good together when everything of hers fitted me.

So much for trying to keep my head out of the river. That hair-do was ruined, the one I'd spent a fortune on ready for the Fun Fest. Not to worry. I sat in front of a mirror while Anita blow-dried and combed out my long curls down onto my shoulders. Then she drew them up into their ponytail, and painstakingly put the braiding back in, the way the Afro-Caribbean girls wore theirs.

'How come you can do this so cleverly, Anita?' I asked. 'Are you a hairdresser?'

'Course not,' she laughed. 'I was a cinema cleaner till our Brendan came along.'

'So where does does this skill come from?'

'Hours and hours with the girls when we were at school. There were posh kids there and no money in our houses to be like them. We read it up in magazines and practised on each other.'

'I haven't had this done since my mum died,' I said.

I enjoyed the attention and the feminine touch of Anita's fingers.

'If only Brendan had been a girl,' she sighed.

'I'm glad he wasn't,' I laughed.

We enjoyed a silent moment, both far away in our own thoughts.

How easily would Mum have learned to get on with Brendan, I wondered. Would she have bought the stuff about his form and jumped straight to the conclusion that he was the one who set fire to the school?

'I wish my real mum and dad had ...'

I stopped. I could have had a little cry. I felt safe enough with Anita, but this was a precious moment and I wanted to protect it.

'Had what, love?'

I shrugged. 'Had been my mum and dad, I suppose.'

Anita understood already, even before I understood myself.

'That must hurt,' she said.

'Why didn't Mum tell me who I am?'

Akinyi

It was a long time before Anita spoke.

'She did her best, Akinyi love. She'd been through a lot before she decided to have you.' She paused for another thoughtful silence between us. 'I'm sure that more than anything she wanted to do what was right for you. I don't know how any mother makes sense of that stuff for a child.'

'How am I going to find out who I am?'

I had my head down and I bubbled through choked-back tears, but Anita understood. She was already asking herself the same question.

'What about your dad?' she said. 'Can you ask him?'

Our eyes met in the mirror and I smiled through my tears.

'It should be easy, but it isn't. It's as if ...'

As if ... as if ... It was as if I was telling him he had no right to be himself.

'He's lost Mum,' I said. 'I don't think he could bear another loss.'

And yet with every day that went by we were losing each other anyway.

'I will speak to him. Honest I will.'

'You'll find a way, Akinyi. A way that will bring you together.'

Hair-braiding was finished and I controlled myself. I sat up straight and met my own eyes in the mirror and told myself I looked pretty good.

'Whatever were you up to?' Downstairs, Anita poured me a mug of steaming tea. 'Some mischief with our Brendan, I'll be bound. Trust him to come home dry, and you frozen and pongy from that filthy river.'

'Not quite how it was,' I laughed, and I told her the story of Marksy's adventure in the pool. Accidentally on purpose forgetting to mention that Brendan had helped him in with a hefty shove.

'Thank goodness our Brendan isn't in trouble for once,' Anita said. 'Hot scrambled eggs and bacon?'

I snuggled up to Brendan on the sofa in front of the gas fire and a black and white film. I still had the shivers but now the warmth was back in my bones and I hadn't a bad thought in my head.

Truanting from school? It never crossed my mind.

Until a visitor turned up.

The afternoon film had finished. Brendan and I were swapping memories of children's TV when Anita showed the Lion in.

'Guessed I'd find you here.'

'Oh no,' I gasped, and my doubts and fears came rushing back.

My sad dad.

The school on fire.

Brendan and his knife.

Legging the afternoon from school.

'Didn't I warn you?' said Brendan. 'You're a truant. It's catching.'

'I've got form.'

It was easy for him to laugh, but I didn't, and neither did the Lion. In fact, she gave me the creeps with those threatening lioness yellow eyes, and her lips gave me just a hint of scorn.

'The Community Constable was asking after you,' she said casually.

I supposed she had switched her attention to Brendan. It gave me quite a jolt when I realised that her eyes, unsympathetic and unblinking, were still on me.

'After me?' I said hotly. 'Why would he do that?'

'Perhaps he's heard you've got form.'

'But I've already spoken to Detective Chief Inspector Cardew.'

'Ah, yes, but as Brendan can tell you, once you've got form you never know when the cops will come knocking.'

Anita poured tea and offered biscuits.

'I can't bear our Brendan to be in any more bother,' she said.

'I gather he's brought you more than your share, Mrs Smart,' said the Lion.

'The cops - they'll have us down at their station again. Bound to.'

Akinyi

We were all quiet, waiting as the helicopter racketed above the street.

'The policewoman was killed with a six-inch knife,' said the Lion.

She spoke so quietly that we had to let the helicopter noise fade before we could continue.

'Every policeman and woman knows it could have been him or her. It scares them, as well as making them sad for their lost young colleague. It hardens them.'

'They turn their cars round outside our house,' Anita said. 'I was just getting into bed last night after Akinyi left.'

'Outside your house?'

'Silly isn't it, Missis Lyon? They could turn round anywhere, but they always choose our house, with their headlights shining full blast. It's bad enough when they do it in the daytime. At night it's really scary. I swear they can see me through the curtains, as if they've come on purpose to watch me undress. It's harassment, that's what.'

She paused and then snapped at Brendan. 'It's you they're really after. You're the troublemaker round here.'

Brendan was back in last night's sullen mood.

'We've been out of bother for so long,' Anita continued. 'It's been like a holiday.'

'Are you settled in Ashbrook?' the Lion asked.

Anita shook her head. 'It'll never be like Rosebud. Friends and neighbours, that's who I miss. Here in

Ashbrook you pass folk in the street, but everybody lives on their own.'

'What about joining a women's group? At the community centre, say?'

Anita looked down. 'I've been meaning to.'

'They'll be pleased to see you, Mrs Smart. What do you find interesting?'

'She makes things,' said Brendan. I squeezed his hand, welcoming the return of his warmth. 'You're clever with your hands, Mam.'

'Look what she's done with my hair,' I said.

'One of these days. Maybe when this - this business of the fire gets sorted.' She laughed. 'OK, I know what you're thinking. If it's not one thing it's another with our Brendan. After the fire, a bit of peace if we're lucky. Then on to the next thing. It's been the same since he first learned to walk.'

'I understand,' said the Lion.

Perhaps she meant to sidetrack Anita. If so, it didn't work. I was struck by the way Anita had taken so quickly to the Lion. She needed a shoulder to cry on, and the best she could find belonged to a schoolteacher. She cradled her teacup and leaned forward, desperate for reassurance - from the school's Lion.

'When I stopped his pocket money ...'

'What did you do that for, Mam?' Brendan quipped.

'Because on top of your asthma you started smoking,' she snapped. 'Can you credit that, Missis Lyon? He can hardly breathe when he has an attack, yet there he was, not ten years years old and smoking like a chimney. Fags paid for by thieving from my handbag till I stopped him. Next it was shoplifting. The security manager from Ashbrook Shopping Centre came to see us. A carton of fags nicked from the paper shop. Could have been anybody but I forked out without arguing. Do you blame me?'

The Lion let her go on.

'Burglary was the worst. I cried in the night about that, I can tell you. My son a burglar! At first he was a hanger-on with older kids off the estate, and there were chats from the police. In one ear and out of the other. So they cautioned him. Then things got out of hand, and we went to court. Burglary was one thing, the judge said, but he had to put his foot down when it came to fire.'

'Yes,' the Lion nodded. 'Fire's in a league of its own.'

'Of course.' Anita hadn't finished yet. 'I could have managed if I'd had a bit of help from his dad.'

'Whose fault was that?' Brendan snarled.

I squeezed his arm.

'Talk about frustration.' Anita said.

'Serves you right for leaving my proper dad.'

Anita's eyes welled up and she wiped them with her sleeve.

'My dad and I were good mates.'

'Oh yes, it's easy enough to be mates with a 6 year-old. As soon as the little devil needed sorting out, Missis

Lyon, where do you think Superdad was? Half a mile away at the allotments. Shut in his shed with his *Composter's Weekly* or counting his racing pigeons. We were supposed to have been trying to get out of Ashbrook to a nice house in Willowbank - or anywhere. Steve, that's Brendan's dad, he lost all interest, gave up the fight. Said we could manage where we were. He got sulky with me. I couldn't do right.'

She paused, and now she and Brendan glared at each other. He had to hold himself back from gagging her.

'That's why,' Anita said, 'it was so good when Eric appeared.'

She caught her breath, and more tears spilled down her cheeks. She tried to wipe them away.

'Anita!' I felt so awful. 'Please don't ...'

'Let her be,' the Lion murmured.

'It was the hardest decision of my life,' Anita blubbered, 'but I did it. Eric and his wife had got this house but she left him. He asked me to come here with him and I did.' She hiccoughed and irritably dashed away more tears. 'Our Brendan refused to agree. It might have been hard for me, but it was plain agony for him. Specially when ... when his dad said he might as well go with me.'

Silence in the room. I didn't know where to look. At uptight Brendan. At lovely Anita with tears streaming down her face. The Lion balanced her empty tea cup on her knees as she managed to signal her concern and at the same time stay watchful.

'So you can understand why Missis Lyon has to come here, can't you?' Through her tears Anita appealed to Brendan with a desperate smile. 'I shouldn't have made you leave your dad. You've been nothing but trouble ever since and it's all my fault.'

We waited for Brendan to accept his mother's apology.

'Burglaries and fires.' Now Anita appealed to the Lion. 'You know, there's been none since he met Akinyi.'

The Lion nodded. 'I'm afraid, Anita, that he might have let you down on Sunday night.'

'You might be right,' Anita moaned, 'but God, I live in hope.'

The Lion stood up. She waited by the door as Anita bundled my wet clothes into a shopping bag.

Then the door bell rang.

'Oh, oh,' said Brendan. 'They have their own special ring. The law.'

Chapter 21

Detective Chief Inspector Cardew was only a thin man but he filled the doorway.

Anita looked haggard. 'OK', she sighed. 'I suppose you'd best come in. And before you ask, yes, our Brendan is at home.'

She pointed at an armchair. Cardew sat down, crossed his legs and faced furious Anita and sullen Brendan.

No one suggested I or the Lion should leave, so I sat beside Brendan. The Lion took the vacant arm chair.

As they had been in my dad's office, Cardew's manners were immaculate. I knew what his game was. He's picture painting again, I thought. This time he wants to size up Brendan's family scene.

'Some questions of fact to begin with, Brendan.'

I would have loved a moment on my own with Brendan. I wanted the chance to warn him - don't be taken in by the quiet voice, the gentle tone.

Akinyi

'How did you spend Sunday afternoon?'

'I've already answered that question of fact I don't know how many times.'

Brendan was looking anywhere but at the policeman. I knew he felt cornered. Trapped.

'Your friends took him down the station as soon as the lady cop was killed,' said Anita. 'This is a waste of time. We've been over this stuff.'

'I can understand your annoyance, Mrs Smart, and I promise you I'll be quick in checking the basic facts.'

'You already know the basic facts. You knew them before you came here,' snarled Brendan. 'So why bother?'

'Tell you what,' said Cardew. 'Humour me.'

'That's what he said to me,' I said, 'word for word.'

'Humour me - what's that supposed to mean?' Brendan muttered. 'Dunno what he's on about.'

'I have nothing to hide and neither do you,' I said, 'so best get it over quickly.'

He remained sullen but he did look at the policeman.

'Sunday afternoon?' said Cardew.

'Mooched about,' Brendan sighed.

'At home?'

'Just here and there.'

'With anybody in particular?'

'Some mates. Can't remember who they were.'

Akinyi

'Time?'

'Can't remember what time I went out. After dinner, I suppose.'

'Twelve o'clock?'

'Maybe. Half past maybe.' Brendan shrugged. 'Could have been quarter to one.'

'You do remember, I hope, that you eventually met up with Akinyi?'

'Went to see her at the school. So what?'

'That was at around 7.15.'

'If you say so.'

'Did anybody come with you?'

'My mates. Can't remember their names.'

Cardew nodded as if he had never heard anything more reasonable.

'Do you like living in Ashbrook?' he asked.

Brendan scowled at him in sudden surprise. I wondered if he had ever met a Cardew, watchful and cunning.

'What's that got to do with anything?'

'Are you a happy lad? You don't look very happy.'

'How in the name of God,' Anita burst out, 'is he going to be happy with cops crawling all over him? Helicopter flapping about. Cars buzzing up and down the street, poking their nasty noses into people's business.'

'Do you miss your father?'

The question stunned both Anita and Brendan. Cardew didn't spare them.

'You're bitter, perhaps, that he's separated from your mother.'

Brendan's head was down. He shrugged, flattened for a moment.

I slipped a hand through his arm and gently persuaded him up.

'When your parents separated,' said Cardew, 'you'd set your heart on staying with your dad. She overruled you.'

'I told him he had to come with me,' said Anita. I could tell she wanted to be calm, but she was finding it hard. 'And when Brendan turned to his dad, he got a big shock.'

'Remember that, Brendan?'

'Course I do.' His voice was hardly above a whisper.

'What exactly did your father say? Do you remember?'

'Told me I had to go with her.' He shrugged towards Anita.

'That was a bad moment for you, wasn't it?'

It could have been a sympathetic question but I knew it was no such thing. It was just a matter of fact statement of the Cardew kind. No emotion. No loading.

I understood.

Cardew is probing, I thought. This is how he works. He wants to learn if anger and frustration might drive Brendan as far as setting fire to the school. Surely, it can't

Akinyi

be fair to poke him like this in places where he's been hurt so badly.

'It was when I found out my dad couldn't care less.'

'I cried when Brendan told me this story,' I butted in. 'It's horrible. Do you have to make him go over it all again?'

Cardew studied me without speaking. He gently rubbed his nose.

'It might help,' he said.

'He felt rejected and hurt,' I persisted. 'I know that because Brendan has taught me to wonder about my own parents. Perhaps they rejected me. In Africa parents like to have boys. They think boys will grow up to own the land and to look after them in their old age. The only use of a girl in tribal societies is for the dowry. The more lovely the young woman, of course, the larger number of cows that can be claimed for her dowry.'

I was out of order, I knew that, and I paused long enough for Cardew to tell me so. Then I remembered that wasn't his way. I saw the corners of his mouth soften into the faintest hint of a satisfied smile. I hardly had time to wonder what that was about when I knew the answer. He's used me to soften Brendan up, I thought.

'My dad was a good mate,' Brendan said.

I nodded. 'You did things together.'

'There was this field of allotments where we lived.' He ignored Cardew and spoke to me instead, still hardly more than a sullen mutter. 'He built a greenhouse on ours. And we had this wooden shed, where we used to go at night in the winter. If you closed the door and pulled a curtain across the window you could make it warm in there. My dad read gardening and fishing magazines and … and told me stuff.'

Cardew tilted his head and made a thoughtful shape with his lips. They were the slightest of movements, but watch out, I thought - here comes another of his menacing questions.

Right on cue.

'Did your dad teach you to be a burglar?'

Brendan glanced angrily at him, then looked away. 'I couldn't get my head round it when Mam and Dad split up,' he said, and it was an obvious attempt to change the subject.

Cardew let him get away with it.

'It didn't seem real. I couldn't imagine not having them both at home.' It was still me he was talking to. 'When I think about it now I can remember that Dad might have had a nasty temper. I don't think Mam knew him all that well when they married.' He looked defiantly at Anita. 'It was a shotgun do.'

The room was silent, a moment of tension as we all waited for Anita to protest. She put her hands across her eyes instead. She shook her head as if she realised she would never make sense of this bloody-minded son of hers.

'Do you care?' Cardew asked.

'Course not. It happens all time, doesn't it?' He challenged me. 'I mean, I wasn't a bastard, was I?'

Akinyi

My stomach lurched. A bastard! Perhaps that's me.

'They'd been married a few months before I stuck my nose into the world,' said Brendan. 'You tell him, Mam.'

'Steve and I paired up when we worked at the Ritz cinema,' said Anita.

'Maybe he should have warned you,' sneered Brendan.

'Warned me what?'

'That his favourite spot was his allotment shed.'

'Would that have made a difference?' asked Cardew.

'Might have. She could have told him to sod off, she'd bring me up as a single mam. Plenty of women do that.'

'You would have missed out,' I said, squeezing his arm.

'Oh, yeah.' His sarcasm was bitter. 'You don't know the end of this story yet, Akinyi.'

'Perhaps my African mum told my real dad to sod off. Perhaps she's better off without him. I hope not. I hope they love each other, even if they've given me away.'

'We were 18 when we got married,' said Anita, 'and the Council gave us a house. Just where I asked to be, five minutes walk from where we both worked at the Ritz. Not far from my mother.'

'And a rotten house it was, by all accounts,' said Brendan.

There was a sudden tightness in Cardew's lips. Oh! oh! I thought, Brendan's his target. That face is his warning for Anita and me. We've to keep our noses out now, thank you. This is between him and Brendan. Well, he can get lost. He's a nosy sod and he's deliberately stirring up trouble.

'Why did your parents decide to bring you to Ashbrook?' I said.

'They couldn't wait to get me out of that grotty house.' Brendan sighed irritably 'It was damp. Doing shocking things to my chest. Giving me asthma. Then they got a letter from the Council and they went to look at houses on Ashbrook, five miles off. It cost expensive bus fares, and there was no saying you liked what they offered. Twice you could say no thank you and the third time you had to like it or tough.'

Now Brendan was vicious, and Cardew's smooth forehead showed a wrinkle or two of concentration.

'My Grandma was the wise one. She got out before ...'

'Got out?' I prompted.

'Passed away. Snuffed it. Kicked the bucket.'

'Steady, Brendan,' I murmured.

'Before my mother started mucking about with ... Why did she have to leave my dad?' Brendan turned from me to challenge Anita. 'You weren't so clever, were you, when you got tangled up with that git?'

Before Cardew could react, I was ahead of him, unruffled, determined to hold him back. 'That git? Who do you mean?'

'I can hardly get my tongue round his sodding name,' said Brendan. 'Him. Hammond. Eric Hammond, my mother's fancy man. Useless git.'

Akinyi

'Ambulance driver, isn't he?' said Cardew.

'You know fine well he is, so what are you asking for?' Brendan didn't even glance his way.

'Your mother's fancy man, I think you called him.'

'Cheeky devil.' Anita snapped. 'I'll fancy man you, our Brendan.'

'I hated the bastard on sight,' Brendan told me.

We waited again. This time not a nerve stirred the smooth skin of Cardew's face.

'I was only 6, but I should have booted him where it hurts.'

I can keep Cardew out of this if I'm lucky, I thought. Though I can't stop him watching Brendan like an attack hawk.

'I wanted to go to the Ritz,' said Brendan. 'Tell my dad about him. It couldn't be right. She was my mam, and I wanted to puke.'

He paused. His fists were clenched, and his face was taut with the rage he could hardly hold back.

'I knew they'd been to look at this house because she came back full of herself. I was mixed up. I liked seeing her happy. This Eric pleased her with soft words and little prezzies. I didn't know what to think.' His rage surged. 'Do you know what she said? My mam? Do you know what she said? "It's taken us years to find a real good house, our Brendan," she said, "but this is it. It might not be Willowbank, but it has a perfect garden for Eric. Not too long at the back, just right for a patch of

Akinyi

veg and a little greenhouse." Jesus! Can you believe she'd say that? I went dead quiet, real hard. "Just right for my dad," I said. She blanked me. She'd made her mind up. She was coming here with her fancy ambulance man. She was set on it. She went on and on about the kitchen and its electric hob and the shower and the three bedrooms upstairs.'

'And what did you say?' I whispered.

His rage had gone. He put his feet on the coffee table and looked at Anita, half in sorrow, half in scorn.

'Told her straight I wasn't going.'

The blue eyes and the pale face were clouded with faraway thoughts.

'My dad didn't put up a fight for me. Mam wanted me, and she was my mam, wasn't she? What was I supposed to do? She got her own way.'

He looked round the room, at the Lion and at Cardew, full of wonder. As if it had just dawned on him they were there. As if he'd thought that all along he was having it out with me. As if something about himself had just clicked.

'I must have been soft in those days, Akinyi,' he laughed. 'It's meeting you that's made me hard.'

I squeezed his hand. 'As if,' I murmured.

'She wasn't so bad,' he went on, 'because she stuck with me. I had no time for her Eric. He'd run off with her, hadn't he? Wrecked our ...'

He hesitated. He didn't want to say anything softer than he'd already said.

'Family,' he said so quietly even I hardly heard him. 'And definitely no time for my dad. Why didn't he fight to keep me?'

Cardew uncrossed his long legs and stood up.

'Oh, Brendan,' he said. He spoke as if it was hardly worth mentioning. 'Perhaps I could borrow your raincoat.'

Brendan stood, too, and faced him. Inches separated their noses. Cardew was in control, smooth, calm. Brendan was braced in fury. I watched, horrified and helpless. In only a second the tension collapsed from his face, replaced by scorn.

'I can't stop you, can I? You know that, and so do I. Borrow the kitchen sink. Borrow the duvet off my bed while you're at it.'

'I could get a warrant.'

'Stuff your warrant. Give yourself a tour of the house. Mam won't mind. She's seen it before.'

'Just the raincoat, thank you, Brendan. For the time being.'

Chapter 22

As soon as we drove away from Brendan's street in the Lion's car, I let rip.

'You've got it all sewn up, haven't you, you and Mr Winter and now that rotten detective fellow. Brendan's guilty and nothing's going to change your minds. That's disgusting. All the kids at school think you're fair. Even Brendan. And you're ...' All my bottled-up confusion, frustration and fear frothed out. 'You're bloody well not.'

I was fuming, but I didn't dare go on. Besides, I was lost for words. Confused. Frustrated. Frightened. That said it all.

Nobody talks to the Lion like this, I thought. After all, she's the Deputy Head. She's entitled to dish out the how-dare-you treatment.

But no, she didn't need to do that. She'd seen too much in her time to be fazed by my feeble brand of cheek. She hardly even took her eye off the road.

Akinyi

'Your father will be glad to have you back,' she said. She pulled up at a crossroads to let some traffic go past. 'He's never had to account to the police for your movements before.'

'And another thing,' I said sulkily. 'Why has he taken away Brendan's favourite raincoat? He carries it with him everywhere. I don't understand.'

'There's a lot we don't understand,' the Lion murmured. 'The raincoat's one of the easy bits.'

'Doesn't make sense to me.'

'Tests. Modern testing. The raincoat will probably tell them what Brendan had for his breakfast.'

'Oh yes,' I muttered.

And I knew it wouldn't be Brendan's breakfast the police were interested in.

The knife. Traces of the knife would make them sit up and take notice.

I wrapped my arms tightly round my school bag. In it were my books, and between the pages of one book was the knife. Now I'd got it I had no idea what to do with it. All I knew for certain was that I didn't want anybody unexpectedly finding it on me. Hide it in my bedroom? Put it in the dustbin? Talk to Frosty?

I was well confused, but then I gave myself a good talking-to. If the Lion can look so trim, so controlled, dammit so glamorous even when she's driving her car, I'll aim for some of that myself.

'You haven't asked why I'm dressed in Anita's clothes.' I pulled a sulky face.

'It was on the tip of my tongue before you mugged me.'

'Sorry.'

'No need. I must say Anita's clothes do suit you. You look good.'

I decided I'd stay sulky, but I did moodily explain how Brendan and I met Marksy at Mog's Swing. How Marksy congratulated Brendan on a fine fire. How he fell into the river.

'Well, actually Brendan pushed him.'

'I see.'

'In front of loads of kids Marksy accused Brendan of lighting the fire. He couldn't get the word out, so he called him an arse.'

'An arse?'

'Arse ... arsonist, what's the difference?' I shrugged. 'Everybody thinks Brendan did the fire, but I don't. Brendan doesn't think Marksy could have done it, but I do. He was there. He was talking big. So why not?'

'Why does Brendan say not?'

'He says Marksy wouldn't have the guts. Calls him a weed. But he had that other boy with him.'

'Leonard Longley? Not an arsonist, according to Mr Winter. Too much sense.'

'You talk exactly like Brendan.'

'Probably. You'll have to face it, Akinyi. Brendan is everybody's favourite. He has the form.'

Hysteria welled inside me and I bawled at the Lion again.

'The form, the form, that's all you ever say. There has to be more to it than that.'

'He's a one-off, Akinyi. What you have no way of understanding is what a tough-nut he is. You heard what Anita said. He's been chased by the police since he was knee high. And by magistrates.'

'Not since I've known him.'

'It's no good crusading for him.'

'I'm not.'

'It's a danger. It'll take more than a nice middle class girl like you to convert him.'

The Lion socked it to me.

'You quarrelled last night. Then you and I both saw him kick Jonathan Marks this morning.'

Amazing woman. I could hardly believe she'd spotted that.

'And now you tell me he's pushed Marksy into the river. It all adds up.'

'To what?' I heard myself scream my protest against her unshakeable certainty.

She'd pulled up to look both ways at another Ashbrook cross roads.

Abandoning reason, I opened the door and jumped out of the car. Holding tight to my school bag.

'Sod you all,' I snarled. I crashed the door shut, nearly knocked a kid off his motorbike in the middle of the road, and dashed along a street.

Chapter 23

I wasn't spoiled for hiding places. The best I could manage was a spiky hedge in somebody's gateway. From there I watched the Lion drive by, turn at the end of the road and drive slowly back.

Looking for me, I thought. Let her look.

I fidgeted as I hid in my gateway.

A kick and a push. Two simple actions to frighten Jonny Marks. And so many ways to make sense of them - enough to drive me crazy.

First the kick. OK, so it was a warning, a painful one at that. A warning, says Brendan, to get off Gloria's back. A warning, says the Lion, to keep quiet about the fire.

Then the push. I'd seen it with my own eyes. Brendan was frustrated that Marksy took it for granted that he lit the fire. That's an innocent girl's nice interpretation, says the Lion, of another naked threat.

I shook my head in sheer frustration.

Akinyi

Marksy, I thought. I'd give anything to talk to Marksy. The police are for ever leaning on Brendan to account for himself. Why not turn the heat on Marksy? It's only fair.

So what are you waiting for? You know where he lives. You've walked past his house with Brendan.

A street corner phone box, camouflaged by graffiti and shattered glass, reminded me that time was passing. It was after six.

Time to check in with doting Daddy.

I took out my iPhone and saw that he had rung me several times. And left text messages.

I didn't speak to doting Daddy as a darling daughter should. He was fretting about my safety ... as well as the company I was choosing to keep.

'Akinyi! You missed half Miss Butler's French lesson ...'

'Ten minutes.'

'The Community Constable came looking for you. PC Philips.'

'That's stupid. The police don't think I lit the fire, do they?'

'They have to make their enquiries, Akinyi. You weren't far away when it was lit.'

'If it comes to that, you weren't far away either, Dad.'

The spite in my impertinence made him take a sharp intake of breath.

'I don't know what's happening to us, Akinyi,' he said. I was really sorry for him. I knew he was struggling to control his anxiety. 'You went out at lunchtime and didn't come back for afternoon school.'

A day ago that would have been as breathtakingly unthinkable to me as it still was to my dad. Not any more.

'I've got to find out who lit the fire,' I said.

'Akinyi!' He was winding himself up. 'Miss Lyon has rung here and told me that you've run away from her. What can you be thinking of, my darling? Where are you? When will you be back? Let me come and pick you up.'

Good idea, I thought. I could go home. Forget about this whole stupid thing, leave it to Cardew, the Lion and Frosty. Make Dad his supper. Stop him worrying that I've gone totally off the rails, up to my eyeballs in stuff neither he nor I understand.

'And your final rehearsal for the festival?'

'Oh heck!'

This was terrible. I hadn't given the rehearsal or the Fun Fest a thought.

And there was so much to worry about. The Hall, for starters. It was a chaotic mess. Where were we going to perform? Where was everybody going to sit?

The acts. I needed to check up on them all. They needed me chivvy them along. To bully them. To make sure they understood that fire or no fire the Fun Fest was going ahead.

Had the Steel Band boys checked their drums and agreed what they were all going to wear?

The pantomime actors. Last time I saw them in rehearsal hardly half of them could remember their lines. I meant to find time today to lean on them.

And the magician. T. Saisha's dad.

Oh God! I needed to get hold of him for a serious chat, but he was such an oddball. I'd rather not. Surely, he must understand that his fire swallowing routine was right off limits now.

My dad interrupted my chaotic thoughts. 'Mrs Siddle and George had to make do without you.'

I didn't like the self-pitying sound of it, and my determination came back in a flash of irritation. No, I've got to do this. Brendan has got to be innocent. And if I don't prove it no one else will.

'Dad.' I spelled it out for him. 'I'm finding out who started the fire.'

'Fortunately, Mrs Siddle, top class Music teacher that she is, has finalised the arrangements and everything is on schedule. Assuming you can be relied upon to be there.'

'Course I'll be there, Dad.'

Unless I forget to press *Save*. Again.

'Miss Lyon has arranged to come here quite soon. She and Mr Winter need to update each other about the fire.'

Clearly, my dad would sooner drift back into his little fantasy that the fire had never happened.

Temptation again. Wonderland temptation. Was it really possible - I enjoyed the thought for a moment - that this time yesterday the fire was still waiting to happen? Was there a time BF - Before The Fire?

Then no, I have to do this.

'Put the kettle on,' I snapped, and I jabbed *End Call*.

I switched my iPhone to silent mode, came out of my hedge-back hiding place, and strode towards Marksy's house.

My poor old dad, I thought, chances are he thinks I've lurched into teenage trauma. Maybe I can talk him into retiring. Soon. Sooner the better. Trouble is he's scared he'll be out of a job at the same time as I leave home for uni.

I wondered if the Lion would help me talk to him.

As I marched, I had to control my rising irritation at the thought of those stupid policemen with nothing better to do than wind Brendan up and give my father grey hairs.

And Dad himself. My anger and my fear gathered as I thought of his helplessness. I need someone like the Lion, I fumed, to help me ask him all the questions I have about myself. He doesn't understand that it's facts I'm after, not pats and cuddles. I'd like to scream at him.

'I'm Akinyi from Kenya,' I'd scream, 'not from wimpy Willowbank!'

For a moment I lost it. Terrifying hidden thoughts surged into my mind, and my pretend scream became a real howl. Right there on an Ashbrook street.

'My parents are dead, aren't they? What did they die of, Dad? Was it AIDS?'

Chapter 24

The privet hedge outside Marksy's house had never been trimmed. It had crisp packets and torn polythene among its stumps. There was enough orange light from the street for me to see that a patch of sad grey lawn was home for seeded dandelions and tough weeds.

I hesitated. I had no plan. Anything could happen to me. As I pushed the front gate, its wooden frame sagged on one hinge. I tried giving the area the Frosty private eye treatment. I was quietly pleased with myself when I spotted next door's lace curtain twitch and a bloodless face draw back into the room. I opened the gate on its one hinge and squeezed through.

Down the side of the house was the dustbin, half buried in the hedge. It smelled of ash and burned cooking fat. I glimpsed a pocket handkerchief of back garden. Cracked paving stones, a cockeyed washing line pole, more grey grass.

Akinyi

My heart was racing, and I was tempted to change my mind. Only for a moment. Then I tapped on the door.

Another surge of panic. I couldn't believe I was doing this. It wasn't too late to scarper.

Then - pull yourself together. Think like the Lion. How does the Lion behave when she makes awkward, frightening home visits to difficult kids? You're not the Lion, but you can be yourself. Think like a proud African. Darker eyes than any white girl could dream of. Beautifully Anita-braided black hair. And you look good in Anita's clothes - the Lion says so.

I stood tall in defiance of curtain twitching neighbours.

For reasons of her own, Mrs Marks wanted her visitor out of sight. She ushered me into her kitchen.

It was my second Ashbrook kitchen and not a bit like Anita's. Mrs Marks had no handyman Eric to fit cupboards and shelves with a glossy modern finish. Her kitchen was as scruffy and as poky as a school stock cupboard, lit by a single weak lightbulb behind a dingy shade.

I had to edge my way through the door, and Mrs Marks rammed it shut behind me. There were five of us in there, and that didn't include Jonny.

Mrs Marks was a small lady. Aged thirty and a bit, I guessed. In other words, she had Marksy when she was 16 or 17. She looked grey and tired, sad and angry. She hadn't brushed her hair. There were angry lines across her forehead and around her eyes and her mouth. She looked sorry for herself.

Akinyi

But I knew she was ready for a fight.

It was a kitchen-dining room. There was a table in the middle, with a floppy tasselled cloth. A half-full bottle of milk stood on it, with an evening paper and a scattering of crumbs. Cups, saucers, plates and dishes, all waiting to be washed up, littered the table.

Sitting up to this mess, chomping away at a monster bag of monster-munchies were two gorgeous 6 or 7-year old boys. Twins. Mixed-race. They had curly hair and huge dark eyes full of wonder. What a contrast to poor Marksy, with his beaten-up eyes in his pasty face - and that weird bullet-shaped head.

And, sitting in a cellophane-wrapped pushchair there was a baby. Boy or girl? I couldn't decide, but it was a Marksy lookalike. It seemed quite content to make miserable chuntering noises, slaver to itself and - no kidding - bend its double-jointed elbow up to its nose and sniff.

Hands on hips, braced for battle, Mrs Marks poked her face at mine.

'I've heard of you,' she said.

She didn't invite me to sit down, though we could both have squashed in beside the boys at the table and been more comfortable.

'You go around with the Smart lad.'

In spite of her slightly disgusting family sniff, she managed to look smug.

'I've told my Jonathan. If ever I hear of him anywhere near that good for nothing, I don't know what I'll do to him. So he knows. He's to stay away from him.'

I was speechless. I only knew I'd been crazy to come here. Help!

'Well then, has he sacked her?' Mrs Marks dipped her head as if she was going to butt me with her sore-from-sniffing nose. 'Half a day's pay I've lost because of her, and that's not money that grows on trees.'

'Sorry,' I stammered. 'Who do you mean?'

'Your father, of course. He's the Headteacher, isn't he? He's sent you here. Why else would you come? What I'm waiting for you to tell me is has he sacked her?'

'Sacked her? Sacked who?'

'Her, of course. The Siddle woman.'

'What? I ...'

'And I say again, it's only right and proper that if she clouted my boy for nothing I should clout her. That's what I'd tell your father and that's what I'd tell the Education. Except it costs me half a day's pay to leave work.'

'But that's none of my business. I haven't come here to talk about Mrs Siddle.'

'Oh? And what have you come for then? What else is there?'

'The fire, of course.'

'Oh that. I don't know about that.' She sniffed. 'He's come home this dinnertime wet through and freezing. I've kept him in bed, wrapped up with hot water bottles. Says he knows who did the fire.'

'I know who he has in mind, and that's what I'd like to talk to him about.' My anger pounded back and with it my determination. To rescue Brendan I'd say whatever I had to say in this house. And I wouldn't leave till I'd said it. 'I bet he's perfectly well enough to come down.'

'I suppose I can see if he's got warmed up.'

Mrs Marks chuntered as she went to the stairs and - hello, what was this? Sitting at the bottom of the stairs, earwigging behind the curtain was none other than Marksy himself. You'd have expected Mrs Marks to be as surprised as I was, but it seemed he'd played that trick before.

'That's your game, is it?'

She grabbed him by the earwigging ear and hurled him at me. I couldn't stagger back because there was nowhere to stagger to. I was jammed between the table and the back door

Marksy whimpered. As I put one hand out to stop him falling onto me I nearly dropped my school bag, which I'd been clutching all this time. I wasn't going to let go of that. Not in this house.

'Not fair,' he snivelled.

'I want a word with you,' I said.

'And since you were lughole-flapping you'll know that I've mentioned no names,' said his mother.

'It was Brendan Smart,' said Marksy.

Just like that.

'What was?' I said.

'Eh?'

'You said it was Brendan. What was?'

'That fire, what do you think? It's what you've come here to pin on him.'

'Pin it on him? Sounds like you're the one doing the pinning, Marksy.'

'He did it, didn't he?'

'Can you prove that?'

'We followed him. Legs Longley and me.'

'You did what?' Mrs Marks swiped a broad flat palm across his ear. 'How many times have I to tell you to stay away from that jail bird?'

'Brendan is not a jail bird,' I said, flashing my indignation.

'Damn soon will be. The whole estate knows that. How many times have you promised me? You snivelling little ...'

'Brendan met me and we went away,' I began.

'We followed you,' said Marksy, rubbing his reddening ear. 'The pair of you had a barney. You went home. We followed Brendan to school.'

I shuffled impatiently. It sounded like a boring jigsaw, beginner's level. 'You followed him to school. Whereabouts?'

'Round the back.'

'Then?'

'He went in.'

'Went in? How?'

A pause.

Aha! So the jigsaw pieces were not a baby's toy after all.

I watched him. Sifting the remaining pieces? Thinking ahead?

Nice try, Marksy, but I'm not letting you get away with this.

'How, Marksy?'

I could imagine the Lion's tone of voice. Detective Chief Inspector Cardew's, too. They could both do it. They could load their voices with gentleness and menace at the same time. OK, if they could do it, why not me? After all, I was going to be a teacher one day.

'He went in, Marksy.' I coughed. Too gentle. A bit of the menace needed. 'You going to tell us how?'

'I dunno. It was dark. Legs and I went home.'

'So you didn't see Brendan go into school?'

Silence. The twins crinkled their monster-munchies bag.

'Or light the fire?'

'No.' Marksy was rattled. He started to panic. 'But it must have been him. He's lit loads of fires.'

If there was one thing I knew fine well it was that I should control my impatience. I should move forward, as the Lion and Cardew did, in careful steps.

Too late.

'That doesn't mean he did it this time,' I said, and my voice was more shriek than menace. 'He says you were talking big. Let's break in and write graffiti. Pathetic talk like that.'

It was an effort, but I managed to come down an octave. 'Did you say that stuff?' I growled.

Marksy nodded.

It was too much for his mother.

'You stupid little so-and-so! You talk like a hooligan. Just wait till I ...'

'You can't have it both ways, Jonny,' I said, and I was close to sounding reasonable. 'If you know Brendan lit the fire you must have been with him. So let's have it - were you with him or weren't you?'

Marksy shook his head, a definite shake this time. As far as I was concerned, that was enough. Fat lot of use it was coming here, I thought. What have I proved? Not a single solitary thing - except that the Lion and Frosty are spot on - Marksy's a little boy and a big liar. He was at home when the fire started. He knows zilch about it or about Brendan's movements. Time to get out of here.

'So you were not in the school last night with Brendan?' I said hopelessly. I couldn't even raise a miserable hint of detective or teacher, and Marksy had no trouble slapping me down.

'Course I wasn't, Stupid. How many more times?'

'And you didn't follow Brendan into the school?'

'No.'

Akinyi

'The last you saw of Brendan last night was - when?' I risked giving Marksy a gentle shove in the chest. 'When? Go on, Marksy, tell me when.'

'Why should I? Who do you think you are, anyway?' he blazed. He pushed me, harder than I'd pushed him, against the kitchen door. 'He buggered off with you.'

'Language!' his mother snapped.

'And you followed us?'

'Course we did. We weren't going to miss you two, were we? Not when you were knocking lumps off each other.'

'How nicely put, Marksy. And now we're somewhere near the truth.'

A nod.

'No more lies, please.'

I was getting a bit of confidence back. Following a new line of thought before I was even conscious of where I'd heard such ideas.

Even less where they might lead.

'Good,' I said. 'Now tell us what you do know about the fire.'

Marksy jerked his bullet head, and specks of dirty pink appeared in his sickly cheeks.

'Nothing. How should I know anything?'

'That's rubbish. Everybody knows something about it. Next, you'll be telling us you didn't even know there was a fire.'

'I'm not that daft'

'Course you're not. So tell me what you know.'

Marksy shrugged. 'I dunno, do I? There was this fire.'

'Have you looked at the hole it burned?'

'Suppose so.'

'Where did it start?'

'In the ...'

Marksy looked straight at me and we shared the faintest of understanding smiles.

'You thought you could con me,' he said. 'I don't know where it started, do I? They say it was the ...'

'Music Room. Who says so?'

Marksy shrugged. 'Mostly everybody.'

'What else does mostly everybody say?'

'Eh? Like what?'

'Like, for example, who did it?'

'I didn't do it.'

'Who did? The truth, mind.'

'How should I know?'

'Mostly everybody is talking about it. I bet mostly everybody in Ashbrook has an idea. What do they say?'

'Never heard anybody mention it.'

'When they catch the person who did it, what do you think will happen to him?'

And now my spirits lifted. Schoolteacher talk. Talk brought home by Dad to Mum at the end of long days at school. Talk I'd heard as I cooked supper after Mum had died and Dad spent hours on the phone to colleagues and parents.

'Dunno. He'll get taken into care maybe. Special school.'

'What's that?'

'I don't know, do I? It's like jail. They get locked up.'

I waited. I tried to pin hope back but it wriggled free inside me. Marksy did it, after all! Brendan was innocent!

'If they won't do drugs they get knacked in the showers.' Marksy, stared at the unwashed pots.

Still I waited. This time it seemed Marksy's imagination had dried up. Lion-style, I weighed my words to disguise my excitement. Featherweight, even lighter.

'Is that what they'd do to you?'

Marksy was not fooled. His eyes shot up, full of protest. His mother was unable to stand by any longer.

'He's told you he didn't do it!'

'I've told you I didn't do it!'

I spread my hands wide in innocence. 'I said if you did.'

'But I didn't.'

'If you did,' I said with a flash of fear. I knew that somehow I had to dig deep for the cheek to ignore Mrs Marks' simmering violence. 'If you did, let me tell you what they'd do. They'd take you to court.'

Akinyi

Now I really was pushing my luck. My understanding was no more than a patchwork of half-overheard conversations. I had to think quickly to piece it all together into something that made sense. And quickly. Mrs Marks was highly likely to know this stuff inside out. Any moment she could swipe me aside in scorn. In violence even.

'Your mother would come along, too, of course, and our Year Head, Mr Winter, would be there to help you as much as he could. There'd be this judge chap. Not one of those blokes with curly wigs that you see on TV. No, this would be the juvenile court, you see. The judge would be an ordinary bloke in a suit and tie. He'd look at your school report, written for you by Mr Winter, and at your police record.'

'I haven't got a police record!'

'He hasn't got a police record!'

Mrs Marks hammered a clenched meat-red fist on the table. Crockery and cutlery bounced. One twin stuck a thumb in his mouth. The other wrapped his arms round his brother's neck, and they rubbed their two munchie-crumbed faces together.

'That's true,' I said, eyeballing Marksy, 'but you see, you would have if you'd lit that fire. On your police record - the one you haven't got but which you would have - the judge reads that you're a good boy. This is your first offence. He can see that you come from a supportive home. That means your mother looks after you. "Poor boy," they say in the court, "we're sorry he hasn't got a dad. Tell you what we'll do," they say, "let's put him on probation." And that's arranged. You have a probation officer to talk to every week.'

I let my gaze saunter round the kitchen. Everywhere except at Marksy's mother. I daren't meet her eye because I knew that any moment she was going to rumble what a con merchant I was.

'I think you'll enjoy having a nice bloke to talk to, won't you, Jonny? It won't take him long to realise that you're a good boy at heart.'

Marksy was mesmerised. Frankly, so was I - mightily impressed by my own performance.

Not so Mrs Marks. She was not so easily taken in. Far from it. She turned on Marksy without mercy.

'Is this true, you …?'

Marksy flinched. 'Is what true?'

'God give me strength!' She flat-handed his ear for the second time. The twins' eyes filled with tears. 'Did you light the fire the way this … this … this schoolteacher's brat says you did?'

'Do I?' I said, but I kept my face cruel and gave Marksy no hope.

He was going to confess the fire. I was breathless with impatience to tell Brendan. Wonderful news!

'I never did,' sobbed Marksy. 'Wasn't even there.'

'You tell so many lies you wouldn't know the truth if it kicked your arse,' said Mrs Marks.

Marksy's terrified eyes skittered between his mother and me.

'Alright, alright. I'll tell you.'

I held my breath. So - somehow - did Mrs Marks. The twins licked yet more monster-munchie crumbs off their lips.

I let myself give Marksy the gentlest smile of encouragement.

'Go for it, Jonny.'

'It has to be a deal.'

'I'll give you a deal, my lad,' said Mrs Marks. She shook her fist. 'I'm good at deals.'

'What's the deal, Jonny?' I said.

'I'll admit I was in the school last night, if you ...'

'Will you listen to him?' Mrs Marks wailed. 'Now what sort of deal can you make, Brainbox?'

'Go on, Jonny. You were in the school last night. And ...'

'I didn't light the fire.'

Chapter 25

I slumped. Served me right. I'd been so sure I'd pushed Marksy into the admission that would clear Brendan. What a letdown!

'You can't blame me for the fire and you can't blame me ...' Such as it was, Marksy's confession came in a rush. 'For pinching the dog.'

We all waited.

There was nothing more.

'What are you on about?' Mrs Marks growled. 'Pinching what dog?'

My inspiration had left me. And just when I'd been looking forward to describing my triumph to Brendan ... and to showing the Lion that I wasn't such an innocent after all. That the fire mystery was solved and all thanks to me.

I felt limp with disappointment

'Poor little Pirate,' I muttered. 'Where did he spend the night?'

'It was his idea,' said Marksy. 'That Newk ... You know him, that Newk ...'

'Newk?' Mrs Marks snarled. 'Now who are you dropping in it?'

'Newcomb,' I sighed..

'That's him,' said Marksy. 'George Newcomb.'

I took in a sharp breath and held it painfully tight. It was incredible.

In more ways than one.

Incredible that it had never occurred to me that George was there, too. In the street with those boys last night. But ... But ... surely, it was off the planet to think that George, silly George, violin prodigy and classroom idiot ... no, it couldn't be true.

Could it?

It had taken Marksy long enough to get started, but now he couldn't wait to give us chapter and verse.

'You were there when we met him one night. That time we were messing around out Fencote way. Me, Legs Longley and that bossy lass, you know who I mean.'

'Saisha.'

'That's her. Legs wanted to know if he had any money on him worth nicking.'

'And he hadn't. Not even 10p. So?'

'So, we went back. Yesterday afternoon.'

'Back to Nether Fencote? What for?'

'To that church. Just Legs and me. We wanted to have a look inside.' Marksy sniggered. 'It was dead easy to get in. There's a key hidden on a shelf in the porch. We went in and ...'

He looked fearfully at his mother. He had every reason to fear the worst. A shadow of rage darkened her face. I did my best to head her off.

'You went in, Marksy. And ... ?'

'We did our tags.'

'On the walls?'

'Tags?' Mrs Marks snarled. 'What are you talking about? Tags?'

'He means they wrote their names,' I translated flatly.

'Your names. You wrote your bloody names,' said Mrs Marks. 'God above grant me patience.'

The sudden dead calm simplicity of her voice was proof that Marksy had pushed his mother into unknown territory. Her exasperation had never been forced to stretch this far without her lashing out.

Marksy nodded and whispered. 'And in the Bible.'

Silence deepened in the gloom of the kitchen. All of us pondered this breathtaking admission of mindless destruction.

Then from somewhere at the back of her throat Mrs Marks let out a gurgle of half-exploding rage.

'You did what? You piece of ...'

'Well then.' Marksy fended her off. His voice rose to a shriek. 'We had a look round. There was nothing worth nicking, was there?'

I let out a hopeless sigh. 'And on your way back you met George at school? And Saisha. Anybody else?'

'Only you and Brendan. You disappeared along the street. Brendan told us to naff off. I was just going to follow you and him when George says to Legs and me, "Do you want to go into school?" Well, we'd just been talking about it, hadn't we?'

'You had,' I said. 'Silly talk about breaking in and ...'

'George said we didn't need to break in.'

'Oh? How come?'

'He said Ma Siddle was still in the Music Room. With her dog. "She's that big fat woman," said Legs. And George goes, "Want to have a laugh with her?" Well, Legs wanted to go home because it was his little sister's birthday, but we got him to come along for the laugh. She was singing a song and feeding her dog. We took the piss out of her.'

'Give me strength.' said Mrs Marks. 'And you have the nerve to bring me to school when I should be at work. All because she's given you a push. It's more than a push you're in for after this, I can tell you, my lad.'

The twins separated their heads. Wordless, they left their seats and ghosted, one this way, one that, round the table.

'Please, Mrs Marks,' I said. 'Let's hear the rest.'

'He was the worst, that George,' said Marksy. 'He's barking, that kid, the things he was saying.'

'Alright, alright, Marksy, everybody knows about George,' I cut in. 'What happened next?'

'While her back was turned George picked the dog up. He shoved it inside Legs's jacket. Then it jumped out and bolted through the door and we scarpered after it.'

'Did you catch him?'

'Legs did. It stopped for a pee on the playing fields.'

'Where is he? You haven't given him back.'

'Legs said he wanted to keep it.'

'Humph. And I thought he was the one with a bit of sense,' I grumbled.

I noticed a movement by my knees, and those amazing twins, thumbs in mouths, took one of my hands each. They've got it sussed, I marveled. They reckon if anyone around here is going to get their head knocked off, it's me. I crouched beside them, and we shared quick high fives.

'To give to his sister for her birthday,' said Marksy. 'She's always wanted a pup.'

'OK,' I said. 'You scarpered. Where to?'

'Home.'

'And George - did he go with you?'

'He lives in Willowbank. Dunno what he did.'

Marksy and his mother were nose to face, ugly with hatred of each other. I used the moment to catch them both off their guard.

'Did you light the fire, Jonny?'

I blinked at my own suicidal cheek. I'd popped my question like a dummy into a baby's mouth. Things had been threateningly quiet. Now Marksy went into a tantrum.

'No! No! No!'

'Were you there when it was lit?'

'We never even heard the fire engines. We ran home with the dog.' He met his mother's furious stare for the first time. He was desperate for her to back him up for a change. 'I was sure Brendan must have lit the fire.'

My heart sank. Back to square one. Again.

'Are you sure?' I spelled it out for Marksy. 'Are you sure that George had already left you by that time?'

Marksy stared at me, frowning out of the mud flats of his eyes.

'This is important, Jonny,' I murmured. 'Think.'

'He lives up the hill in Willowbank. He'll have run home in case somebody stopped us with the dog. He's a wuss.'

Can you believe it? Marksy thought George was a wuss.

Ugh! I couldn't look at him close-up any more. I couldn't bear it. He was horrible, but I knew I had to insist. Even if it meant gazing into his creepy eyes.

'Did you see George run home or are you guessing?'

Akinyi

Marksy was at full stretch. I could see it there in his shifty eyes and the way he dipped his bullet-shaped head as he sifted truth from giant porkies.

'Think about this, Jonny,' I pressed. 'Might George have been in the Music Room after you left him?'

Marksy elbow-wiped his nose. 'Might have.'

I'd outstayed a welcome I'd never had. If I was going to get out of there in one piece I'd need to choose my words.

Too late. Again.

I stamped my great hoof.

'What time did you get home?' I demanded.

That was it for Mrs Marks. She'd had enough.

'You might be the Headteacher's daughter,' she hissed, 'but we don't have to answer your questions, young lady.'

I had one muddled thought left in my stupid head, and that was the last shadow of a possibility that Marksy lit the fire. I turned on him and went bonkers. The twins clung to my dress.

'I don't buy your stories,' I shouted. 'You lit the fire. If you'd been back here in Ashbrook as early as you say, your mother would back you up. I think you're the arsonist.'

I got what I deserved. And how! The only surprise was that it hadn't come earlier. A fearsome ear-bashing. Fortissimo.

'Just you wait, young lady, till I see your father. I'll let him know what I think about you. Just you wait … next time I lose half a day's pay and I come up to that school. I'll give him what for. And you. You cheeky madam.'

She grabbed a weapon from the kitchen stove and rushed at me.

'Accusing my lad of I don't know what. And where's your proof, that's what I'd like to know. Saying he lit the fire. Saying he pinched the dog. Telling us he's going to court. All lies and no proof. It's you that's lying through your teeth. You that needs a probation officer. You'd better get out of here before I wrap this round your ears. And I'm not talking about one day next week, either. The minute I catch hold of you, I'm gonna …'

I'd witnessed the Mrs Marks line in ear-smacking and I didn't fancy it. Not one little bit. I ducked under whatever it was she was swinging - a frying pan. There was hardly room for me to turn round, untangle myself from the twins and scrape the kitchen door open before the frying pan came whizzing at me again. I shot out into the dark.

If she'd wanted my arrival to be hush-hush, Mrs Marks did everything to report my departure on the evening News.

I scarpered, dropping the rotten front gate off its hinge. Recklessly, I waved to the twins as they flat-nosed an upstairs window. Then I was glad to be chasing my shadow between gloomy orange street lights.

Chapter 26

I trembled as I headed homeward along dark Ashbrook streets. Behind drawn curtains shadows flickered from TVs. I envied these homes where it was the end of a working day and life was about the simple things. Tidy the supper dishes into the dishwasher. Put the kettle on. Switch TV channel. Go on Facebook and You Tube.

Oh well, at least Marksy let slip about George and the dog.

So I knew he was in school after all.

But - and it was a big but - I'd blown it.

Accused Marksy of being a liar.

In front of his mother.

In their own kitchen.

No wonder she wanted to smack my head with her frying pan.

Akinyi

In the gloomy orange light of a street lamp I recognised the Lion's car parked outside somebody's house. I didn't know whether to be relieved or to continue with my stroppy sulk.

After all, I hadn't changed anything, had I? I couldn't tell the Lion that I was right and she'd got it all wrong, that Marksy had lit the fire and Brendan hadn't even been there.

Dream on.

I was back to where I was before I jumped out of her car.

I didn't feel like admitting it, and I decided I'd get away from her. Quickly.

Just as quickly I found my mind had changed itself and I was sitting down to wait on a low brick garden wall.

A cold wind gusted along the street. On the pavement a pile of grey plastic bags had been loosely stuffed with old armchair cushions, pieces of carpet and torn wallpaper. A woman, overweight and shapeless, crossed the road. Her lookalike Labrador stopped to squirt its scent onto one of the front wheels of the Lion's car.

'Nice,' I murmured.

A chance to chill. I couldn't have walked home anyway. Twenty four hours of action had stormed past, and I was ready to drop. My feet were sore, my legs were aching and my head was buzzing. I'd done things and seen things I'd never have believed.

And tomorrow it was the Fun Fest. I'd been planning it for weeks. Then two days ahead of the great event I go and turn my back on it.

Did it matter?

Not as much as the fire.

Correction. Not as much as the fire if the fire was lit by Brendan. The fire I could live with. If it was lit by Marksy or Legs Longley.

George? No, forget that.

Hang on, though. Maybe it was time to think again about my friend George. To have some second thoughts. To listen to some nagging doubts.

One. Take George the angel - violinist and model pupil on his own with Gloria. Him and arson? Forget it.

But two. Take George the demon - classroom buffoon. Worse. Classroom vandal. Classroom thug. Driven by a need to prove himself to other boys.

Look. This George meets up with Marksy and Legs Longley, and what happens? Imagine it. There's talk of break and entry. Graffiti. Anti-school tearaways, shouting their mouths off. There's backslappingly noisy self-congratulation. Crazy laughter. Dare devils, all safe inside the mob.

For George these are blissful moments, as he kids himself that he's accepted, that he belongs, that he really is one of the boys.

Let's face it. This George could easily flip.

What - and take those kids back to Gloria's room, where the three of us worked all afternoon at our music?

He might do, yes.

And be mean enough to steal Gloria's beloved puppy?

Afraid so, yes.

And setting fire to the school - might he ...?

Yikes, what a bombshell if that was true!

Yes, but people get over shocks, and that was one I had a feeling I could live with.

So, I thought, this matters more than George. It matters more than the Fun Fest. More than anything, it matters that Brendan is innocent of the fire.

And - I faced this, in that quiet moment in a cold wind down a dark street - Brendan was close to the school when the fire started. He'd only just left me. He was certain he was followed. But he was wrong.

For once in their lives those boys didn't traipse along behind him. They got mixed up with George instead. They couldn't give Brendan an alibi.

So it was possible that he, as well as they, went into the school building.

Brendan promised me this wasn't so, and I said I believed him. What if it turned out that he'd lied ... ?

It was a horrible thought. I didn't think I had it in me to make my Fun Fest a success. People would be disappointed. My dad would be appalled. My idea of twinning with an African school would flop.

I closed my eyes tight and prayed that I was right to trust Brendan. He and I, I prayed, God knows how but we must come through this. Together.

Chapter 27

I was miles away when the car locks sprang open and the Lion bundled a bouncy Jack Russell puppy onto the back seat.

'Joining us, Akinyi,' she asked, 'or still doing your own thing?'

'Sorry.'

The Lion shrugged my half apology away. 'Perhaps,' she said. 'Best get into the car anyway. Your father will be out of his mind with worry.'

The puppy leaped forward onto my lap and licked my nose with his warm tongue. Somebody loves me, I thought, and I tickled his ears gratefully.

'You missed a treat,' said the Lion, starting up the car.

I was keen to hear. Anything for a bit of hope.

'Legs wouldn't speak,' she said. 'Not a dicky bird.'

I groaned. 'This is Legs Longley's house?'

'Yes, I thought you'd be grateful if I called in,' said the Lion casually. 'You were in my face, you know. Telling me I should double-check your suspicions.'

'But it's still Brendan you're after?'

'I learned one thing, and it rules out ...'

The Lion broke off to lower the window on my side.

A man poked his head into the car. I got a squinted close-up of the whiskers on his cheeks, and he grinned at me in the glow of the street light. He was a big, friendly fellow, a bit like a human version of Gloria's Pirate. If he'd had a tail he'd have wagged it.

'Saw you sitting out there, love, and I thought I'd have a word. My lad tells me you're Mr Macdonald's daughter. A gentleman, your father. You to can tell him from me, Stan Longley - all my kids say this - Missis Lyon is the best teacher in England.'

'Alright, Mr Longley,' laughed the Lion and she touched the window button.

'I agree,' I told the friendly man.

'You do understand, Missis Lyon, don't you?' He looked past me and Pirate and spoke to the Lion. 'I mean - why our Len can't speak.'

'Yes, Mr Longley. You've made it quite clear, thank you.'

I detected the first hint of weariness in the Lion. And why not? After all, I wasn't the only one who'd been going flat-out for twenty four hours. In fact, she'd probably been up all night. Keen to make sure it was business as usual on Monday morning. No wonder she was a bit ratty with well-meaning Mr Longley.

'They've always been the best of mates, those two,' Stan Longley said. 'Through thick and thin. More thick than thin, you might say, they've got into that much trouble. His friend more than our Len.'

'OK, Mr Longley. We'll be off then.'

She wanted to close the window, but he was through it beyond his neck, and he was in no hurry.

'So,' he said. 'The fire. I know who. You know who. And our Len knows who. It's just - I'm sorry he can't help you with the name. Young devils, the pair of them. I've always had high hopes of our Len. He's never been what you'd call a real bad lad. You can check that with Mr Winter. I've told him this time, though. "Your mate's landed himself in it good and proper, my lad." That's what I've told him. "Forget about how good he might have been when he was a little lad. Nobody's going to set him on with form as a fire-raiser." Our Len clams up, Missis Lyon, but you can take it from me he understands what's happened and how bad it is.' He sighed. 'That doesn't mean he can shop his mate. The estate wouldn't understand, you see.'

'Listen, Mr Longley.' The Lion seized her chance. 'It's too soon to be certain, but I believe you've given me the information I came for.'

'Eh?' He jerked his head back in fright. 'See here, don't go saying I've fingered anybody. Not me.'

'Alright, take it easy,' said the Lion. 'The time. Remember? You told me the time Leonard got home.'

'Did I?'

'For the end of his little sister's birthday party, you said.'

'That's right. Eight o'clock their mums and dads collected them. '

'And he was home by then. You told me so.'

'Oh, a good while before. Quarter of an hour maybe. He came home, puffed out from running with the dog. Lying young devil told us he'd run all the way from the kennels. Now we know better, don't we?' He tickled Pirate's ears with his huge hands. 'Oh, it was a good while before eight because all the kids were on the floor playing with the dog when their mams and dads came to take them home.'

'Well done, Mr Longley. You can relax. I'm pretty sure Len's in the clear.'

'What? No fire-raising?'

'Not this time,' said the Lion. 'The fire service timed my 999 call at seventeen minutes past 8. What is it for a fit lad up here from school, carrying a dog - fifteen minutes? That puts him out of the school by ... what? Twenty five to?'

'Missis Lyon! You might not be very old but you've got a head on your shoulders, you have.' To me - 'You tell your father that, young woman.' To Pirate - 'Bye, dog.'

The Lion pressed the window button and pulled away from the kerb.

'Imagine,' she chuckled, 'an Ashbrook full of Stan Longleys.'

Typical of the Lion. She was a blend of contrasts. Gratitude. Affection. And downright exasperation.

And exasperation was something I had my own share of.

'Do you mean to tell me,' I said, 'that Legs was going to sit there in silence and take the blame?'

'That's the code of the estate. He'd rather do that than shop his friend.'

'Yes,' I grumbled. 'And I thought that was what Brendan was doing. Now it appears there's no one left for him to protect.'

'I have to agree, I'm afraid.'

'Mr Longley gives Legs an alibi.'

'And by implication Marksy, too.'

'I suppose so.' I was moaning again.

'I'm going to suppose that when Legs came home to Ashbrook, so did Marksy.'

'I've been to see him.'

'You have?' The Lion took her eye off the road to give me a sharp look.

'Yes,' I said, quietly satisfied.

'I should have known your little wobble wouldn't take you home to your father. Goodness knows what he'll think now.'

'Mrs Marks could have put her darling Jonathan in the clear. She could have told me what time he got home.'

'She could, could she?' said the Lion. 'Am I right in thinking Miss Tantrum didn't give her the chance?'

Chapter 28

The Lion and I were laughing when we reached my house. It was exhausted laughter, giddy you might say. Pirate was still with us. We wanted to give him back to Gloria, but she wasn't at home when we called. I was glad. I scribbled a note to say I was looking after him.

'He can spend the night with me,' I said. 'I've often asked Dad to let us have a little dog.'

The Lion yawned as she drove.

'Mrs Siddle and George were all for calling off your Fun Fest when you didn't turn up after school.'

'I know. That was terrible.'

'I talked them into giving you another chance.'

And we giggled together, so that my dad and Frosty looked at us as if we were crazy. Two crazy females and a pirate pup. The men were watching *Coronation Street* in the front room. I was glad to see some cups and a milk jug on the table between them. The teapot was on top of the filing cabinet. Oh well, I thought, you can't have everything. It would have been just like my dad to forget the creature comforts altogether.

Frosty was funny. He'd had his hair cut. And I could swear he'd had his suit pressed. How funny. For the first time ever, I felt slightly sorry for him.

Feeling sorry for Frosty. How weird was that! It was like I was noticing for the first time that he was a real person. A man, not some kind of superman.

I guessed the Lion fancied him just as much in his usual crumpled mode.

I kissed my dad's forehead and told him he'd done well. The Lion went to the bathroom and I to the kitchen to find a water bowl and make a bed for Pirate. Then it was time to rustle up supper. My dad was anything but a soaps fan, not even of *Corry*, and he was soon checking up on me.

'Careful not to tread on Pirate,' I warned him. 'You can slice the apples, stir in sultanas and put them on the hob to stew.'

They were little jobs I could trust him to manage while he did what he was itching to do. I didn't mind.

In fact, I gave him the answers before he even asked his nosy questions.

'Yes, Dad, what your minders have told you is true. I've spent today with Brendan Smart. Yes, I truanted. And no, I haven't forgotten that I promised Mr Winter not to see Brendan again till after GCSEs.'

My white sauce boiled and I stirred in grated cheese.

'I've broken that promise, Dad. I'm seeing him again.'

My sauce thickened smoothly. I sprinkled pepper.

'Have you noticed I'm wearing his mother's clothes?'

He shook his head without understanding. I'd been doing really well with him - giving him that little kiss and talking nice and friendly - but suddenly my weariness flared into irritation. I just managed not to yell at him. Instead, I took his glasses off, polished them on a kitchen towel and slapped them back on his face.

'Now can you see?'

'You feel a lot for this boy, don't you, darling?'

I held back a scream, but my voice was menacing. 'Yes I do.'

'You've always had lots of friends, Akinyi.'

'I'm glad you think so,' I said bitterly. 'Would you mind telling me who they are exactly, these friends you have in mind?'

'You have a whole class full of high quality friends.'

'Name them for me, Dad. Name one.'

'There are ... boys and girls.'

I spoke through clenched teeth. 'Have you the remotest idea what it's like being the daughter of the Headteacher in a stonking great high school full of ... boys and girls?'

'But, Akinyi, you've always been popular.'

'Name me these kids I've been so popular with. I can't wait.'

Akinyi

'Well, there's George.'

'Dad! Do me a favour.'

'Then there's Justin, Leroy, Michael ...'

I found this hard to believe. He rattled off the names of all the boys in my class, all sixteen of them, without tripping over one.

'You're sure it's not just because Brendan is very good-looking?' he added. 'Girls of your age are bound to be tempted to impress their friends.'

Ouch! I didn't expect that. He might be the Headteacher, but I'd always thought of him as a headteacher who knew more about the inside of his headteacherly office than he did about kids. He didn't come out into the corridors and mix with them, that's for sure. He had the Lion and Mr Frosty Winter, among others, to do that for him.

'I suppose you can recite the names of all the girls, too, can you?' I said sarcastically.

'Well, there's Megan and there's Chrissie ...'

For the first time, he hesitated. In fact, he came to a grinding halt. I could have ranted at him. I settled for a second helping of sarcasm.

'Bet you wish you had my Brendan, don't you, Megan and Chrissie?'

I turned on him, armed with a saucepan of boiling cauliflower.

'If I ever did have this thought, Dad, it didn't taken me long to ditch it.' I tipped the cauliflower into a colander and flushed the boiling water furiously down the sink.' I can tell you there's far more to Brendan than a model to show off with.'

He peered at me through rising steam. 'Such as, Akinyi? What is it about him that attracts you so deeply?'

I pulled a furious face.

'It was exciting at first to be seen with an Ashbrook boy.'

Damn, damn, damn! He'd only just accused me of wanting to impress my friends by parading Brendan, and here I was proving him right.

'And then you realised that was phony.' He was understanding and forgiving.

'It was phony, of course it was. Especially compared with the welcome I had from Brendan and Anita. Then Mr Winter got me to make that stupid promise not to see him. That screwed everything up with both him and Anita. The best chance I've ever had for a real friend. '

'Along came the fire,' said my dad.

He was in control, and I was furious. If we're going to row I wanted it out in the open, rowdy, with no rules, the way rows were among the kids at school. How could I row with him when he was so reasonable?

And what if he was right?

'It seems,' he went on, 'that there is every chance that your Brendan lit the fire.'

Now I shrieked. 'What proof is there?'

'His record …'

'Don't give me that stuff about his form. I'm sick of hearing it.'

'He doesn't have a proper alibi, Akinyi. Not one that will stand scrutiny by Mr Winter ... or by the police.'

'OK, OK, so according to his form, it's cut and dried that he lit the fire. He has no alibi. I know that. I should hate him. He's set fire to our school. Your school. I should hate him.'

'But what if he did it out of deep frustration?'

'Stop it, Dad,' I shouted. It was the pan of hot sauce that I was wielding now. If my dad saw that it could become a weapon at any moment he didn't flinch. 'You're not Gandhi. We've been learning about him in History, and he's really inspired me. Now the pacifist bit is getting me down. What do you mean he's frustrated? That's my argument.'

'I'm waiting for you argue it, my darling. If you did I might understand.'

'OK. Look, Dad. Brendan had a best friend, his dad. His name was Steve. Things went pear-shaped. Brendan's dad left him without looking back. Brendan had always been naughty. Now he became downright bad. Brendan loved a girl. She had other things to do. She strolled off without looking back. Brendan did a bad thing - maybe.'

'A bad thing? What he did was an outrage. Terrorism.'

'Dad ...'

My dad held up his hands to silence me.

Akinyi

'But perhaps it was an understandable thing,' he said softy. 'A forgivable thing?'

Our row was over. It had flashed and blown itself out.

I poured my white sauce over the cauliflower.

My dad has outmanoeuvred me, I thought. He can argue for me and against me in the same bust-up. His face is haggard. He looks old. His hair has turned from silver to white. His eyes are tired but full of tolerance for me and my funny ways. The cheeky old sod!

'I hope,' he said, 'that once tomorrow's Fun Fest is over you'll be able to concentrate on your GCSEs.'

I pushed his glasses up and kissed his face. 'Try stopping me, Dad.'

'He's not from an academic background, Akinyi.'

'That's true, but you should have heard what he said about my friends who fool about in Mrs Siddle's music lessons. I love him, Dad.'

Wow! I'd blurted it out.

Out loud.

And I felt wonderful. I'd spelled it out for my dad, after all.

And while I was at it, I'd put myself straight.

'You're very, very young, Akinyi,' he said.

He was an old dear. He would say that, wouldn't he?

'I know, Dad, but I'm not stupid. Listen. If I've got Brendan, I'll be happy. I'll get on with my schoolwork. Without him I don't know what will happen.'

We enjoyed each other's company for a peaceful moment.

'Two minutes till supper,' I said. 'Pour our guests a sherry.'

Chapter 29

The guests were bound to have heard me scream at my dad. No doubt Frosty gave his eyebrow a workout, but he was all innocence when Dad and I came into the room. He and the Lion were sitting together on the sofa and she was tactfully asleep with her head on his shoulder.

Dad and I took the arm chairs.

'Summarise the situation for Mr Winter, Akinyi,' the Lion mumbled without waking up.

Frosty looked at her, with just a hint of the raised eyebrow. I stifled a giggle.

'Miss Lyon and I have visited the homes of three boys, Brendan Smart, Jonathan Marks and Leonard Longley.'

I stopped for a moment. Just long enough to go to the piano and bring the stool across so that I could sit beside my dad. Feeling guilty for doing so many things all in one day that were enough to give him nightmares? For shouting at him about Brendan? For telling him I loved Brendan when he had Brendan down as his favourite for the fire?

Some of that, no doubt. Along with just a little feeling that he needed protection when his familiar world had suddenly gone crazy on him.

'Legs Longley's father gives him a passable alibi,' I went on. 'Miss Lyon believes it also covers Marksy.'

'Mr Winter,' the Lion sleep-mumbled, 'works to timetables.'

He gave her a special look, her hair spread across his suit. 'No flies on Miss Lyon,' he said, as if he needed to apologise to me and my dad for his admiration and love.

'Akinyi,' the Lion said, still mumbling, 'do a timetable of movements. It'll help you. Me too.'

Frosty helped me on my way with the raised eyebrow and an Uncle Frosty wink.

'OK.' I began. 'I'm thinking aloud here, you realise. On this time-and-movements grid, there are a few definite points. One is the start: 7.15 when George and I leave Mrs Siddle in the Music Room. She told us we'd had a long day and it was time to go home. The other fixed point is 8.17 when Miss Lyon dials 999. And if you like, you can count 8 o'clock, when Legs Longley's sister's birthday party is scheduled to end and parents arrive to collect their kids.'

I paused to think. Pirate was at my feet. How good to have a little dog all of my own, with his unconditional love. One day perhaps.

'Yes, then there's the fireman, Mr Evans. He estimates that the fire was started between ten to 8 and eight o'clock. He might have a more precise suggestion by now, of course. Anyway, the rest is guesswork.'

I paused again to gather the logic of it all.

'Seven fifteen · George and I leave the Music Room. Mrs Siddle is packing up and Pirate is feeding.'

The pup caught his name and gazed adoringly up at me.

'Seven twenty - in the street we meet Brendan, with Marksy and Legs. Mmm: they had a girl with them. Her name is Saisha. Seven twenty two - the others buzz off. Brendan and I quarrel. Seven twenty five - we go our separate ways.'

'Did you notice,' Frosty said, 'which way his way was?'

'Sorry, no. Detective Chief Inspector Cardew asked me that. I was in a strop - too proud to look back.'

Frosty's eyebrow behaved itself, but he pulled a face.

'Seven twenty eight - I arrive home. Around the same time George, Legs, Marksy and, presumably, Saisha reach the Music Room.'

'Humph!' said Frosty. 'We can imagine, can't we, what the cops will make of this when they get round to interviewing all the kids? "These three lads," they'll say, "and a girl, go into the school, yet you say they have an alibi. Can't wait to hear what it is". What were they playing at?'

'Winding up Mrs Siddle.'

My dad gasped, and I was glad I was sitting with him.

Akinyi

'Seven thirty five-ish,' I hurried on, 'they set off home.'

'With the possible exception of George,' yawned the Lion, sitting up, 'who might still have been in school. We don't know. One of them had Mrs Siddle's dog in his pocket.'

My dad started to speak, then changed his mind.

'Tell them about Pirate,' said the Lion.

Pirate sat up, ready for anything. I bent down to stroke his ears.

'If you believe Marksy,' I said, 'George stole the pup and pushed him into Legs' jacket.'

Frosty understood. 'Palmed him. Got rid of the evidence. Dropped Legs in the brown stuff.'

'Legs took Pirate home as a birthday present for his little sister,' said the Lion.

Frosty scowled. 'If you hadn't tipped me off, I'd have these charmers down as the fire-raisers. No question.'

'Tough, mate,' said the Lion. 'By the time I dialled 999 at 8.17 Legs had already topped the bill at the kiddies' party, entertained them all with Pirate's party tricks and handed them over to their mummies and daddies at 8 o'clock. Estimated time of his arrival home: quarter to 8, ten to maybe. Ahead of Fireman Evans's guesstimate of the fire's start-up time.'

'OK, so that's Legs out of the frame,' said Frosty. 'What about Jonny Marks?'

'Akinyi and I don't see eye to eye. For me, it's a dead cert that when Legs ran for home he had Pirate in his pocket, and Marksy ran with him. You've told me yourself that he rarely, if ever, acts on his own. He went home to his mother.'

The Lion interrupted herself with a dry cough and an unsmiling glance at me.

'Akinyi has paid her a little visit.'

'She wouldn't give me the exact time Marksy got home,' I said.

I shuddered as I remembered my undignified retreat in the face of Mrs Marks' frying pan.

Frosty frowned at me.

'So,' he said, 'Brendan Smart? Last seen by Akinyi at 7.24. He's perfectly placed for the job.'

'Yep.' The Lion as good as smacked her lips. 'Unless,' she added as an afterthought.

'Unless?' The eyebrow.

'Unless Anita comes up with a more exact time of arrival home, when you visit her in the morning.'

'Sounds like fun,' Frosty chuckled.

'And another thing. Pin Brendan on what he was up to on Sunday afternoon. The Detective Chief Inspector, for reasons of his own, was soft on him about that.'

I led them into our kitchen dining room and served hot cauliflower cheese. I muttered my annoyance when I found that my once-smooth cheese sauce had gone lumpy. Should have served it straightaway instead of playing detectives.

Akinyi

Apparently, Frosty didn't notice the lumps. He ate hungrily.

'My turn to report,' he said. 'Nice meal, Akinyi. Didn't expect it.'

He wiped his mouth with the back of his hand and put his fork down on the table beside his plate.

'I spent some of the day with Martin Philips, the Community Constable,' he said. 'A chap from forensics rang to confirm the Music Room as the seat of the fire.'

I stared at him, my mouth suddenly dry with anxiety. He wiped his lips with the back of his hand. Mum wouldn't have approved. I'd provided napkins. If he needed to wipe his mouth he ought to have used the one I gave him. Then he put his fork down. Mum had views about that, too. Knife and fork should be placed side by side on the empty plate.

Now look. Frosty had picked his knife up again. He was concentrating hard and must have lost all track of good manners because he pointed it straight at the Lion.

Something panicky lurched in my stomach. Sunday afternoon, I thought. The policewoman was killed with a knife. The Lion told us so. Brendan cut the rope at Mog's Swing with a knife. Then Anita's words last night. "He wasn't even at the football match, were you Brendan?" Followed by the bitter accusation that Brendan was playing dumb. Then Brendan's claim that he was mooching about. No times. No names. No alibi.

The policewoman was killed with a six inch knife. How many inches was the knife Brendan produced from his raincoat pocket?

The one we rowed about.

The one which right at that very moment was hiding in my school bag.

OK, so it saved Jonny Marks at Mog's Swing. OK, so its handle was in friendly yellow rubber. But its blade was long, thin and scary. Six inches? I'd hardly dared look.

For long seconds more of panic the fire was not important. It was not as a mere arsonist that I must defend my Brendan, but - impossible, horrible thought - as a murderer. The murderer of a policewoman.

Frosty held me with a terrible fascination. He was still waving that damned table knife.

'As Dafyd Evans told us in the school yard last night,' he said, 'an arsonist might kick-start his fire with something highly inflammable, petrol, say. The fire department use dogs to sniff it out. This time, there's nothing so obvious. No, the fire smouldered quietly. It built up heat and smoke over a bit of time, like a quarter of an hour or twenty minutes. In the heat, the window gave way and a fireball shot across the hall just as the firemen were arriving. It's the window that has got the cops and the fire investigators wondering. The window that looked from the Music Room down onto the hall.'

'Curtains,' said the Lion.

Again Frosty aimed his knife at her. 'Got it in one.'

'Tatty old things, not a flame-retardant stitch between them.'

'Exactly. Should have been free-cycled years ago.'

He's explaining fire, I gasped, not a murderous stabbing. Brendan was with me when the policewoman was stabbed. I was desperate to leave the room and get a grip of myself, but Frosty was on a roll.

'Martin confirms no school door was forced. And no window. So somebody got into the school with a key. I went with Martin to talk to Mrs Siddle. She said it was impossible she left either the main front door or the Music Room door open.' Frosty shook his head. 'I believe her. She's paranoid about her precious equipment. Good thing too. There's thousands of quids' worth. Was.'

'Then the most likely thing,' said the Lion, 'is that Brendan magicked the doors. You tell me he's perfectly capable.'

I touched my father's shoulder before he could gasp. It didn't stop me feeling my own stab of annoyance and fear.

Frosty went on. 'Mrs Siddle told us she assumed the novelty of the dog would wear off pretty quickly and the kids would get rid of him. She had no chance of catching them but she rushed out into the street in the hope of finding him quickly. What we don't know, then, is whether the fire was already alight when she left the room. She says she didn't smell smoke.'

'Or whether somebody with a key went in there after she left, and started it,' said the Lion.

'Cops' territory,' said Frosty. 'They'll be looking more closely.'

'More about our take on George,' said the Lion

They all looked at each other. I shrugged. I didn't know where to start.

Frosty summed him up. 'A professional musician in the making. A childish little boy desperate to mix with tougher kids because he sees his own talents in their terms ...'

'It's true,' I said. 'He'd much rather be a footballer than a violinist.'

'OK, well, I've had enough for one day,' said the Lion. She yawned and stood up. 'Time for my beauty sleep.'

You and me both, I thought. I was too tired to think straight. I picked Pirate up from under my feet and gave him a tight hug.

My dad went with Frosty and the Lion to the front door.

'I wish I had a fiver for every time his dad has bent my ear about George's genius,' I heard Frosty say. 'Can't wait to hear what he says when he gets to grips with this little lot.'

'I'm leaving Mrs Siddle's Pirate with you, Mr Mac,' said the Lion. 'I'd guess you could have a visitor any minute: Mrs S in person.'

Chapter 30

I thought it was a bit funny that Frosty didn't leave, too. He came back into the kitchen with my dad and he showed no sign of going away.

I made coffee and tried to relax, but Frosty was soon back on the case.

'Interesting about that little rat catcher,' he said, nodding at Pirate stretched out asleep in my lap. 'Martin Philips couldn't get hold of Mrs Siddle last night. She wasn't at home when he called. Today she told us she spent the night with her sister and her brother-in-law. They live downtown. Mrs Siddle went there and waited for Pirate.'

'Waited for him?' I said. 'How weird is that!'

'She wasn't to know that Legs had done a runner with him, was she? Like I said, she dashed out of school assuming the kids would get rid of him. When she didn't find him she went to her sister's and waited there.'

'But downtown? That's miles away.'

'True, but when he gets the urge your little friend Pirate makes a habit of legging it down there. Seems brother-in-law feeds him scraps from his fish and chips.'

'That must be where Mrs Siddle is tonight,' I said. 'Still waiting for him. How horrible for her.'

Frosty nodded.

'I've been thinking,' I said. 'When you and PC Philips spoke to her today, did Mrs Siddle say what time she left school? And can we assume she's right when she says she locked the doors?'

'Tell you what, Akinyi,' said Frosty. 'That grid of yours. I'm not saying you've got it wrong, but I'll play devil's advocate, OK?'

If you must, I thought. I was too tired to argue.

'OK,' said Frosty, 'so we're reasonably sure that two of the lads, probably the girl, too, are away from the Music Room by 7.35. Needless to say, that also means George. We know he won't hang around without the other kids to give him courage. I want to turn your reasoning upside down. Suppose that before they leave they've started the fire. They've used no explosive accelerant so it takes a while to get going, even with the help of the curtains. Forty two minutes till Miss Lyon sees smoke and dials 999. See what I'm getting at?'

'Maybe those kids aren't so innocent after all.'

'OK. Wait a minute. Legs and Marksy have the dog. They get a move on because Legs wants to be home for his sister's party. For George it's a doddle. He strolls onto the patio in plenty of time to admire the pretty fire engines with his dad. Mrs Siddle blissfully locks up behind her, and the firemen have to smash their way in to put out the fire the kids have lit.'

Silence in the room. I glanced at my dad. He was nodding off in his chair. Worn out.

I knew as well as anybody that George had some tricks for getting his father off his back. But to start a fire, stroll home and play the wide-eyed innocent? Surely, that was totally incredible.

But what if …?

'Oh well,' I said, 'that's everybody's alibi knacked.'

'Just looking at the possibilities, that's all.'

Oh, no you're not, I thought. I know you, Frosty Winter.

'You don't believe that stuff,' I said. 'George an arsonist? Marksy and Legs? I might think that but you don't.'

Brendan, I thought. He just won't let go of Brendan.

'Unless Brendan was with them.' I looked straight at him. Challenged him. 'This is just your polite way, isn't it, of saying nothing will change your mind about Brendan?'

Frosty raised the eyebrow and let out a sigh. 'I'm sorry, Akinyi,' he said, 'but you know Brendan .'

'Yes, yes, I do know. He has the form.'

'If I had my way I'd get Martin Philips on the job and we'd put the frighteners on them all tonight,' said Frosty. 'George first. Then Marksy, Legs and Brendan. Oh, and

Mrs Siddle. Pity I don't know her sister's address. I could have dropped Pirate off.'

'Poor lady,' I said, 'she'll probably grieve all night for him. I would if he was mine and somebody ran off with him.'

'Fair enough. Best leave them all till tomorrow.'

Frosty's mobile rang.

'Excuse me,' he said and went into the hall.

I relaxed and drifted into a doze. It probably wasn't more than twenty seconds, but I woke to realise that Frosty was speaking urgently with my dad. I jolted myself back into action.

'Got that did you?' said Frosty.

I joined them in the hall. 'No, sorry. I nodded off.'

'That was a neighbour of mine. Do you know Nether Fencote Church?' Frosty was opening the front door.

'Of course,' I said 'We often walk out there through the woods, don't we, Dad?

'Charming little church in the fields,' he said.

'Right at the end of my garden,' said Frosty. 'And it's on fire.'

The church Marksy and his friends broke into. The church with the Bible. The Bible Marksy wrote in.

We walked with Frosty to his car in the street.

'Another fire.' I groaned. 'Don't tell me it's another disaster.'

'Especially not at your home,' said my dad.

'Just what I'm about to find out,' said Frosty. He revved his engine. 'Sweet dreams.'

We watched the red lights of his car disappear along the street.

I hugged Pirate, and I was gutted.

Chapter 31

Sweet dreams! I don't think so.

Mine were the half-waking kind, hardly dreams at all. I tried hopelessly to make sense of the sound bites and pictures that came tumbling through my mind like a waterfall.

There was fire - no surprises there. Fire and smoke. Smoke rolled into Kenya's Great Rift Valley, across the tea plantations and the banana trees to the Lake. I ran to flap it away, but found myself escaping Miss Butler's French lesson. I turned over in bed and moaned in protest, only to go for a spectacular swing with Jonny Marks and plunge on my back into the Willow. I seized the slashed rope of Mog's Swing and flapped its knotted end at Gloria in her fight to control her Music class.

More than half awake, I turned over again, closed my eyes tightly and begged my mind to blank out this confusion. Whichever way I wriggled, Brendan's yellow-handled knife came for me with its sickeningly sharp edge and its hideous point. It was six inches long. It was twenty feet long, huge and vicious. No, no, it was determined to be six inches long.

I shook myself free, sat up and read for a while. Pirate whimpered in his sleep in my arms. Useless. I turned over two pages without understanding a word.

Anxious not to wake my dad, I groped among my scattered clothes on the floor, couldn't find anything warm and tiptoed downstairs in my night dress.

He was waiting for me in the kitchen, grey, haggard and wide awake. Thrust together into our own company, we were both clueless.

'Your big day tomorrow, my darling. I'm afraid you've had the worst possible preparation for it.'

'You're worn out, too, Dad.'

Hint, hint. Go to bed, Dad, and leave me to wind down in front of the TV. Please!

Instead, he put into words my own chaotic thoughts.

'George,' he said. 'A unique talent. A boy with the world at his feet. Comes from a thoroughly respectable home. We've known him since he was a babe in arms. Surely ...'

I was torn by my love and my pity for him. I was ashamed of the impatience I had to choke back.

'You do realise, Akinyi,' he went on, holding my hand to soften his nosey-parkering, 'that not only is your ... er, your friend Brendan ... not only is he Suspect A for the arson attack on our school ...'

'Yes, Dad, I do realise it.'

'But, Akinyi my darling, you surely share my shock that the young man is an accomplished burglar.'

'According to the Lion,' I retorted.

'Indeed. And Miss Lyon is an experienced professional teacher of the highest integrity.'

'Yes, Dad. I know that, too.'

'And Mr Winter. Teachers who know and understand young people of this kind. They agree that your Brendan is capable of getting into and out of school without being detected by the police. That is truly shocking, Akinyi.'

'He's not guilty until it's proved. And at this moment, Mr Winter isn't proving anything, and neither is Miss Lyon.'

I stomped back to my bed.

Sleep wouldn't come. Anita was in my mind. She was kind. She understood. She accepted me as plain Akinyi, not as Akinyi the Headteacher's daughter.

I felt bonded to her in gratitude and affection.

And Brendan. If only I could work on him. Get him to settle down into proper behaviour. The kind that would give Anita a break. My hold on him was neither here nor there. Look at that knife. Would he carry that in his pocket if my opinion really mattered to him? School rules? He couldn't care less. As for the police helicopter, for all he cared it could buzz as much as it liked in its fury at the murder of an innocent policewoman.

Thank goodness it wasn't him that knifed her - couldn't have been, because I was with him at the time of the stabbing.

Then - oh no! The realisation came with a furious middle-of-the-night lurch.

Oh, no! Oh, pillow-thumping no!

I crouched in bed and held myself in arch-backed tension. With one hand to my mouth I choked on the certainty that I would throw up.

At the time of the stabbing? How did I know what time the policewoman was stabbed?

What made me so confident that Brendan was with me?

Get real for God's sake. On Sunday evening we were only together the time it took to swap a couple of snarled insults. Then we stropped our separate ways off into the night.

When did the policewoman die? How did she die?

I swore at myself.

You know nothing, I snarled. You've been wrapped up in proving Brendan innocent of the fire. You're pleased with the time grid you worked out for Frosty. There's been no room in your head for anything else.

Oh God! You didn't even ask yourself where the death of the policewoman would fit into your oh so smart grid.

I brought the knife out of its hiding place in my school bag and stared at it in dread. There was no need to find a ruler. The thing was 6 inches long. It was foul in its tapered, polished beauty. Sickening.

Pirate woke up, came out of his basket and put his front paws up onto my bed. I scooped him into my arms and hugged him tightly.

Tiptoeing downstairs to my dad's study with Pirate in my arms, I found the day's paper. He'd been too busy to read it. It was hardly creased. There on the front page was the story and the policewoman's photo. A 22 year-old woman on duty at the football match in town. Stabbed in the throat.

'Football?' I asked Pirate. 'Isn't football played on Saturday afternoons?

I turned to the sports page at the back, and there were the screaming headlines. *Rovers Ambushed.*

The story of the game was a jumble of names and football chatter. Meaningless. Yet there was no escaping the truth. The match was played on Sunday. But when, that was the question. What time? It didn't matter to the reporter.

'I'll find out at school in the morning,' I told Pirate. 'George will know. I don't suppose he could kick a football for you to chase across his garden lawn, but it's part of his macho hopes that he knows the teams, the players, the scores. George will put me straight.'

I was jolted from my panic. My iPhone's call tune.

Dashing to the kitchen I found the phone on the table and saw that it was after midnight. Who? Who on earth? I had a moment's excited hope. Brendan! Then - no, he'd never asked for my number.

'Yes?'

Akinyi

The voice was young and female. 'I'm on the front doorstep.'

'I don't know what you mean. Whose front doorstep? And who are you?'

'It's Saisha. Are you letting me in?'

'I don't know anybody called ... Of course I do. You're the girl who ...'

'Two minutes. That's all I'm giving you. You need to hear what I'm going to tell you. It's about your Brendan.

It was enough. I opened the door cautiously and Saisha pushed her way into the house.

'What's it all about?' I hissed. 'Whatever you do, don't you dare wake my dad. And your face, what's happened to your face? It's filthy.'

'I'm allergic to dogs,' she said. 'They make me sneeze and go all spotty.'

'This is a special dog,' I said shortly. 'He lives here.'

'Looks like Ma Siddle's mutt to me.'

We tiptoed to the kitchen. 'Get your head round this quickly,' said Saisha. 'I'm on the run.'

It was incredible. I looked her up and down without knowing where to begin understanding what was happening. A slender, good-looking girl, as tall as me. Eyes dark. Not as dark as mine, but pretty dark all the same, and flashing with pent-up energy.

And what looked suspiciously like scorched cheeks.

Bewilderment or fear? None.

Nervousness then? Not a sign of it.

This girl, I marvelled, she comes crashing into the Headteacher's house in the middle of the night. She isn't scared. She doesn't even hesitate. The nerve of it!

One thing was for sure. Whatever Saisha was thinking, it wasn't for debate. She'd made up her mind.

So much to cope with. I was worn out. But I can play have-things-my-own way games, too. Just as well as her. Get a grip, I told myself.

'On the run?' I snapped. 'What you're talking about? And what's it got to do with me?

'From my old man and the cops.'

'I'm up to my eyeballs in cops. Which cops are you talking about?'

'When they get hold of me they'll take me to the station downtown. After that my dad will kill me.'

Saisha sneezed. Then she sneezed again.

I told Pirate he was a good boy and told him to wait in the passage. To stay put.

'They must have their reasons,' I said to Saisha. 'What did you run away for? And why here of all places?'

She calmly walked to the sink, ran the tap and washed her hands and face in running water.

'Washing that dusty dog off me,' she said. 'Stops me sneezing.'

I gave her a hand towel.

Akinyi

'My old man wouldn't put up a fight,' she said as she dried her face. 'He'd make me tell them everything.'

We sat side by side at the kitchen table.

'So I came to you. You need to know that I was at the football match and it wasn't Brendan who killed the copper lady.'

I totally forgot myself.

'Do me a favour!' I stood up and shrieked. 'Of course it wasn't him. He wasn't even there.'

'Sssh! Your dad, remember.' Saisha touched my arm gently. 'Listen. If you think the cops aren't closing in on Brendan, you must believe in Father Christmas.'

'You've got this all wrong,' I spoke in a fierce whisper. 'Brendan wasn't even at the football.'

'You do believe in Father Christmas.' Saisha jumped up. 'Time I was out of here. Your old man ... Listen, take it from me. There were hundreds of us. Fists and boots everywhere. Lumps of brick flying in all directions. Cops on massive horses. Cops with shields. It was mad.'

'But ...'

'We haven't got time. Listen. I'm giving you my mobile. And I'm out of here.'

She tossed a phone onto the table.

'There's a video. Download it onto a flash drive and get rid of the mobile.'

She was already in the passage and on her way out.

'For God's sake come back,' I said. 'Why are you doing this? And where are you going?'

'I think you understand better than anybody,' said Saisha. 'I'm going home. To my old man.'

'T.'

'T ... bloody T. Him who gets the 6th Form to paint mind-boggling pictures. Coaches football. Tells oh such funny jokes. Does tricks, swallows swords, makes things disappear into thin air. Wonderful, isn't he? What you might not know is he's also as mad as hell. Pissed off with my mother because she pissed off with another bloke and never came back. Spitting blood because I'm a normal kid who wears jeans and plays with the boys.' She glared at me. 'If on top of that he finds out I support Rovers and go to matches, he'll murder me.'

I stared back into her deep dark eyes, lost for words.

'He kids himself I spend match days shopping with my mother. And he doesn't know the half.'

She'd have been down the steps and away into the darkness but I wasn't having that. I pulled her back. We struggled. Beneath our feet, Pirate squealed and scurried for cover.

'Don't let the dog out,' I panted. 'He'll do a runner.'

Thank goodness Saisha was light enough to push away. Breathing angrily, we faced each other.

'You're not leaving here till I make sense of this,' I said. I closed the door and turned the key. I picked Pirate up. He licked my face, and Saisha sneezed. 'You were at the football match. Brendan was, too. Is that what you're telling me?'

'The Boot Boys were right in there where it was roughest, and so was Brendan. And so was that woman cop.'

'This is scary, Saisha.'

'Just give the cops the video. I promise you you're best off not saying a word.'

I stirred myself.

'I can do promises, too,' I snapped. 'Here's mine. You don't leave here till I get to the bottom of what's going on. Now listen. Either I ring for the police or you and I sit down to a cup of cocoa and you tell all. What's happened tonight?'

I picked up the hall telephone.

'Deal or no deal?'

'Don't blame me when you regret this.'

'Sounds to me like a deal. Back to the kitchen then. I'm keeping between you and the door, so don't bother making a dash for it. Your face is still filthy, Saisha ... in fact it's burned. What's happened?'

I closed the door again on poor Pirate.

Saisha sniffed. 'You said we were having some cocoa.'

'All in good time. You've come to my house in the middle of the night. Now, what gives?'

'Well, don't say I didn't warn you to keep out of this.'

'Get on with it.'

'OK, you asked for it. I've been playing with fire.'

Her seen-it-all eyes were on my face. 'There you are. Told you so. You're going to panic, aren't you?'

'Fire?'

'At Nether Fencote Church.'

'What! I don't believe it. There was a fire there tonight. It's where Mr Winter ... Playing with fire, what's this got to do with the football match? The murdered police lady?'

'I went there and started it.'

'You have to be joking. It was you who ... You started a fire on purpose!'

'Only because of the Bible.'

'The Bible?'

Oh my God, I know what's coming, I thought. Marksy and Legs, they wrote in the Bible. Now Saisha has ...

'How could you do that, Saisha? You know what it's like. It's a lovely tiny country church. There's only a service once every two months.' I whispered. 'You set fire to ... ?'

No, I couldn't finish.

'I got the kerosene from that kid George,' said Saisha.

'You don't mean George Newcomb.'

'Genius, that's what we call him. You've heard him. Says he is one.'

'Are you telling me George was with you when you ...?

Akinyi

'Course not, no.'

The rough edge of Saisha's street cunning made my heart race.

'So how does he come into it?'

Saisha was the cool one.

'A few weeks ago George said he would give us twenty quid, remember. I went to get it off him at his house one afternoon. You were there. He showed us his dad's posh workshop.'

'He didn't give you the money.'

'No, but he said if I came another time I could nick anything I liked. There was loads of stuff worth the twenty.'

'You mean you'd go into Mr Newcomb's workshop and …'

'George said I could.'

'I don't know how you'd dare.'

'Course I'd dare. Give me a break.'

'Saisha! What about your father?'

'Come off it, Akinyi. I went to George's house after tea tonight. He was already in bed when I whistled in the garden. He rushed to his bedroom window. It was too dark for him to see anything, but I whistled again, and waved to let him know it was me.'

'Wow, I wouldn't fancy that. Somebody whistling outside my window after I'd gone to bed.'

'Yes, well. At first I thought he would get back into bed and pull the duvet over his head. That would have made things more difficult. I'd have had to go to the front door and speak to his dad.'

'Saisha! Are you crazy?'

'I knew George really wanted to come out.'

'But his dad ... You can't mess about with people's dads like that. Specially not Mr Newcomb.'

'He fancies me, you know - George, I mean. He couldn't say no, and he pushed his bedroom window open. I could tell he was nearly wee-ing himself with fright. "Climb out of the window," I told him. He was all excuses. Said he was wearing his pyjamas. Said it was the middle of the night. I told him he was a scaredy cat and I dared him. He came out with a bunch more excuses.'

'I bet he did,' I said. 'Like what if he broke one of his fingers?'

'Yes, that was one of them.'

'I should hope it was. Just before the Fun Fest.'

'Don't worry, he had all that stuff off pat.'

'And you bullied him.'

'You're having a laugh. I told him to cock his leg over the window sill, hang onto a tree and climb down the drainpipe.'

I took a deep breath and switched into school teacher mode.

Akinyi

'Saisha!' I said severely. 'You haven't told me about your mother. I wonder what she's going to make of all this.'

'My mam,' Saisha snarled. 'Oh yes, she knows a thing or two about what to do with her legs.' There was vicious scorn in her glance. 'Mams. Dads. Who'd have them? Specially teacher-dads.'

I couldn't meet her bold dark eyes.

'No,' I murmured.

So much for school teacher mode. It might work with feeble characters like Jonny Marks. Not Saisha. Saisha was something else. She was in charge.

'Say no more,' she said. 'Listen. George was pathetic. I had to tell him where to put his feet and which branch to hold onto with his arms. If I hadn't been there he might have jumped and done himself an injury. He'd have been fun at your Fun Fest then, wouldn't he? I got him down in the end and had to calm him. He'd forgotten all about his mummy and daddy and was whooping as if he'd won the Lottery or something. Then he noticed burning where his precious fingers had scraped down the rusting drainpipe. You should have seen him panic.'

'I can imagine.'

'Anyway, we went up the garden. The geese were shut in but they cackled a bit. We went past them and into the workshop.'

'Cheeky or what!'

'We made sure the door was shut, then switched on the lights. There's tools in there, every kind you can think of, hundreds of them.'

'Go on, tell me,' I said. 'What did you steal?'

'There's a fancy kerosene heater on wheels. I saw it last time.'

'Kerosene? You used kerosene to light a fire at Nether Fencote Church?'

'Sort of. I was fire-eating.'

You'd think she was an A-grade celebrity, the way I stared at her.

'Why shouldn't I? My dad can do it, so I decided it was a good time for me to learn.'

'But ... isn't it horrendously dangerous?'

'Course it is. That's why he's made me promise to wait till ... you know, like dads do. Till I'm a teenager. I'm nearly that now, in case he hasn't noticed.'

'Nearly? What do you mean - nearly? How old are you?'

Saisha gave me a filthy look.

'Could have done it there in George's garden or that tool shed, but his dad would have seen the lights and spoiled the fun. My dad was right about the angles, I'll say that much for him.'

'Angles?' I mumbled.

'You have a mouthful of kerosene,' said Saisha as patiently as an Infants teacher. 'If you breathe it out at the wrong angle un-ignited fuel can fall back in your face. It's all about the angle. It takes hours and hours of practice with water and a professional instructor. My dad would tell you I was lucky I didn't set fire to my hair or my clothes.'

'How big was the fire?' My voice was hoarse. 'Don't tell me it was like the one at school.'

'The neighbours must have seen shadows jumping about behind the stained glass windows.' She had the cheek to giggle. 'They weren't to know, were they, that it was only a learner-driver fire-breather. Probably rang 999.'

'What about the Bible?'

'I had to burn that,' said Saisha simply. 'Those stupid boys. It's their fault. I told them never to go back there without me, but they must have. They wrote their names in the Bible. Their names! I mean how stupid can you get? It would have been dead easy for any cop to track them down if I hadn't got rid of the evidence. And now you know why I've given you the mobile.'

I frowned. 'No, I don't,' I said.

'I've got to get home. The cops will be waiting. And my dad. I'll tell them what I like about the fire but not a word about the video. Sweet FA.'

'But ...'

'They'll never know who made it. The cops won't and my dad won't. So long as it's you that hands it over. I mean, they're not going to suspect you, are they?'

She was itching to be on the move again.

'Did you help George climb back in through the bedroom window?' I said.

'Nah, didn't bother. I pushed him towards his front door and legged it.'

We were silent. I was gob-smacked. The cool of this kid was awesome.

'You were at the school's fire last night, weren't you?' I said suddenly.

'No.' Saisha flashed me a look of surprise and dark-eyed resentment.

I was pleased with myself to get ahead of her for the first time.

'With Jonathan Marks and Leonard Longley,' I pressed.

'We went home before the fire.'

'Who can confirm that?'

'Nobody. The house was empty when I got home. Susan has a new fancy man and she's hardly ever in. That's my mam.'

'Listen, Saisha,' I said. 'You've got to tell the truth. Seriously. Did you take part in lighting the school fire?'

'No, Akinyi. No. I didn't even know there was a fire until we were on our way to school this morning. I walked home with those two boys. Legs went to his sister's birthday party. I came home, watched the telly and went to bed.'

I brought my face close up to Saisha's.

'You didn't light the school fire.'

Saisha stared, wide-eyed but unafraid. For me it was a really nervous moment. We were inches apart. Wow!

She's one tough lady, I thought. She's shaped her world and left no one in doubt who's in charge.

'No, I never.'

'And you don't know who did?'

'No.'

'It wasn't you and it wasn't ...' I gave her chance to interrupt. She didn't. 'Leonard Longley.'

'No.'

'Not Marks, Jonathan Marks?'

'Nah, course not.'

'How can you be so sure?'

'I've told you. I was with them.'

'Who else was there?'

'I've told you that as well. George Newcomb and Mrs Siddle. And her dusty puppy.'

'Anybody else?'

She shook her head.

'Smart. Brendan Smart?'

'Give over. Everybody knows him.'

'And was he there?'

'He was out in the street with you. Akinyi how come Mr Macdonald has a black daughter?'

'Good question, Saisha. I'll work on it.'

I leaned closer still. I needed to claw back the contact her special brand of cunning had broken.

'Brendan.' I said. 'Was he in Mrs Siddle's room?'

'I never saw him.'

She must have seen the tiniest veins in my eyes, but she didn't back off. Instead she gave a piercing screech.

'That's it!'

She broke past me, heading for the front door.

'The dog!' I shouted. 'Don't let him escape.'

'Play cops on someone your own age.'

She turned the key and let herself out.

'Download that video. You won't regret it when the cops corner you.'

She was away into the darkness.

'And don't kid yourself that it won't be soon.'

She'd gone.

The power of her personality was amazing. She'd told me to do it, and obediently I did it. Downloaded the video from her mobile onto my own hard drive. Then I sat at the laptop.

I wrapped myself in my duvet and hugged Pirate. First I had goose pimples, then I broke out in a prickly sweat as I stared at a wild scene of violence that filled me with sickening confusion.

I watched the scene over and over again until I thought I understood.

Akinyi

At last I fell into bed, but sleep was never going to find its way into my over-worked brain. Saisha on the doorstep. Brendan at the football match. Lines of policemen. Kids fall over each other in a mad rush. Saisha coolly clicks the video button on her mobile phone. A whirl of fighting, truncheons and stones.

The knife.

The knife and the video.

Brendan again. He was at the football. I'd been naïve to kid myself that he wasn't. Amid all the confusion one thing was clear. Sharp and in focus, the knife in Brendan's hand.

I must see him in the morning. First thing.

My mind was made up. The fire and the knife - I would thrash the truth out with Brendan

Chapter 32
Tuesday 20*th* October

Before school started on Tuesday morning I joined the Lion in checking that everything was in place for the Fun Fest. I had to admit that while I'd been busy truanting, all the stops had been pulled out. The assembly hall was hardly better than a smelly, filthy hole full of bent metal frames and dangling cables. It had been taped off, out of bounds. All the arrangements had been transferred to the hall in the Ashbrook Block.

The entrance hall was a picture. It had a brand new rust-coloured carpet. It wasn't going to win any prizes for charm, but at least it was practical. The walls had been painted and the award boards re-hung. The Art Department had put up a fantastic new display of sculptures, pottery and paintings.

Outstanding among them, vivid, unmistakable - the Gaffer, the Rovers Boot Boy with his shaved skull, his red and white stripes, the lurid scar across his cheek. My stomach lurched.

Akinyi

I controlled myself. After all, it was very decent of T and his 6th Formers to put up a new display, and who was I to nit-pick about their choice of pictures?

'The hall in the Ashbrook Block?' I said. 'But isn't that tiny? Surely we can't get everybody ...'

'Take it easy,' said the Lion. 'Everything's under control. Years 7 and 8 are going home at lunchtime.'

'Hang about! That means they'll miss everything. And after they've worked so hard.'

'Quite right. And now they're on a promise.'

'A promise? What promise?'

'You're going to do a special Fun Fest for them. Not tomorrow perhaps, not next week, but I'm sure you won't be backward in coming forward with suggestions.'

'Wow! I wonder what my dad will say about that. I told him that after today I'd focus on my GCSEs.'

'About time, too,' said the Lion as if she hadn't a care in the world.

The fire had been brushed-and-panned out of sight. The only clue it left for the afternoon's visitors, even in the Ashbrook Block, was that stubborn background stench of smoke.

Gloria had thought of everything. The Lion confirmed it with a finger ends checklist.

'Team of Year 11s to direct traffic. Year 10s to escort visitors. Room allocated for performers. Changing facilities. Trophies. Refreshments team organised. Flowers for the stage, and bouquet for Lady Mayoress.

Media ... they'll please themselves, anyway. Feeling good?'

Good? I was a bag of nerves. I was sick with pumping adrenalin. The Fun Fest - who cared? It belonged to another world. A child's play world.

In the real world, in her very own bag the daughter of the Headteacher of Willowbank High School was carrying a flash drive with Saisha's video on it. And a knife. Not just any old knife.

The video, the knife, all those kids and men fighting with the police. The sooner I passed the flash drive and the knife to Detective Chief Inspector Cardew the better. That much was obvious.

Yet I was reluctant. And pig-headed. It was Brendan I wanted to speak to, not the policeman. Not that I knew what I wanted to say to him. Only - stop messing me about. I'm desperate to keep you as the best really good friend I have. I want you to be innocent. Give me it straight. Am I being a sucker?

I wasn't thinking straight, but then what was the straight way to think? I hadn't the foggiest. Arson and murder. Till only a couple of days ago I hadn't given a passing thought to either.

I must find Brendan.

'OK.' The Lion was sharp. 'Normal lessons. Have a relaxed morning. If we need you or George we'll come for you.'

I knew I had to find Brendan. There was no time to waste. Yet where to look? The duty teachers were already chivvying everybody into class.

Chemistry for me. Chemistry experiments. One of my favourite lessons. Today I hardly knew what they were about. I wasn't in ambitious teacher mood. My mind was everywhere else.

From the chemistry lab I drifted along to Mrs Siddle's lesson. The class was a bit better prepared for music theory, and things started quietly. One boy even helped her plug in the portable keyboard she'd brought with her to the unfamiliar classroom.

'Manuscript pads ready,' said Gloria.

We all fumbled in our bags. To write music you need a pencil with a sharp point. Try writing a bar of quavers with a blunt stub. People needed time to scrounge and fumble. Gloria waited as we got ourselves sorted.

'Now,' she said when we'd arrived at something like a decent atmosphere, 'let us continue our work in the Key of B Minor in three-four time. I suggest you begin by writing your key signature.'

She ignored the blank faces in front of her.

'My starting note is C-sharp. Transcribe, please.'

And she tinkled a melody on the keyboard.

I wrote the key signature. I could do that much. And the first few notes. Then I was stuck. I glanced at the rest of the class and saw everything I suspected. They were hopeless.

Akinyi

I wished Gloria would explain, but the old woman wouldn't even play the tune again. Who could blame her? She'd tried often enough through a babble of impertinence.

She looked tired and ill. Her face was heavily powdered. Around her eyes she might just as well have used a worn-out tennis ball to apply her bruise-coloured make-up. She sat at her desk and watched us without interest.

Stalemate. Gloria knew everything and was not telling. We knew nothing and were ashamed to ask.

That would have been that, if it hadn't been for George.

On this day of all days I did think he might at least stay in his seat.

Not George.

He stood, as if this was any other Gloria lesson, and ambled across the room. Behind her teacher's desk Gloria tracked him in hoity-toity silence. George put his manuscript pad beside mine and squinted through his thick glasses at my work ... or rather, my lack of it.

'Akinyi! I didn't know you were useless at music theory.'

'What do you expect?' I hissed. 'I haven't done a stroke in Gloria's lessons. Go back to your seat, George, and let everybody get on.'

'But you're wonderful on the clarinet.'

'Fat chance of that when I've never been allowed to get on with my theory.'

'I'll help you catch up.'

Akinyi

'You help me, George! Thanks but no thanks.' I probably showered spit into his face. 'You're the worst idiot of us all.'

My fierceness shocked George. 'That doesn't mean I haven't done the work,' he said. 'My music theory's as good as Gloria Siddle's any day.'

Just like that.

'George. You'll spoil everything. Get away from me before Mrs Siddle kicks you out as usual.'

I stood up and pushed him roughly. George was too shocked to argue, and he stumbled towards the door. Our classmates tittered and jeered. I ignored them and gave him another good shove.

'Go on, George, get out.' I gave Mrs Siddle a glance. 'Excuse us,' I said, and I slammed the door.

In the corridor I squared up to George. Not that it was difficult. He lost about ten years in the face of my anger and scorn. For two pins I'd murder him. And he knew it.

'George, I want to know what happened when you went back to the Music Room on Sunday night. With those kids, Marksy and Legs. And Saisha.'

'I ...'

'And I'm sick of cover-ups and lies. Even if nobody else will, you can tell me the truth.'

'It was only a bit of fun.'

'Oh, yeah. The school catches fire, but it's only a bit of fun.'

Akinyi

'Akinyi ...' George fumbled in his blazer pocket. He looked miserable and about 6 years old. 'I wrote you this,' he said, and he offered me a scruffy piece of paper.

It was crumpled and sweaty-pawed.

'What's this?' I said. 'A signed confession?'

'No, of course not. It's a ...' He was blushing and lost for words.

I unfolded the note and read.

'*Darling*,' it began.

I frowned. I peered at the note. He'd written something, crossed it out and written "*Akinyi*" over it. I peered harder. *Saisha?* Was it possible that he had actually written *Saisha?*

Will you go out with me? Do you want to go to the Town Hall concert with me on Saturday night. xxx, George

OK, so where was I supposed to start?

We've just walked out of class.

We're in a school corridor at lesson time.

The teacher hasn't got what it takes to tell us to get back to our desks.

I'm in a love scene with a serious Oscar contender for a starring role in the horror movie, *Mixed-up Kid of All Time*.

It's Fun Fest day, planned for weeks.

One half of my brain is fire-addled, the other half Brendan-obsessed.

Without giving him the brush-off, how could I show George he was OK as a music partner and utterly pathetic with his babyish need to show off to other boys?

What was I supposed to say? I have a boyfriend. Brendan is a real man. You, George, are a baby. And, by the way, what the hell were you playing at on Sunday night?

'What about Saisha?' I snarled. 'She was with you on Sunday. You took her to see Mrs Siddle as soon as I turned my back.'

George and Saisha!

Saisha - whose dad played the clown and disappeared behind a pile of books. Saisha, who came to my house in the middle of the night. Saisha, who went to the football match on Sunday afternoon. Saisha, who had the nous to video the street battle.

Saisha, the one who'd dropped me right in it with the police.

And all the time she was getting her act together with George. Nah - it didn't make sense. Not with George.

'Come to the concert,' he said. It was the spoiled little boy touch.

'Oh, God!' I moaned. 'I give up. I've torn a strip off everybody in this class, and they're not going to be impressed that I'm the only one not working. Get back to your desk and shut up, George.'

Shutting up was beyond him - at least until I'd given him an answer.

'Is that Brendan ... Are you and that Brendan ... ? Can't you and I ... ?'

'Can't we what, George?'

'Don't be cross, Akinyi please. I only want to know if that boy ... you know.'

'I know, George, that I want to get on with my music theory.'

'It's that Brendan from Ashbrook. You were with him all day yesterday. He's my rival.'

This is a soap scene, I thought, and George has no off switch.

'My father says,' he began, as if his father was the prime minister or something, 'that it's been downhill for you ever since you met that Ashbrook lout.'

'Typical. Well, for your information, George, and for your father's, Brendan is not a lout.'

'My father told me last night there was only one thing for it.'

'Break it to me gently, George.'

'He told me I'd have to compose a new piece for this afternoon's festival.'

'Oh yeah,' I sneered. 'And I suppose you went right ahead.'

'I did, yes. A violin solo.'

'Great. I'm sure Saisha will be star-struck when you give her a command performance.'

Akinyi

'I had to do it, Akinyi. The television will be there. My father says it's a great career opportunity for me and I mustn't throw it away because of a ... ' He hesitated.

'Don't mind me, George. Let's hear what your darling daddy says about me.'

'When you didn't turn up for rehearsal with me and Mrs Siddle last night he called you feather-headed.'

'He'd be stretched to find matching insults if he could see you now.'

I'd known George all my life. All his life, too. I knew he was fighting back tears.

'Are you seriously going to let me down, Akinyi? After all our weeks of practice?'

He dragged his forehead and his cheeks and his chin into an ugly mask. 'Yes, I know, don't tell me,' he said. 'Brendan Smart has taken away your common sense. I don't suppose you'll ever come back to me, will you? He's as tall and as handsome as you deserve your boyfriend to be.'

He took off his glasses and wiped his face with his blazer sleeve.

'There wouldn't be much point in me coming back to you, would there?' I said. 'You've got a girl friend. Her name's Saisha. Don't forget you're taking her to the Town Hall concert. It wouldn't do to stand her up.'

'I can't imagine what you and Brendan have to say to each other.'

'While you and Saisha, I suppose, bill and coo like mating doves.'

He was silent for a moment, struck by some wonderful truth. 'She knew the name of the William the Conqueror's mate. Remember?'

'What's so amazing about that, George?'

'I didn't realise that Ashbrook kids had ...' He dried up.

'Been to school?' I said, spitting sarcasm.

'She's spooky, Akinyi - so self-confident and a leader, even among the boys who are much older.'

'How old is she?'

George looked away, couldn't meet my eyes. 'She's 12,' he whispered, and now a tear escaped onto his hot cheeks.

Twelve. I frowned.

Twelve? Weird or what!

She barges into the Headteacher's house in the middle of the night. Coolly announces she's made a video that might rescue Brendan from the police. Gives George's father's workshop the once-over to see what's worth nicking. She drags George out of bed and gets him to climb out of his own bedroom window. Then, if that's not enough, she swallows fire, burns a Bible and sets fire to a church.

And she's 12.

Some 12-year-old!

Akinyi

'I thought she must be at least 14,' said George, 'specially the way she bosses the boys about.'

He was the nearest I had to a friend. We'd shared so much and had loads of good times together. I felt horribly sorry for him, the poor, silly little boy. To fall on the re-bound for a 12 year-old. Wasn't that just George?

Then he helped me from my moment of weakness by trotting out his manly announcement.

'You hate me,' he said, 'and I won't take part in the Fun Fest this afternoon.'

I sighed. When I spoke I sounded like a greasy politician I once saw on TV. I think she was opening a garden fete and fighting off a massive yawn.

'I can't manage the Fun Fest without you, George. You're the greatest musician since Mozart.'

His face brightened. 'I sat up all night, Akinyi, thinking how beautiful you are.'

I did my best not to pull a face. 'Go back to your seat and think about the applause you're going to get this afternoon.'

I opened the door and marched back to my seat. There was a shout of rough laughter from the class.

He told me nothing, I thought. I'm not one bit the wiser.

Chapter 33

Away George pranced. He was so full of himself it would have been a miracle if he'd sat quietly. He squirmed in his seat. He was sitting next to a boy called Eddie Fitzgerald, who moved away, spread his elbows, dropped his chin onto his desk, and squinted at his music.

'You've got that wrong, Steady,' said George, pointing at a page of smudges. 'You've done it with no sharps. That's A minor, not B.'

Eddie snatched the manuscript away. George grabbed it. They scuffled and the pad fell on the floor.

'Stop messing about, Newcomb.'

'You're a dumbo, Steady.'

Gloria lost her nerve. She lumbered to her feet, dragging one leg like a loaded shopping bag.

'George Newcomb, you naughty boy, go outside at once.'

Business as usual - but wait for it.

'Yes, Mrs Siddle,' said George. 'One.'

Oh great! Everything was back to normal in his silly little mind. With his smug grin, he bounced towards the door - and came to a sudden stop.

Gloria blocked his way. She waved a long thick stick.

George's mouth hung open and he stared. The whole class did.

I did.

Gloria limped menacingly forward. 'Where do you think you're going, George Newcomb?'

She could hardly gasp the words out. Her chest heaved.

She looked terrifyingly ill.

But there was more to it than that. I could see it in the way she held her head upright. She suddenly looked like a determined woman. Determined to make one last stand.

She looked awesome.

She's planned this moment, I thought, as I held my breath along with everybody else in the room. She knows what she's about.

She and George might be within a few hours of performing together in a great whole-school occasion, but that's not going to stop her whacking him one.

With that humungous stick.

George knew it, too. He ducked away from her in panic. She blocked his way. There was nowhere for him to go.

Then in a burst of brilliant thinking, he dodged sideways, flung open a window and scrambled onto the sill. The class rumbled, part cheer, part jeer. I was on my feet. Gloria and I shouted simultaneously.

'George Newcomb, sit down immediately' - Gloria digging deep for the energy to let loose her rage.

'Please, Mrs Siddle, no' - me pleading for common sense.

Gloria worked her flabby neck muscles in an exhausted attempt to give her head one last arrogant toss, and she glared from George to me with the whole of the planet's supply of scorn.

'It's just that ...' I began. I meant to say something nice to her. Honestly, I did. Then weary impatience took over. 'Well, for God's sake,' I screamed. 'You can't hit him with a bloody stick.'

From some unimaginable store of energy Gloria found the shriek of a death-defying witch.

'You are telling me what to do, Akinyi.'

Wow! she was mad, and who could blame her?

'No, of course I'm not,' I said. I knew I ought to be reasonable. No chance. I was too tired to hold back my anger. 'Why do you always fall for silly George's dumb tricks?'

Gloria dug again for energy and hauled up her massive body.

Akinyi

'I am glad, Akinyi Macdonald, to receive your advice on how to run my class.'

She flourished her stick so that it whipped the air within millimetres of my face.

I heard it. I felt its closeness. I ducked away and I screamed.

Mrs Siddle didn't care. She had other things on her mind. Like using that stick on George. She turned towards him, where he crouched frog-like on the window sill.

'This way, George Newcomb.'

The class allowed a little of its breath to escape.

George took one look at the glint in Gloria's eye, another at the stick.

'Just leaving, Mrs Siddle,' he said and jumped into the yard.

The bell rang. With a bellow of merriment, the class would have stormed into the corridor amid the usual chaos.

Except that the Lion blocked the doorway.

Silence, sudden and terrifying.

The class shuffled past her. Nobody risked making eye contact. I made a point of being last. I passed Gloria, close enough to catch her expensive scent as it fought its losing battle with the foul stink of ancient tobacco.

I had in mind to flounce out, but the Lion twitched one finger. Red traffic light. I stopped.

Not so Gloria. She elbowed past. In the doorway she turned on me.

'Patronising advice from the Headteacher's daughter. Now I've seen everything.'

She stomped off.

'What was all that about?' The Lion looked grim.

'Wow! I tried to help her. She threatened to hit George with a horrendous stick.'

'It's high time your class settled down.'

'I thought we might today. Poor Mrs Siddle, she's frightened.'

'Yes?'

'And furious.'

I looked at the Lion and wondered if I dared go on. Her face was scarily grim. Her lioness eyes were fierce. She was waiting, and I was cornered. I had to go on.

'She sees herself as a great teacher. She's having sleepless nights and nightmares about uncontrollable classes.'

She raised her eyebrows, almost Frosty-style.

'What makes you think this?' she snapped. Her voice was icy.

'She's told Brendan.'

It was an interesting moment. In the last day I'd seen the Lion puzzled. I'd never expected to see her amazed.

'That's right,' I said, and I had to stop a self-satisfied giggle. 'Brendan Smart.'

'When? How?'

'Oh you and Mr Winter think your precious form tells you all there is to say about Brendan. But you didn't know, did you, that he has a cosy meeting with Mrs Siddle every morning.'

'Meeting? What sort of meeting? Where?'

'Surprising, isn't it? They have a smoke and a chat together. And she tells him her problems.'

'Clearly,' said the Lion stiffly, 'I shall have to follow this up.'

She strode away to her room, and I dashed off in search of Brendan.

I knew this wasn't the time to congratulate myself. It was already morning break. I had to find him. And quickly. Should have found him hours ago.

Chapter 34

There was no tell-tale smoke signal to bring me to the car park that morning. I didn't get there before Brendan came hurtling towards me. Bang went all my plans.

'Fetch the Lion.' he shouted. 'Mrs Siddle's out cold in her car.'

'She's what?'

'Get a move on. If we don't get her into hospital she could snuff it.'

No point in asking him if he was sure. One look at him was enough - the crazy way he was waving his arms, the wildness in his face, the panic in his voice.

The Lion thought so, too. I dragged her from her consultation with some other harassed teacher in her room. As we dashed together across the school yard, I gave myself a heated lecture.

Akinyi

'You knew it,' I muttered. 'Why didn't you see this coming?'

Brendan had done well. He'd lowered the driving seat and turned Mrs Siddle as far as possible in onto her side. He'd tilted her head back to open the airway. So there was one teacher in the school who had taught him something.

A glimpse of Gloria's bloodless face was enough for me. Last time I'd seen a face like that it was my mum's. I was beating my sobbing mouth against Dad's chest and clamouring that Mum couldn't be dead because how were we going to live without her.

I wasn't about to look any closer at Mrs Siddle. Frankly, I didn't want to be told that Gloria had anything in common with my mum.

The Lion didn't hesitate. She climbed into the passenger's side and got her face down next to Mrs Siddle's.

'OK, Akinyi,' she called. 'Nine-nine-nine for an ambulance. Report that the patient is breathing, but unconscious. Ask them to make it snappy.'

To be given a job! It was sweet relief. Especially a job that let me turn my back on Gloria.

The ambulance's siren was already sounding in the valley bottom by the time I'd keyed in the number, gabbled my message, answered the telephonist's ten thousand niggling questions and turned in search of Brendan. It wailed across Willow Bridge and up the hill to school. Some of the teachers had got wind of what was going on.

As they hurried towards the scene, they shooed at a tide of kids in a hopeless attempt to keep them back.

The Lion and Brendan were eyeball to eyeball, both their faces furious. She waved a finger under his nose. I'd never seen that before. I could tell she was giving him a piece of her mind and Brendan was coughing. His asthma!

He stomped off, and I buffeted kids out of my way in protest.

'I expected you to have more about you than this, Brendan,' the Lion called. 'I backed you to face up to what you've done.'

He flipped her the finger.

The ambulance sped along the school drive. It was between me and Brendan, and I stepped onto the grass to let it pass. When it stopped beside Mrs Siddle's car, Brendan had disappeared. I shouted his name, once, twice.

It was pointless. He'd gone. The school gate was just a few yards away. Beyond it - the road down to Willow Bridge and the path to Mog's Swing. Brendan would expect me.

As the ambulance whisked Mrs Siddle away, the Lion took my arm.

'Don't even think about it. You've done your lifetime's legging.'

We walked together to the Den. I was shivering the way I'd shivered when I was wet through from rescuing Marksy.

I'm so mixed-up, I thought. It's awful. My thoughtless, arrogant interference might have killed Mrs Siddle. The old woman's last feeling was the humiliation of me shouting at her.

Then I was furious all over again. The stupid cow, why did she allow George to make such a fool of her? Waving a stick in his face like that. What came over her?

In George's face? George! George deserved everything that was coming to him. Bloody hell, what about my face?

I could hear and feel the whoosh as the tip of that vicious thing flashed past the end of my nose. Imagine if it had whiplashed a ferocious scar across my face. Then Gloria really would have had reason to be stressed and to be carted off to hospital in a state of collapse.

'Have I killed her?' I moaned. 'I want my dad. I want to tell him I didn't mean to kill her.'

The Lion handed me a mug of tea. I wrapped my ice-block hands round it, soaking its heat into my shaking body.

'Drink,' she said. 'It's hot. Your father will be here in a minute.'

Then Brendan. I felt such a traitor. He was out there. Waiting for me. And here I was, a good little girl, afraid to join him, afraid to stand with him when it seemed certain his game was up.

'I wanted to tell him,' I said, half laughing with love, half crying with frustration that he was so near and yet so far, 'that the police could could catch him at any moment.'

'Brendan knows that. He and I were discussing that very point.'

'And I wanted to confess to him.'

'What now?'

'About the time and movements grid I made for Mr Winter.'

The Lion laughed, and I scowled through tears that scalded my freezing cheeks.

'With Brendan smack in the middle of it.'

'No point in blaming yourself,' the Lion said. 'Mr Winter is quite clever, you know. Even his garden is laid out in a grid.'

'So it's hopeless?'

The Lion nodded. 'Let's just wait and see,' she offered, 'what Anita has told Mr Winter.'

We didn't have long to wait. The phone rang, and the Lion listened to a hysterical voice. Then she passed me the receiver.

'Anita for you.'

Anita had blown her storm of grief out on the Lion. She spoke simply.

'It's no good, Akinyi. Mr Winter has been here, and I know now. I should never have taken our Brendan away from his dad. It's all my fault, and the only way I can help him is to find Steve. I'm going to look for him.'

I shook the phone, but Anita had rung off.

Chapter 35

It was only when the Lion checked her watch that it dawned on me.

The Fun Fest!

I'd been so stressed-out about Brendan that I'd clean forgotten.

The Fun Fest without Gloria. How were George and I going to manage without her to accompany us on the piano? Without Gloria the Fun Fest ... well, it couldn't be done. Simple as that.

In seconds the Lion reached the opposite conclusion.

'There's only one person who can take over,' she said.

I tried but I couldn't think who.

'Your father, of course.'

Dad? Master of ceremonies? On the piano?

'No way ... You have to be joking. My dad couldn't ...'

The Lion was impatient.

'He hasn't been Headteacher all these years for nothing,' she snapped.

'Of course not, but ...'

'Other suggestions?'

I had none.

My dad was shuffling papers at his desk when the Lion and I barged in. As soon we told him about Gloria, he was all for contacting the hospital. The Lion eased the phone from his hand and reminded him about the Fun Fest.

'It's a great opportunity for you,' she said.

He met her eye with an understanding smile. 'My swansong, you mean.'

Then he straightened his shoulders. He was back in the Army, and I knew he was not a deserter.

I didn't tell him or the Lion that I was legging-it again. Instead of back to my next lesson, I dashed down the road, crossed Willow Bridge and clambered over the downtrodden fence onto the riverside footpath.

You're crazy, I told myself, off your trolley, lost your marbles. In case it's escaped what passes for your mind your Fun Fest is hardly three hours away. You've planned it, you've rehearsed it ... and you've dropped your dad in it. And now you're in a blind panic.

There was no sign of Brendan at Mog's Swing. I was desperate. I could have sworn he'd wait for me there.

Akinyi

There was no time to look anywhere else. Besides, where would I begin?

Anita was in the queue at an Ashbrook bus stop. In high-heeled shoes and her best skirt, blouse and jacket, didn't she just stand out among the shopping bags and cigarette smoke. People fell silent when I appeared.

Again I was gutted.

'Brendan,' I stammered. 'He isn't with you? He didn't come home then?'

'Of course not, Akinyi. He's at school. Mr Winter has told me everything. And I'm going to find Steve.'

'I'm coming with you,' I said. 'But what's Brendan playing at?'

Anita had made her face up, put on lipstick and mascara. She looked like a 17 year-old, a lovely one at that. As we climbed onto the bus I took one last wild look around, desperate for Brendan to appear.

'Where to?' said the driver.

'Tell him where we're going, Anita.'

'Rosebud Lane,' said Anita. 'It's where the Ritz is,' she said. 'You know - the cinema.'

'Showing your age, love,' the driver laughed. 'My missis worked at the Ritz. It shut down years ago.' His machine spewed out our tickets. 'It's Greenhills Industrial Estate now.'

I don't believe this is happening, I thought as we took our seats. The hysteria of the phone call had completely gone. Anita was calm. Her eyes weren't meeting mine.

They were looking somewhere in the far distance. A distant place and a different time.

'What have you in mind?' I asked. 'Will Brendan's dad be there?'

'He'll have gone back to his mother's.'

The bus growled through city traffic.

'She'll be long gone now, of course. He'll have the house to himself.' She laughed bitterly. 'I shouldn't wonder if he's got himself another woman.'

'Anita - have you thought that things will be different?'

'Steve's the only person in the world who can help our Brendan and there's only one place I know to look for him.'

Downtown, we crossed City Bridge where our Willow plunged into the big river, with its silent current sweeping between blackened brick wharves. As we climbed away from the city centre, Anita peered ahead.

'Look, there's the Ritz clock tower. We're here.'

'Like I told you,' said the driver. 'Greenhills.'

The bus left the fast out-of-town dual carriageway and ran beside warehouses, where state-of-the-art businesses had sprung up since Anita's time. Then it was the Ritz. I saw it with a sinking heart. An old fashioned brick building with a tall white clock tower. It was like something out of a museum.

'Stop!' Anita called. The bus was already slowing but she rang the bell frantically. 'Pull up.'

Akinyi

We were at the bottom of a sweeping brick stairway.

'To think of the years that I went to work through that door. The last time I came out, I was ...' Anita giggled as she sketched a swollen belly, 'huge with our Brendan.'

'I hope you two women know what you're doing,' the driver laughed.

He didn't hope or laugh long enough for us to reply. His doors swished closed and his bus roared away in a trail of diesel fumes.

It might have been the glass palace car showroom with its landscaped lawn dotted with shiny BMWs. Or the giant backlit screen running a video display of modern kitchens on now or never sale. Or the delivery wagon with a million wheels nosing its way out of a builders' warehouse. Whatever, the party balloon of Anita's excitement was suddenly pricked.

The doors to the Ritz shouted the truth in tall letters. It was home to an electrical goods company. Anita went rigid, knuckles white on the straps of her handbag. She tottered on her high-heels among the pavement's soot-smudged willowherb. She was a panicky visitor to a foreign country looking for something comfortingly familiar. She didn't speak the language. Hadn't read the brochures.

'I'm lost.'

I hovered. No, of course we weren't sure what we were doing. The only thing I was sure about was that I should be at school, psyching myself up for ... no point now in fretting about the Fun Fest. I'd blown it. Blown everything.

And Brendan, where was he? Was he waiting for me to find him? Did he think I'd let him down again by siding with his enemies, the teachers and the police?

Fifty yards away, a grass bank was a shoulder for the dual carriageway. In each direction the line of traffic was as continuous as its din. I pulled my scarf round my mouth and nose to protect them from the stench of fumes and windblown dust.

I was on edge. Ready to flip. This is totally crazy, I thought.

'This way, I suppose,' Anita said.

She checked her bearings against the Ritz's redundant clock tower, and set off.

We ghost-walked into a sea of parked cars.

My iPhone call tune played.

'Now what are you up to?' the Lion demanded. 'You're out of school again. How long do you suppose it is till the start of your Fun Fest?'

'I'm with Anita. We're across the town, outside the Ritz ... where the Ritz used to be.'

'Akinyi! Are you out of your mind? Any street name I can head for?'

'Rosebud Terrace, but we haven't found it yet.'

'Look,' said the Lion. 'Stay with Anita. I'll collect you as soon as I can.' Her voice betrayed her weariness and exasperation. 'It might not have occurred to you Akinyi but you father and I have other important work to do today. For goodness sake, have some sense and stay put just this once.'

Anita shuffled forward, and we clung to each other's arms. A homing instinct worked on her. She weaved her way between parked cars. Gusting litter was ankle-deep. Flying grit from the dual carriageway stung our cheeks.

Again Anita lined herself up on the old cinema clock tower.

Beyond the car park we found the streets. Rosebud Grove. Rosebud Way. Rosebud Crescent. And at last Rosebud Terrace.

Stay put, the Lion had advised.

Easier said than done.

Anita stared along the street.

'I wouldn't have known it,' she murmured. 'It's all done up. All prissy. What's happened to the yard?'

The yard, I guessed, must have been where each pebble-dashed house now had its square of garden neatly separated from the neighbours by a knee-high brick wall.

'I knew everybody in this street. My mam pushed me along here in my pram. I ran for sweets and pop at Wilsons' corner shop. I did a paper round. We were married in the church.'

She spoke as if she saw only beauty. No way was it the beauty of the modern prissified street she and I were standing in.

'Our Brendan could have lived here,' she said quietly. 'Except we were crazy enough to cart him off to Ashbrook. Until today I kidded myself I could always come back and find his dad. I'd send them out to their shed again. I'd call on Steve to stand with me when the cops knocked on our door.'

'Shall we knock now?' I said.

Anita looked blankly at me. She's totally forgotten who I am, I thought.

'At your house,' I prompted.

'No, no. This isn't our street.' She shook her head. 'Not any more.'

'What about Steve? Where's his mother's house?'

'Nah.' She shook her head again. 'Steve isn't here.'

There was nothing more to be said.

We stood in a gap torn by vandals in the fence next to the dual carriageway and looked out across the lines of speeding nose-to-tail vehicles. The traffic tossed our dresses. Choked us. Deafened us.

Anita took my arm.

'We'll have to face the cops without Brendan's dad. Will you face them with me?'

Happiness took me by surprise. We hadn't found Brendan's dad, but it hadn't been a waste of time, and I didn't want to leave. I wanted to stay there with Anita. I hadn't been this close to anybody since Mum died. Not to my dad. Not to any friend.

My best-remembered childhood song came into my mind, the song Mum and I sang and played together when I was just a primary school kid. I longed to be that kid again. I longed for my mum. I clung to Anita and sang for her. As I sang I turned her away from the traffic-packed road so that we could look along Rosebud Terrace.

'Down by the riverside the green grass grows,

Where Mary Nelson washes her clothes.

She sings, she sings, she sings so sweet,

She calls to her playmates across the street.

Playmates, playmates, won't you come to tea?

Come next Sunday at half past three.

Teacakes, pancakes, everything you see,

Won't we have a jolly time at half past three!'

'I'll find out from my dad,' I said. 'I'll ask him who I am and if my parents are alive. Will you ... ?'

It didn't seem possible Anita could hear through the traffic din, yet she nodded. She nodded again and again.

'Together,' she said. 'We'll face him together.'

We turned for home.

A moment later and I would have been getting into the cushioned warmth of the Lion's car and speeding away. Instead, I stared at a gigantic truck hurtling along the main road.

'Luxury Curtains.'

I read the giant icon splashed across the lorry's side, and I spoke aloud my sudden clear understanding. It was down to the lorry driver, because at the same moment he flicked his cigarette butt out of his window.

That's it, I thought. I can't believe it. It's as simple as that.

In the back seat of the Lion's car I frowned.

Can it really be so simple, I thought.

Guesswork. It's still only guesswork.

Can I convince them? The Lion? Frosty? Detective Chief Inspector Cardew?

'Anita and I have made a promise,' I told the Lion. 'We're standing by Brendan whatever happens.'

The Lion eyeballed me in the driving mirror.

'It could be a detention centre this time,' said Anita. 'That's if we ever find him.'

'No need to worry about that,' said the Lion, crisp, certain.

She'd been, she told us, to the hospital to check on Mrs Siddle.

'How is she?' I asked. I hardly even pretended to be polite.

'You know hospitals.' the Lion shrugged. 'I'm not a relative, but they did tell me her son was with her. That's all I needed to know.'

'Her son? Does she have a son?'

'It was you,' said the Lion, 'who told us she has the next best thing.'

I clapped my hands in excitement.

The Lion pulled off the road to ring Frosty on her mobile.

'Tell Mr Mac,' she said, 'that his globe-trotting daughter will be back with him inside twenty minutes.'

She listened, and I watched her happy smile. The Lion and Frosty, I thought. They're my secret. No more kids' gossip games for me.

'Naughty of you,' said the Lion into her mobile. 'I'll have to consult my social appointments secretary.' She worked hard to control her delight. Then she was businesslike again. 'Oh, and another favour, please. Collect Brendan from the city hospital. Coronary care unit. Too complicated to explain now. All will be revealed.'

And you don't know the half, I thought. I could tell you - but not till I know what Brendan thinks.

It was just so good to know where he was and that I would be with him again soon. He could count on me. I'd make sure he knew that.

'Would it be too much to ask,' said the Lion, 'for you to concentrate on your Fun Fest now?'

I smiled. I was tired. Tired and almost past caring.

The Fun Fest - yes, alright.

Chapter 36

Backstage, I was in a proper tizz. This wasn't the way it was supposed to be. I'd had weeks to plan for this moment and now everything was a mad rush. There was loads of stuff that should have been planned down to the last second and I hadn't even checked up on it. I was winging it.

I'd got rid of my school uniform to put on a smart new waistcoat in a deep chestnut and a pair of calf length jeans with silver flashings. Not what Dad would expect, far from it. Not George and his parents either.

Tough. I'd made my mind up to do my own thing. As I combed out Anita's braiding, I promised myself I'd soon ask her to do it her way again. I let my long curls part, Lion-style, and drop forward and back across my shoulders. With a special touch - my stylish silk headband ordered for just this occasion in Kenyan colours from a Kenyan web site.

Akinyi

What was worrying me most? That my dad might make a mess of things? Not a bad guess.

Well, I needn't have worried about that. He welcomed the visitors, told everybody what a terrific occasion this was, how thrilled, how proud ... I didn't miss a syllable, and if things had got out of hand I had it in me to dash into the limelight and drag him off the stage.

It's your clarinet piece you should be worrying about, I lectured myself. After all, you haven't practised for a single minute since Sunday. You've hardly slept since Sunday. And, in case you haven't noticed, you're not exactly soul mates with your partner George. I wouldn't put it past you to harmonise on different melodies.

Luckily, there was no need to make polite chat. George sat with his mum and dad in the audience until the last minute.

I was worried silly about the other acts. This whole occasion, after all, was my baby, and, before the fire, I'd spent weeks on making it happen.

The hall was packed with kids who'd raised good money, many with clever ideas. They were stars. They'd walked, run, danced, biked and swum unbelievable miles. Painted their faces. Held a bring-and-buy sale and an auction of promises. Sat in silence for endless sponsored hours. Valeted cars. Begged money, scrounged money, borrowed money. Now it was their turn to be entertained.

I'd got together highly-rated artists and now I could only hope they'd be well received.

Akinyi

They were.

My dad introduced the first turn, the Afro-Caribbean steel band. I was proud of him - yes, why not? His introduction was a revelation. He had buttonholed the band leader, and could not only introduce each player by name but make a little joke about him and her. It was more than Gloria would have done. Kids wriggled in their seats, and waves of warm chuckles spread through the hall.

Chuckles for the Headteacher, no less.

Good old Dad, he had given the festival a lovely send-off. Then the band had them stamping and clapping. Marvellous stuff.

From the backstage door I could see down the school drive. Frosty's car, with Brendan in it, hadn't come.

And that, no prizes for guessing, was what I was seriously twitchy about. Let him arrive soon, I thought. I'm desperate to see him arrive. To know he's in the audience. I want him to hear me play. As soon as all this is over I shall run to him, to tell him that I know he's told me the truth about the fire.

And the other business. I want to tell him that Anita and I will stand with him.

And that he must … it's a tough ask, but I won't take no for an answer.

After the steel band, the pantomime scene. Everyone remembered their lines. Macho boys played dame and ugly sisters, and they soon had the hall howling. 'He's behind you' and 'Oh no, he isn't'. Follow that. An interval was the only possibility, for stretching and ice cream.

No Frosty. No Brendan. What was happening? I prowled the backstage, willing them to appear.

Gloria and I had fretted about the interval. Cramming so many kids into the hall had been a headache in the first place. They couldn't be allowed to leave their seats. It would be impossible to get them back. Ice cream was the Lion's idea.

'Tell them to stay put and give them a Cornetto,' she said.

It worked. I peeped into the hall, where I could see my friends from Gloria's music class. Troublemaking innocents one and all, they were working hard to dish out the goodies.

My dad introduced the magician. And Saisha, his assistant.

Oh, jeepers! Saisha!

Fire? Surely, she isn't going to swallow fire. Not here in the brand new hall.

I felt dizzy. How had I allowed this to happen?

Too late. To stop them I'd have needed a plan. Plans take time. I hadn't made the time to stop and think.

It was too late.

They juggled balls, three, then four. They juggled skittles, four, six, then eight. Every kid in the school had seen some of T's tricks and now they called for their favourites.

'The rabbit, T. The rabbit from the hat.'

T wound them up. He teased them. He poked fun at them. He led them on. Then he delighted everyone by producing not a rabbit but a cooing white dove, which perched on his hand, flew high into the hall, came back to his hand and disappeared. Thunderous whistles and catcalls.

The moment arrived for lighting the kerosene torch. My heart was pounding. Should I run onto the stage and stop him? Tell him not to be so stupid as to light a fire when we'd just had the fire to end all fires?

Magnificent in his smiling mischief, T turned to face his audience.

'Fire?' he laughed. The hall was silent. I didn't dare look. 'Some other time perhaps.'

Before a groan of disappointment could form he lifted his show forward, sweeping the air with a flashing sword.

'Swallow! Swallow!' the audience howled.

I let my breath out in a painful gasp of relief. Then - what will Detective Chief Inspector Cardew make of Saisha's video, I wondered.

T made them happy. He brought his act to a stunning climax by swallowing the sword.

I knew for certain I would be a flop if Brendan didn't arrive.

I hardly heard the stand-up comic's gags because by now my stomach was seriously queasy. George appeared backstage and began tuning his violin.

I took one last look along the drive - and saw Frosty park on the double yellow lines by the front steps..

'Thank you,' I sighed.

George and I stood side by side in the wings. The laughter faded. The stand-up comic took an encore. He might have taken half a dozen encores for all I knew. I focused, at long last, on my clarinet piece.

My dad introduced us. He made a joke about his daughter. Something about everybody knowing who was the real boss. He had to do that, of course, to cover his love and his pride. Then he sat at the piano, twirled his wrists and began to play.

George and I stepped forward into the lights and the applause.

George, naturally, was outstanding. He and Gloria had composed our piece, for violin and clarinet, weaving it through the melody line of a pop hit. Every kid in the hall could hum along.

Even after weeks of practice I hadn't heard what the music said. Keyed up for their great moment, George and his violin told the clarinet how much they loved her. Tears came to his eyes as he played, and for a while he drew me along with him. The audience, hyped by an afternoon of belly laughter, was up for it, too. Everybody recognises a genius.

George played on, and bar by bar I abandoned him.

The cheek of it. To fool about. To show off. To torture Mrs Siddle. To talk to me like a baby. To give me a love letter written for another girl.

Then to use his violin to express everlasting love.

Not for me, mate.

The clarinet's response to the violin's sweet-talk became more and more wooden. George knew it, too, but he stuck to his task, and if people in the hall rumbled how deeply he'd failed, they certainly didn't show it.

They clapped.

A lot.

My dad thanked everyone for coming. He told them he was setting up a partnership between Willowbank and a school close to Lake Victoria in Kenya. He mentioned the size of the cheque that was going to my chosen charity, Build Africa. He laughed one more time with them and they gave him one more mighty cheer.

The hall seethed with excitement. Kids danced and they clapped as they went back over the acts. They shrieked and groaned as they re-told the jokes and added their own. They did contortions as they tried to re-hash T's magic. And they blasted out the original lyrics of our pop song.

The TV cameraman was busy. Proud parents hugged their stars. Very carefully I packed my clarinet case. Then I took out my iPhone, found a contact and keyed it in.

'City Police.'

'Detective Chief Inspector Cardew, please. It's urgent.'

Chapter 37

He said he was very interested to hear from me, but I cut him short. I hadn't rung for a polite chat, and my picture painting days with Mr Cardew were over.

'Come to the school,' I said, 'and you'll be interested. I'll meet you in the entrance hall. If you're there before me, there's an art display that won't disappoint.'

Before he could get a word in I hit *End Call* and picked up my clarinet case. Then I bobbed through the excitement to the group gathering in a quiet corner of the hall. Anita was there, Frosty, the Lion.

And Brendan.

Frosty and the Lion wanted to shake my hand in congratulation, but they were too late. There was no holding Anita back.

'I wanted your dad to be here, our Brendan,' she began. 'The cops, they were waiting when I got home. They've searched the house.'

Brendan turned on her. 'Did you let them in, mother?'

'I couldn't stop them, Brendan. They had a warrant.'

'What were they looking for? I bet you never even asked.'

'They wouldn't tell me.'

'And what did they find?'

'Nothing, Brendan, honest. They left without taking anything.'

This was awful. I had to talk to him, just the two of us. Before Detective Chief Inspector Cardew arrived. As always, there was so much to say, so much we needed to sort out together, just him and me.

Yet it seemed he was public property now.

'I could wring your neck for lighting that fire,' Anita said. 'They'll take you away this time, son. Bound to. But I know it's my fault and I'll stand beside you.'

As near as he could with that lopsided stance of his, Brendan stood tall. I knew how much anger he was controlling because his left hand was clenched till his knuckles were bloodless. He was missing the comfort of his black raincoat.

I couldn't stand back. I wrapped both arms round his middle and put my head against his chest.

'I'm standing by you too,' I said.

Brendan was rigid.

George chose that moment to join us. I didn't look at him. Couldn't bear to. Frosty and the Lion pumped his hand, told him how wonderfully he'd played. Without letting go of Brendan I told him, too, that he'd done well. I knew he had in mind high fives, but I'd given him all I had to offer.

Next, George's father and mother arrived, purple-faced, beaming, puffed with pride and triumph. They had a right to be, I gave them that. George had played brilliantly. More congratulations. Then Mr Newcomb gave a formal cough. An announcement was due. Time to cut the cackle.

'People may be interested to know that Mr Winter visited my offices this morning,' he began, directing himself at Frosty, who raised the eyebrow.

Things were grim, but I giggled. I couldn't help it. He'd had his hair cut yet again. How many days in a row was that?

'As a result of our consultation my solicitor and I have spent some time at police headquarters.'

'So I understand, Mr Newcomb.' All-watching Frosty.

'You may also know then that we shall make strong play of the fact that there are no signs of break-in. That rules out an amateur. In other words, George could not have lit the fire.'

'Later, Mr Newcomb,' suggested the Lion. 'In private, OK?'

It was news to me that Frosty had tackled George's father. It was news to George, too, anybody could see that. He went pale. He grabbed his mother's hand and, through his thick glasses, peered in trembling amazement at his father. Mr Newcomb's fury was in a twitching vein in his purple face.

With terrible timing, the Headteacher arrived. Understandably enough, he was glowing. He had covered himself with glory, and everybody took time to tell him so. I let go of Brendan, and allowed my dad to peck my cheek. He told me I'd played beautifully. So it's true, I thought, that only George is aware of my wooden performance.

My dad turned to George, seized his hand from his mother's and shook him, too.

'A marvellous, marvellous performance, George. I've come from telling the television people how proud the school is.'

Wan smiles all round. Everybody's mind elsewhere.

Mr Newcomb repeated his aggressive cough, but Frosty got in first.

'As I understand it, Mr Newcomb, George didn't need to break in. He was already inside the school.'

Mr Newcomb turned on unsuspecting George. Pathetic as he was, I pitied him. Poor kid. One minute the glittering star, the next accused of being the baddy.

Worse followed, for now Brendan was standing beside George and gave him a sudden push. For second or two they scuffled till Frosty coolly pushed them apart.

'He didn't need to break in,' Brendan snarled. 'Mrs Siddle let him go in and out any time he fancied.'

'That's preposterous,' my dad spluttered.

'Oh, yeah?' said Brendan, and he tossed him two keys on a ring. 'I bet one of those once fitted your lousy Music Room. Try the other on your school's front door.'

Dad's hour of triumph was over.

'I think you'll find George has just had his pocket picked,' said Frosty cheerfully.

'So what are you waiting for?' Brendan turned on him. 'He was there on Sunday night and he had the keys. He could do what he liked with them.'

I gaped at George.

The purple of Mr Newcomb's face had darkened.

'Who is this unspeakable lout?' Then he turned all pompous. 'I shall sue if a syllable of this nonsense appears in the media.'

It was true that the TV cameraman had got wind of a disturbance and came pushing through the crowds.

'Miss Lyon,' said Frosty. 'Let's take George and his parents to your room. Private there.'

It was too much for Mr Newcomb. He turned on George.

'This is horrifying, George. Whatever did you mean by it?'

It was Brendan who stopped him exploding.

'Let's get real,' he told Frosty. 'This kid couldn't even light a match.'

'Alright, Brendan,' said the Lion, moving to calm him.

Brendan shrugged her off.

'If that's your best shot, you might as well hand me over to the cops. That's been your idea all along, so get on with it.'

The Lion tried again.

'Ever since the hospital told me Mrs Siddle's son was with her I've been wondering,' she said. 'Are you going to explain, Brendan?'

'Went there to sit with her,' said Brendan. He flashed into fury. 'Let's face it, none of you bastards got into the ambulance, did you? Nobody was with her when it carted her away.'

We all glanced at each other in shame and we knew he was right.

'Busy day,' my dad muttered. 'The fire. The Fun Fest - and everything.'

'Sod the lot of you then,' Brendan snarled. 'I went to the hospital. Told the nurses I was her son, and I'm glad they let me see her.'

He was a wonderful boy. I glowed with pride. Who would have thought that he, of all kids, would set up such a special relationship with Mrs Siddle of all schoolteachers?

And suddenly I knew I was right. Forget his form. Forget Marksy and Legs. Forget George.

The curtains. The cigarette.

Better still, I understood Brendan's game. I didn't need to doubt him any more.

Of course. Of course. Mrs Siddle ...

'Mrs Siddle!'

It was true. He was protecting ...

'Mrs Siddle!' My voice rose in my excitement. 'Don't you understand? He was protecting Mrs Siddle.'

Chapter 38

Brendan put his arms round me, and the rigidness went. He sobbed. Rage and scorn, frustration and sadness juddered through his whole body.

'About time too,' he said, and he turned his grief-shattered face to Frosty and the Lion and my dad. 'She's the best teacher in this school. She's had heart trouble for years and none of you couldn't-care-less bastards even knew. Kids were awful to her.'

'It's true,' I said. 'In my class we've been so horrible she even threatened George with a massive stick this morning.'

'I gave her that,' said Brendan. 'I wouldn't have blamed her if she'd smacked Newcomb's arse with it.'

'That's it,' I said. 'Tell them.'

'Last week,' he said , 'Mrs Siddle told me she was going out of her mind with the interference of the ... Miss Lyon ... in her work. How horrible her classes were. How scared stiff she was of having a real big heart attack and dying in front of a class of kids. You're all lucky, every one of you, that it was morning break when it happened. Not even the hospital could save her.'

He raised his voice till he was howling his fury. A terrified silence fell in the hall, with everyone's face turned in horror.

'She was lying on her own in her car. She never recognised me. Her face was dark blue. A proper mess that would have been in front of smart-arse George and all his toffee-gobbed mates.'

He went into a bout of coughing.

'His inhaler,' said Anita.

In a moment or two of her special calm firmness she had him under control. He gave a few last weak coughs and could straighten his back.

'You knew all along, didn't you?' I said. 'Why didn't you tell me? Alright, alright, I know. You couldn't shop her, even to me. And then she gave you permission, didn't she?'

Brendan shook his head and spoke through the remains of his coughing.

'That's daft. I wouldn't shop Mrs Siddle. I promised her that. When she was dying in the hospital.'

Across the hall a post-Fun Fest racket had started up again as people moved towards the doors. Among the group gathered round Brendan there was another moment of shocked silence as the awful truth sank in. It stunned us all. That poor old woman. Dead!

Silence. They all shuffled and looked at their feet.

Not me. Not likely. I wasn't looking at my feet for Mrs stupid Siddle. How dare she die? Dying belonged to my mum. Mum died and left me - what? I didn't know the words to describe what I felt. Mum's dying was in every vein of my body, waiting to come out from the hidden parts of my mind when I wasn't occupying myself with - with what? With Brendan and my dad, with my GCSEs, with George and my clarinet and the Fun Fest ... and ... and ...

The hardest thing was to imagine Mum's face, the way it was in that photograph in our front room at home. I knew it was a happy face, a smiley face. She was a mum who took control. She took charge. She made everybody happy. All that was in her face.

But I couldn't picture her face. I'd lost it. It was blotted out by what I'd glimpsed of frazzled Gloria, bloodless, lifeless, caked with white powder, plastered with make-up. Damn Gloria. How dare she?

Mr Newcomb spoke.

'Naturally,' he said, 'we regret this distressing news, but the living must come first. Can we take it that George is innocent of all charges? In that case, my solicitor ...'

'Brendan won't tell us what happened,' I said. 'He'd rather accept the blame than shop Mrs Siddle, so you'll have to take it from me.'

Brendan gave me the faintest of smiles.

'I thought you'd never get there. I thought you were handing me over to the cops.'

It was no more than a trace of his wicked small boy grin, but I was thrilled to see it again.

'I think I have got there, though, haven't I? Brainbox that I am. You told her to clip Marksy's ear, didn't you?'

'Not before time.'

'And she did. You gave her your thick stick and told her to use it on George. And she tried.'

Mr Newcomb's nightmare might be over, but he was still in a bad dream. He tried to shake himself back into control.

His George upsetting Mrs Siddle. His George beaten with a stick. By Mrs Siddle. What sort of nonsense was this?

He started to speak, but Frosty glared at him and eyebrowed me to continue.

'What did you tell her to do about bombing the school?' I said.

'Me?' said Brendan. 'Never said a word. She'd sussed it herself.'

'How did it go? Toss a cigarette end into the wastepaper bin and go home?'

Brendan nodded. 'A bin stuffed full of paper. Kick it over to the window, right under the tatty curtains.'

'There was cupboard with racks of fancy dress costumes,' I said. 'And painted scenery. Stacks of it from old shows. Wooden boards daubed inches thick with oil-based paint.'

'A dozen or more tins left lying about,' said Brendan. 'Some of them half full of old paint. Mrs Siddle laughed when I told her what a great bonfire it would all make. Never thought she'd go ahead and light it.'

'I bet she did, though,' I said. 'At the end of her long weekend preparing for the Fun Fest those boys torment her. She flings a cigarette into a waste bin and deliberately doesn't stub it out. Kids were awful to her. You were the worst, George. You humiliated her, and she must have been furious. Stealing her beloved Pirate was the last straw.'

'Didn't mean those kids to keep him,' blubbered George into his mother's bosom.

People looked away.

'She must have been exhausted and out of her mind,' I went on. 'And I don't suppose my performance today helped. I can't believe that she's ...' Fury surged again. 'The cheeky cow. How dare she die?'

Anita shuffled forward, took me away from Brendan and held me, tight and warm.

'I can't see Mum's face,' I whispered. 'I want to see her face, and it won't come back.'

'It'll come back, love,' Anita murmured, 'as soon as you relax. Trust me.'

I clung to her. I needed her with her understanding and her love more even than George needed his mother.

Frosty was downright smug.

'So,' he said. 'Opportunity. You told us on Sunday evening she pretty well lived in the Music Room.'

'Means,' said the Lion. 'Chain smoking.'

'Motive,' said Frosty. 'Akinyi and Brendan have socked us with that.'

'Of course,' said the Lion, 'Detective Chief Inspector Cardew will need to satisfy himself we're right.'

'He'll be here pretty soon,' I said. 'If he hasn't arrived already.'

The TV crew were organised. Microphone and camera, ready to go.

'Can we get the star into shot, please?' bustled the reporter.

Mr and Mrs Newcomb brushed George down, straightened his bow tie, dabbed the tears from his eyes, ushered him forward.

The reporter addressed the camera.

'I have Akinyi Macdonald with me now. She is the remarkable young lady who not only conceived this successful Fun Fest but graced it with such a beautiful performance.'

I kept hold of Brendan's hand and pulled my dad close on the other side. I didn't want to glance at George, or at his silly parents. I didn't even wonder if they were in the picture.

When the cameraman had finished I turned to my dad and Frosty.

'Excuse us for a moment, everybody, please,' I said. 'Give us five minutes. Ten at the most.'

I eased Brendan ahead of me.

'Now what's going on?' he asked. 'Where ... ?'

'We aren't out of the woods yet,' I said. 'There's still the small matter of a knife and a murdered policewoman.'

Chapter 39

The Rovers Boot Boy had a generous space of his own in the entrance hall. My knees quivered with fright as I stood defiantly beside him, with my back pressed against the wall. Brendan faced me. A new flush was rising in his pale cheeks. His eyes were still damp with the tears of his rage.

The helicopter was overhead. A siren whined far away down the valley bottom as a fast moving police car came out of the city. Soon enough it would turn to cross Willow Bridge and head uphill, bringing Detective Chief Inspector Cardew to the school.

Minutes, I thought. Perhaps as many as five or six.

I spoke in that almost-whisper the Lion used when she meant business. 'I know about the knife,' I said. 'I don't care how bad it is. Just tell me the truth.'

Silence stretched between us, a tense, rebellious silence for Brendan.

Not for me. My mind was clear. Silence I'd visualised. Fury. Perhaps even a blow.

'I wasn't me that killed her,' he said.

I nodded. 'Go on.'

'What's the point? You don't believe me.'

'I didn't say that. You swore you didn't light the fire, and that was true.'

'When have I lied to you?'

'You were at the football. You didn't tell me that.'

'You never asked.'

'Detective Chief Inspector Cardew asked. You didn't tell him. You said you were mooching about.'

'He's a cop.' Brendan was scornful. 'He knew fine well where I'd been. He was just asking for the fun of it.'

'I don't understand that, but I do know that you didn't want to tell me.'

'I didn't need your permission. You and Frosty gave me the elbow.'

It was true and wounding. I felt the pain, and I hardened myself against it. 'That's no excuse. Just tell me what happened.'

'You don't want to know this stuff. You're better off keeping out of it.'

'Too late. I'm in it already. Up to the eyeballs.'

'Why should you be?'

'Because you are, Brendan. That's why.'

'The less you know the better.

I stared angrily at him.

Brendan sighed. 'There was a fight,' he said. 'With the pigs, I mean. They came for us. The cop was in charge of videoing. She was using a camera on a pole when she could have done with coshing a few people. She got stabbed.'

I waited.

He shrugged. 'And now they've got the knife.'

I shrugged too. 'Could be,' I said carelessly.

'That Cardew bloke, remember. He took my raincoat.'

I waited.

'They'll have done their tests on it. Looking for something to tie me to the fire. Which they didn't find.'

'And the knife?'

'It was in the coat, wasn't it?' He shrugged. 'So - he's waited till he's got his result on the fire and all his test results on the knife. Now he'll run me in for the woman cop.'

'There are police all over the city,' I said, 'all over the country, all over the planet, probably, looking for that knife. How come it was your coat it was hiding in?'

He didn't reply. The awful hopelessness of it all was too much for him.

'So tell me about it,' I said. 'The knife.'

'There was a crowd of Rovers Boot Boys,' he sighed. 'The cops surrounded us. We were scratting about on the ground.'

'I don't get it. What were you doing that for?'

'You wouldn't understand.'

'I've learned to understand a lot of things since I met you, Brendan.'

We locked eyes in an unblinking search for shared understanding.

'You were scratting,' I prompted. 'On the ground.'

'For stones, bits of brick. Anything we could skim at the cops.'

'Skim?'

'I said you wouldn't ... A cop carries a body shield in a riot. Rocks ping off it. But you can bust his ankles if you skim one close to the ground and hit him below the shield, above his boots.'

'Ouch! And all for the sake of a football match. You're right, I don't understand.'

'Football doesn't come into it.'

'I give up. Among all this chaos some nutter stabs a policewoman innocently doing her job, then ...'

Brendan and I faced each other. Oh boy, was he beautiful, his blue eyes storm-clouded now by trouble. I was desperate for him to explain. Just to tell me what it was all about. Where was the sense in him being up to his neck in this rubbish?

'Brendan, how come you kept the knife? Why didn't you ... ?'

'Palm it?' he said.

'No, of course not - not that. But if it's not yours, why didn't you get rid of it?'

'It was a good knife.' He shrugged. 'You never know when you might need a knife like that.'

'Brendan!'

He waved my outrage away.

'They'd find it, Akinyi,' he said. 'If I'd buried it or posted it through somebody's letterbox or chucked it in the river, they'd have found it and come knocking. And then it would be just like I'd pleaded guilty. Listen. They've had it for a day now and done all their tests on it. They know it's the knife they're looking for. So, you see, I'm better off walking out there now and letting them pick me up.'

'What if they found the knife wasn't in your raincoat pocket?'

'Like in the fairy tales you mam used to tell you?' Brendan tried a laugh. 'Course it was in my pocket. Where else would it be?'

'How about this, Brendan?'

I flicked open the catches on the lid of my clarinet case.

Neither of us breathed into the stunned silence between us. As I watched him I saw his face run a slideshow of his reactions. He was astonished. He darted a flickering glance of admiration at me. He was puzzled. Much more than puzzled, he was ... Then fear took over. I'd never seen it in him before, and it wasn't even fear.

It was panic.

'Bloody hell!' he whispered. 'What are you doing with that?'

I laughed. 'Amazing, eh? Nearly as good as one of T's conjuring tricks.'

Panic became rage. And hostility.

'Yeah,' he snarled, 'but nowhere near as funny. Akinyi, how come?'

'Come on, Brendan, it wasn't so hard. You gave me your raincoat, remember? From your pocket to my bag - it wasn't exactly a dove from a hat, was it?'

'OK, so now let me have the knife back.'

'Why would I do that, Brendan?'

'Get real, Akinyi. The cops aren't going to take kindly to you being involved.' He held his hand out. 'Give.'

I backed away.

'For Godssake, Akinyi. This isn't your scene. Give me the knife.'

He moved threateningly. I held the knife up and warned him off.

'This is crazy,' he shouted. 'I'm doing my best to keep you out of trouble.'

'Funny. I thought I was doing that for you.'

Akinyi

'It doesn't matter what you do. OK so the cops didn't find the knife in my coat pocket. But they sure as hell found plenty of DNA to tell them it had been there.'

'And what if I can show them somebody gave you the knife?'

'Fairy tales,' he scoffed. 'Listen, Akinyi, for God's sake get real. I've told you enough times. You've got to stay out of this.'

'And I've told you. I'm in it. Up to the eyeballs. Because I know who palmed you the knife.'

I turned to stare at the painting of the football fan and for the first time Brendan took in what it meant. It shocked him. He was motionless. Every muscle in his body was tensed.

Suddenly he turned to face me. Moved in clumsily, threatening me.

'Give me the knife,' he whispered.

I was quick. I was very quick. I held the knife out. Warning him to back off.

And right at that moment the swing doors to the entrance hall were kicked open. Kicked by a wildly swung boot.

The police, I thought. Detective Chief Inspector Cardew. I never thought I'd be so relieved to see him.

Before I could relax I saw the awfulness of my mistake.

Through the doorway, shoulders first and intent on nothing but naked violence, came a big man. In seconds he took in the scene.

Me fiercely determined.

The knife.

Brendan wide eyed in horror.

And it wasn't me who horrified him. And not the knife I was pointing at him.

It was the shaved head. The scarred cheek. The eyes.

Brendan's horror turned again to terror.

It was the painting that saved us.

It had taken the Gaffer those short seconds to size up the situation. He would grab the knife. Use it if necessary. Issue some blood-curdling threats. Then get out of there.

He hadn't bargained on the painting.

It stopped him dead in his tracks. He stared. The fanaticism died from his eyes. His brow furrowed and his eyes narrowed.

'What the fuck?' he said hardly above a painful croak. He looked from Brendan to me, then back to the picture. His face softened. The muscles weren't used to such a thing, and I thought how clever the female artist had been when she admired the slender outline, the delicately arched eyebrows and the eyes with their sexy invitation,

The shaved head, the slender cheeks, the extra-special eyes belonged to a man enjoying parties and the pub, not to a thuggish football hooligan.

'Who the fuck did that?'

My heart hadn't stopped pounding for a million years. I felt sick with fright. Yet I drew on all that schoolteacherly pomposity I'd practised and was beginning to pride myself on.

'What is your business here?' I demanded.

Brendan pushed me aside.'

'It's me he's come for,' he said.

The Gaffer turned away from the painting. Turned his attention to me, and my knees were weak as I saw in his face that the fun had gone and the thuggery was back. How wonderful it would be if the front doors would swing open again and let in Detective Chief Inspector Cardew. Or if Frosty would appear from the new hall, where I'd pretty well ordered him to stay put until Brendan and I came back.

'Right first time,' the Gaffer snarled.

With the flat of one palm he pushed me away. It was a violent push, and I staggered. The Gaffer pointed an aggressive finger into Brendan's face.

'I heard you were mixing with Willowbank lasses,' he snarled. 'The Headteacher's own, I heard. And I'm here with a friendly reminder that you keep your gob well closed.'

He took hold of Brendan's face with one massive paw and squeezed till Brendan's eyes were staring. An ugly metal ring on one claw dug into Brendan's pale cheek till blood oozed.

In a haze of rage and fear I went forward.

'Wait a minute,' I shouted. 'You can't come here assaulting people.'

I didn't deflect the Gaffer a millimetre.

'Tell your little woman to back off,' he breathed into Brendan's face.

'I told you to keep out of this, Akinyi.' Brendan's voice was strangled and he continued to stare into the Gaffer's eyes. 'Now you know why.'

'Oh, do I indeed?' I said. 'Well, let me tell you this. I've learned to accept that you can't shop your mates because the estate wouldn't understand. You wouldn't even have shopped Mrs Siddle. You'd have let them pin the fire on you. You'd have left me to think it was you and I'd have hated you for the rest of my life.'

'What's she on about?' growled the Gaffer.

'Shut it, Akinyi, or we won't get out of here alive.'

'I will not stand by and allow Brendan to take the blame for murder.' I spoke to the Gaffer's shoulder as he squeezed Brendan's upturned face. I dropped my voice into a Lion-style whisper. 'Specially as I know who palmed the knife onto him.'

'Jesus, Akinyi! Shut it.'

The Gaffer chuckled.

'I was a bit late, eh?' He transferred his paw from Brendan's face to his collar and dragged him towards me. 'Looks like I'll have to sort the pair of you. Two for the price of one.'

'I wanted to keep you out of this,' Brendan shouted. 'I tried to tell you. He'll murder us.'

'And I tried to tell you,' I said. 'I can look after myself.'

'Not in this company, you can't.'

'Maybe not with fists. Certainly not with knives, but this might do the trick.'

Suddenly I was holding out the open palm of one hand.

'See this,' I said. 'A four gigabyte flash drive. There's a video on it. As pretty pictures go, it's naff. There's the ground, the sky and a lot of cartwheeling bits in between. Some of the people could be cops and they might be wielding truncheons. Some of the people could be young men and they do look suspiciously as if they're throwing stuff. Skimming perhaps. You're all scarpering down the road.'

The Gaffer made a grab for the flash drive. I was ready for him and snapped my hand back.

'Not so fast, Gaffer,' I said. 'This video is on my laptop's hard drive so don't bother mugging me. It might be a naff video but it has a few frames a professional might have filmed. Clear as HD TV, somebody passes Brendan a knife. Big guy. Massive boots.' The Gaffer was staring at me now.

Ha! I thought. The playboy and the hooligan - they've both disappeared.

'A Union Jack daubed onto his scalp. A pink scar across one cheek.' Perhaps I showed a trace of smugness as I stole Frosty's words. 'Gets rid of the evidence. Drops Brendan in the brown stuff.'

A police siren suddenly shrieked on the school drive outside, and the helicopter was overhead.

The Gaffer dived for the doors. It was beyond him to resist a snarl at the "little woman" who had done for him. 'You bitch,' he snarled. 'I'll see to you.'

He was huge and he was quick, but the two police constables who blocked his way were huger and quicker.

'Not your cleverest moment, Gaffer,' Detective Chief Inspector Cardew remarked, strolling in behind his colleagues. 'I'm surprised at you.'

He waited and watched without moving a muscle.

'You've seen nothing yet,' I told him. I tossed him the flash drive. 'Stick that into your nearest USB port and feast your eyes.'

Cardew spoke into his mobile. The background chatter of police radios ceased and a powerful car engine was switched off. The helicopter climbed from its hovering position over the school and flew away down the Willow Valley. A siren began to shriek, changed its mind and mournfully wound down to a whimper.

Willowbank and Ashbrook were suddenly silent.

END